Happy Endings

Off The

Vegas Strip

Or more formally known as

W.I.M.P.S.

WORLD INTERNATIONAL MORAL PROTECTION SOCIETY™

A Novel by

John Alexander Haskett

Happy Endings Off The Vegas Strip
Copyright © 2020 by John Alexander Haskett

Published by:
Durango Publishing Corp.®
Suite 36 – 747 Princess Ave.
Victoria, B.C., Canada V8T 1K5
www.DurangoPublishing.com
Email: Support@DurangoPublishing.com

Happy Endings Off The Vegas Strip

Or more formally known as

W.I.M.P.S.

WORLD INTERNATIONAL MORAL PROTECTION SOCIETY™

A Novel by

John Alexander Haskett

This is book #4 in The Mike Shant Mystery series.

<u>Previous titles</u>:

#1 Policy Terminated
#2 The Conversion
#3 The "Lose Weight" Scam

Also by John A. Haskett

Highly controversial political satire novel:
>> The Day B.C. Quit Canada. Co-author.

Financial:
>> How to Make Money Beating Horse Races

Consumer:
>> Mexico – Your Complete Guidebook

All are in print and can be purchased from your favorite bookseller or Amazon.

DEDICATION

*To Sandra, Michael, and Roger,
my three wonderful children.*

About the Author

John Alexander Haskett has been a freelance writer for many years. He has written hundreds of magazine articles, financial documents, promotion copy, and five novels. As a publisher, he has published newsletters, magazines, manuals, and numerous commissioned surveys. He has now entered the fascinating realm of book publishing, and has published 4 novels in the Mike Shant mystery series, 2 novels in the satire/political areas (The Day BC Quit Canada, co-authored with son Michael, and The God Franchise) and several other books on horse racing betting and freelance writing.

His line of mystery novels, starring Mike Shant, are gaining fans fast! To receive automatic updates about new and upcoming novels, send an email to Books@DurangoPublishing.com. You can also visit his Amazon author page to keep track of his latest novels.

Prologue

Her secretary smiled. "Go right in, Mr. Shant. She's expecting you."

"Thanks." He opened the large door with its impressive lion's-head knob, and walked in. The office was large and square, with windows on two sides showcasing Vancouver's lush green Stanley Park and the Inner Harbor, with the North Shore Mountains gleaming with their white caps in the background. The harbor bustled with traffic: ferries arrived and quickly departed from their landing slips, open-sided launches gave tourists a watery tour of one of the world's most spectacular harbors, and work boats ignored all that frivolity to load and unload their goods from exotic ports.

"Hi, Mike. You look great." She moved out from behind her desk, long legs quickly taking her to him. She proffered her cheek. He gently turned her head and planted a firm and lengthy kiss on her sensuous lips.

"Do I look like your uncle? What's all this cheek kissing?"

She laughed. "Okay, I guess I wasn't thinking. It's been so long since I last saw you, I couldn't remember whether we were friends, relations, or...." Her voice trailed off.

"We sure aren't kissing cousins. And it hasn't been all that long. We met in, what, October? Your memory doesn't go back that far?

She laughed again, a tinkly sound that seemed to cover about three octaves. "You're right. It just seems longer."

She disengaged from his embrace and returned to her chair and sat down. She gestured at the comfortable leather chair off to her left side. "Plant it, bud."

Shant sat down, crossed his legs. "What's new, kiddo?"

Patricia Morgan reached down to her right, slid open the bottom desk drawer, and withdrew a bright red file folder. She placed it on her desk, then sat back in her high back swivel chair which looked like hand rubbed leather.

"A couple of things, Mike. First, we've had very good reactions to your series on Las Vegas shakers and movers."

[Reported on in Mike Shant #3, The "Lose Weight" Scam".]

"Glad to hear it, Pat. No bomb threats? While it wasn't really an expose series I did probably piss off a few Vegas fakers."

"Not even an irate letter." She smiled. "You're settling down in your old age."

"What do you mean old age? I still have a few good years left, and given the opportunity"—he affected a Groucho Marx leer— "I may be able to show you a couple of new moves."

"Promises, promises, that's all I get." She turned serious. "Anyway, the series was good, and I hear from the sales people that both our circulation and big display ads from Vegas advertisers have zoomed since it was published. The results were so good, Mike, that the publisher of Your Money Magazine wants you to go back into that den of iniquity for another story."

"Not another 'Gee whiz, look how successful I am now' article? I can only stand so much of that syrupy stuff before I clog up."

She opened the folder and took out a handful of printed sheets.

"No, not another gee whiz story, Mike. In fact, quite a bit different. In your Vegas travels did you ever come across a guy named Gilbert Rheambault?"

Shant thought for a moment. "That name rings a very faint bell. There was somebody something like that name who seemed to be on all the radio stations nearly all the time, selling, if I remember correctly, heaven and other paradise real estate. It was pronounced sorta like you did, but I saw it once or ten times in ads, and it was spelled more like..."

"Rambow?"

"Exactly."

"Same guy, Mike. He was a Frenchie from Quebec, his parents never even learned English, and after he moved to Toronto, he got tired of the anti-French feeling almost everywhere, so he bastardized the spelling of his surname to what he thought was a more English name."

"And you know all this lovely detail about our Frenchie preacher how?"

"Because my illustrious boss, god, or better known as the publisher, has already had our researchers working on this story. Apparently one of his aunts was literally cleaned out by one of these phony radio or TV preachers, and ever since he's had an urge to expose one or more of them."

"So how did he hit on Senor Rambow?"

"One of his kids got a freebie Vegas trip as a college grad present. One night after he got back, and he and his old man were sharing a glass or two, he let slip that while in Sin City he'd had an especially satisfactory 'massage' in Vegas."

"So what? Nothing illegal about that. Or he got one of the good massages, and enjoyed either a hand or blow job?"

"He claimed both. But that's not the angle."

Shant got up and went over to the north facing windows. "You sure have a great view of the mountains. Ever go snow skiing up there?"

"Quite often", Patricia said. "There's quite a bit of development up there now, lifts, cozy bars, cabins, all that stuff. Do you ever ski?"

"I grew up in Winnipeg. I had enough snow and cold by the time I was 10 to never again voluntarily get close to either one." He turned back to face her. "So what's the hook, the angle, with Rambow?"

"Well, according to his son, the publisher learned that the massage clinic was actually owned by the preacher man himself."

"You mean Rambow?"

"None other. And the publisher concluded we could do a sort of expose article on this 'servant of god' who also ministers to somewhat baser needs. As you so succinctly put it, hand and blow jobs."

"You don't expect me to roll into Vegas and tell Rambow I want to do an article for a national magazine on how he successfully combines the good book and the good mouth. Or hands, if that's your preference."

"Fortunately, neither are in my list of preferences, Mike. And no, that's not what we want. We figured you could get to Rambow, with a straight magazine article. Based on all we know about him, he'd bite on that offer immediately. Then you could do some investigative type sleuthing and end up with the real story. In short, use your renowned imagination to create a bellringer story."

Shant grinned. "By imagination you mean deception? Lying? Bullshitting?"

"There. See how quickly that imaginative mind of yours is able to cut right to the heart of the matter?"

"How long would you want it?"

"Basically as long as necessary. When we have a publisher's pet underway length is no problem."

"That's what all the girls say. How about pix?"

"Again, as many as required."

"Can I use Pap again, and pay his healthy rates?"

"Absolutely, we were very pleased with the bunch he did for the Vegas feature."

"And my minuscule remuneration?"

She smiled. "That comes in two parts. The first, you get your top rate, and all expenses, even for massages if essential, and if delivered on time I'm authorized to promise you a $5,000 bonus."

Mentally adding up these various dollar items, Shant hesitated, then grinned.

"Sounds barely reasonable, but okay. What's the second part?"

"That will be delivered to you this evening, at about 9 p.m., at 357 Broughton Crescent, Suite 1108."

Shant looked puzzled. "Wait a minute, I think I know that address...that's your apartment."

Patricia Morgan, the very successful and highly paid editor of Your Money Magazine, stretched, putting almost unfair pressure on the long sleeved but tight sweater she was wearing, and smiled.

"Yes, it is. Will you be wanting bacon and eggs or cereal for breakfast?"

CHAPTER 1

"Don't tell me. That four-legged nag went to sleep again?"

"Okay, so I won't tell you." Big Bobby Trumbull—Biggy to his many enemies and very few friends-- swiveled around on his bar stool, along with a great deal of creaking as the ancient seat struggled to stay the course, and waved his empty glass at Joe the bartender to signal another vodka.

"Don't get cute, Biggy. Who the fuck won?"

"Let's just say you don't have to worry about cashing a ticket. Your selection-that-couldn't-lose managed to do just that. By 11 lengths. In short, dead ass last."

"Jesus H Christ! I had it right from a jock's lips that SatinSheets was primed and his connections were going to let him go. Those bastards." The last was said in resignation; he'd had a lot of experience with races going sideways. And backwards, for that matter.

Biggy slid off his stool, standing very erect to maximize all of his 62 inches. "Do you want anything on today's card? Santa Anita goes off at one."

"Yeah, put 50 on Mongooser in the third. That mother is due. He hasn't crossed the line first since Noah."

"Doesn't seem like too great a reason to bet him but it's your money. Incidentally, you owe me 150 from yesterday, plus 50 today, so cross my palm with two C's, amigo."

Rambow reached into his side pocket, pulled out a healthy fold of creased bills, and peeled off two hundreds. "Here, shove them where the sun don't shine. And I expect you to pay me just as fast when Mongooser strolls home first."

"I always do, amigo. Couldn't stay long in the sportsbet receiving and distributing business if I didn't. Don't worry. You'll get any payoff so fast the ink will still be wet on the bills."

Rambow frowned, then turned away just as somebody said, "Hey, you old fart. Where's all the pussy?"

"Where it usually is, asshole. Stuck to the top of all the broads' legs. Haven't you ever looked up there?"

"Not for at least ten minutes. When was the last time you looked, Rambow? Or are you still having one of your choir girls jerk you off to 'Nearer my God to Thee'?"

Rambow grimaced, then stuck out his hand. "Well, it is true. Bad pennies do keep coming back. How you been, Georgie? Out on a day pass?"

"Naw, I ain't been in the can for a long time, at least a month or so." He laughed, exposing a mouthful of chipped and misshapen teeth. "You still trying to beat the ponies?"

"I do very well at handicapping," Rambow said, his mouth tightening like a virgin schoolteacher's vagina. "I am way ahead of the game, something that few players can say."

"Yeah, well, it seems every time I see you, you're tearing up losing tickets. But maybe I just see you on those rare"—he laughed— "losing days. Just how do you pick your winners anyway, Rambow? Some kind of system, or just the ones with cute jockeys?"

Rambow frowned. "I use a scientific method, Georgie, to pick the most logical contenders in the race. Then I narrow those two or three horses down, based on past performances on today's track, the distance of the race, and how the horse performed in its last race. When I have considered all those factors, and factored in the trainer and the jockey, then I make my choice."

"Seems like a hell of a lot of work just to pick a loser, Rambow."

"I'm afraid people like you will never understand the intricacies of thoroughbred race handicapping. You're so used to making choices because some great white father on TV or even the radio tells you what to do, that when you're faced with a problem not resolved by some advertising huckster you're screwed."

Georgie burst out laughing. "That's rich, Rambow. Here you are, the biggest TV faker in Vegas, running down other fakers. If you didn't have an endless supply of rubes looking for some kind of salvation easily handed out by somebody like you with an impressive voice, with nothing behind it, you'd have to get an honest job. Maybe slinging burgers in some greasy spoon."

"Each of us is entitled to his own opinion, Georgie. Even when it's completely fucking stupid. And on the subject of salvation, why don't you try getting some yourself. If you did, you might be able to stay out of the can for more than a week at a time."

"And then how would I be able to keep up with all my good friends, Gibbie? As a matter a fact, partner, most of the hookers I run into there ask how come you haven't visited for a while. Not getting some Uptown manners, are you, Rev?"

Rambow grimaced and turned away. He hated running into locals who were aware of both his TV ministry, and the fact that he also hung around bars, race books, and massage parlors. At least most of those deadbeats were unaware that he also had entrepreneurial interests in all those areas.

Georgie saw an old acquaintance who he might be able to touch for a sawbuck or two. As he moved away, he gave Rambow a friendly punch on the shoulder. "See you in church, Gibbie. But don't expect me to kick in on the collection plate like the other rubes. I'll be like you, taking it out."

These fucking morons. Not one of them had the brains to get financially involved in as many enterprises—he liked that word—as he had, since he first arrived in Vegas with barely enough cash to cover a week's rent in a sleazy by-the-hour motel on North Las Vegas Blvd.

To hell with them.

He opened tomorrow's Racing Form and started his scientific handicapping. In reality he picked the race favorite as selected by the morning line handicapper. His selections didn't win that often, about a third of the time, and when they did they often paid less than 2/1 odds, but Rambow, a privateer in his varied business enterprises, was extremely conservative in his horse racing activities. He was prepared to live on the edge when involved in saving souls, or publishing world tomorrow newsletters, even when interviewing in depth young women for his body massaging 'enterprises', but when horse race betting? He needed the most scientific approach possible.

CHAPTER 2

"I want to welcome you all to my permanent part-time temporary sub-office here at Cindy's fine hostelry and imbibing establishment."

Shant paused to sample the liquid refreshments.

"It's also known by its regulars as simply Cindy's Bar. Under either name, however, welcome.

"And as we have newcomers, perhaps I should introduce everyone.

"On my left, or right, depending on which way I'm facing, is Pap. He's over the age of consent, actually quite a few years past that marker, and he is undoubtedly the finest photographer this side of the Rockies. Or the Alps, for that matter."

Shant had another sample.

"Unfortunately, he is a very poor imbiber of fermented beverages, so under no condishuns, conditions, should you permit him to have more than six or seven at one sitting.

"I have had the opportunity of engaging his professional services quite recently, right here in the city of Love. He did a sterling job. So good, in fact, that my esteemed editor, far away in the True North, inshisted, insisted, that I again employ his talents on this new assignment. And without further ado, whatever that is, let me introduce him. Please stand up, if you can, Pap, and take a bow. But give it back when you're done."

Shant sort of fell backwards onto his seat and looked at his friend.

"Unprepared as I am with public speaking, I thank my great friend and benefactor of the bucks for this opportunity to address this crowd, all three of us. I'm Pap, I take pix. And I think, old friend, that Vegas is the city of Sin, not Love.

"Finally, in the interests of allowing more time for drinking, I would like to introduce my lifelong buddy, Alison, who I met just twenty minutes ago. You can all see that she's beautiful, female, and friendly, and I will ask her to take—seize, if she likes—the podium and tell us a little about her life so far."

He made a courtly bow, handed the imaginary mike to her, and sat down, almost gracefully.

"Thank you all so much for that tremendous intro. Please save your applause for later." She smiled widely.

"My name us Alison, with just one l. My momma did not believe in using two letters when one worked just as well. For the past couple of years, I have lived here in beautiful Vas Legas, and yes, Pap, you were correct, it's formally known as Sin City, although there can even be a little love thrown in sometimes.

"I'm what's known as an unpublished author, a woman who so far has slaved over a hot computer to no avail. But I will persevere and in time my name will be as familiar as John Doe.

"Until that wonderful time I labor in the vineyards of manual labor, doing research of exotic types for people like our well-known writer", she nodded to Shant, "but I just can't recall his name at the moment. I also slave away for reporters, even private dicks sometimes, performing interesting research jobs for guys who are too lazy to do it themselves."

"More! More!" Shant made it to his feet and began clapping, causing the three drinkers at the bar to look up for a split second, then return to their slot machines. "Give us the whole scoop, my dear."

Alison curtsied in his direction.

"My public calls and I respond. Here is Alison Adams in one paragraph.

"I'm over 25, under 30. As Pap said, I am female. My hair hangs down, and when it's brushed well it's auburn. My face has been called passable. My dear mother passed away some years ago, my very alive papa lives in Panama City. The canal place, not Florida. I had a nice boyfriend for a couple of years but he got transferred to New York—New York! —and I declined to accompany him to that sewer so I'm on the loose." She glanced at Pap and smiled. "But I'm not loose. I dislike all loud rock music, enjoy an occasional Jack D on the rocks, and I'm not really an a.m. person."

She took a sip of what looked like Jack D.

"And I want to say how thrilled I am to be involved in this project with you two guys. I think so, because I really know zip about it, other than there's research involved, and I will actually be paid for my efforts."

Alison sat down and both men rose and clapped enthusiastically.

"That was excellent, Alison. Succinct and extensive simultaneously, which is an outstanding ability for a researcher."

Both Pap and the researcher looked at Shant.

"Okay, you guys. I guess you want me to spill the beans. Or at least enlighten you a little. So I will.

"The project involves a little skullduggery. One of LV's most eminent citizens, a Gilbert Rheambault, or Gibbie Rambow as he likes to be called, is the target."

Alison groaned. "I truly hope, Mr. Shant, that you're not going to say this will be a "What a wonderful person he is" article."

"Not to worry, Alison. And my name is Michael, or Mike, whatever you prefer. No, this article will be quite a distance from that saccharine crapola you referred to. What it is to be, friends and colleagues, is an expose of our fraudulent and perhaps even flatulent Mr. Rambow."

This time Alison clapped. Pap joined in.

"A mite more detail, O most excellent employer."

"As you wish, Pap. Here's the secret plan.

"I am going to contact Rambow, apparently to do an article just as you first mentioned, Alison. But meanwhile your talents will be put to use—and paid for--uncovering some of the less elegant aspects of Rambow's life. I know of these slightly from my previous assignment here, helped most ably by colleague Pap and a researcher who is now enjoying a wonderful Old-World vacation for her fine efforts in the boat race of the century.

"Don't fret, my pet, all will be explained to you in good time. And that info, as well as all we're discussing here now, are in strict confidence among the three of us. Agreed?

Two heads nodded as one.

"Fine. Moving on, then. I heard rumors that Rambow, besides saving souls for hard cash, had interests in other ventures. Like very enthusiastic body massages. And some publishing activities that apparently strayed somewhat from reasonable journalistic principles.

"So your job, Alison, is to find out what exactly Rambow is doing. Hard info, hard facts, because that's what our employers, those True North folks I mentioned earlier, are very skittish about publishing articles that would make an ambulance chasing lawyer happier than the proverbial pig in a waste product.

"And Pap will be in circulation, getting some "Mr. Nice Guy" pix, but also other photos to illustrate the interesting aspects of Rambow's business operations."

He took a healthy swallow of what obviously wasn't a soft drink.

"Any questions?"

"I imagine you'll provide a little more hard data on what you are finding, Master?"

"Yes, Pap, you both will be kept right up to date as soon as I have anything tangible. This is a partnership, not a one-man performance. Alison, as a good standing citizen of Las Vegas, do you have any suggestions for how I might best proceed?"

The auburn-haired young woman crinkled up her eyes, gently rubbed her quite elegant nose, looked at Pap, then nodded.

"Not really a suggestion, boss. More a hint. Vegas is really a small town, and if you try to sneak up on Rambow about all you'll accomplish is to alert him. I'm pretty certain he has listening posts in every imaginable spot in the valley, and even a few unimaginable."

"What you're saying, my partner, is that I should make a bold frontal attack?"

"Exactly, my leader." She clicked her heels together and struck a pretty accurate at-attention stance. "Phone him right off the bat and tell him the part about wanting to feature him as a leading LV citizen. Once you've talked with him, my guess is you'll have a much better idea of which rocks we all should start uncovering."

"You see, leader-man, she not only looks like someone from your most erotic dream, but she's also smart. Marry me, Alison."

"Gladly, Pap, if you were only a little older. I prefer really mature men."

"Older? If Pap were any older, he'd qualify as the oldest member of the Old Farts Club."

"Now, exalted leader and bread provider, there's no need to not only stretch but completely break the truth. I do admit that I have passed my fif...fortieth birthday, but I still run 10K every morning."

"10K? As you are obviously referring to centimeters, not kilometers, the correct letter should be C, not K. But never mind, Pap, you have your memories. And boy do you have lots of those."

Alison burst out laughing. "Should we start earning our minuscule fees? I don't want to be fired on my first day."

"You are absolutely right, Alison." He frowned and gave all the appearance of serious thinking.

Pap wasn't a believer, he figured Shant was looking at Alison's butt. Or something else.

"Let's add a little class to this melodrama, folks. How be you phone the good Mr. Rambow, Alison? You can play the part of the dedicated and virtuous secretary that I have retained to assist me in this monumental undertaking. Actually, just about the truth. See if you can do a meeting, as the Hollywood important people are fond of doing. Just Rambow and me, unless he offers to have auxiliary help. The more people of his I meet the better the chances of one of them being an open mouth."

"Sounds good, boss. How soon do you want to get together?"

"ASAP, Alison."

She went to the bar and returned with an artifact of an earlier age. A telephone directory.

"I'm pretty sure his religious thing has an office not far from Cindy's, where we are right now."

Pap looked surprised. "Are you sure, my dear? I thought we were in the public library."

She flicked her hand casually at Pap and continued. "I'll check under the church listings in the back. I haven't used one of these things"—she held aloft the old directory in her hand— "for a long time. Everything's cell now and if you don't have a number you're SOL."

She thumbed through the torn and disfigured book. "Yes! I thought so. Here it is. It's right around the corner on LV Blvd, you guys. If you nail him in that office you can walk to it, boss, just up a block then probably on the other side of LVB in the first, maybe second, block."

"Walk? Are you hallucinating, Alison? No one walks in Vegas. Except street walkers, of course, and that's their storefronts. No, I'll travel first class in this metropolis, as befits a big-time magazine writer from the exotic west coast.

"See if you can set it up, Alison. And wake up, Pap."

"Wake up? I'm far more awake and alert than any other male member at this table."

Alison shook her hand vigorously to shut them up.

"Yes, that will be fine. His name? It's Michael Shant, and the magazine, with world-wide paid circulation, incidentally, is "It's Your Money". He'll see Mr. Rambow...what, oh he prefers to be referred to as reverend? Well, I'll pass that tidbit on to Mr. Shant. Goodbye."

"What an old crow. Sounded about 80 and just about gagged when I called Rambow a mister. 'Oh, my dear, that's Reverend Rambow.' Anyway, boss, you've been granted a papal audience in half an hour, although the rev may have to cut it short in order to meet with a few of his flock who need his reassuring words."

"Well done on your first trial flight, Alison. You have done the sisterhood of secretaries proud, and I will be sending a letter of extreme unction, or thanks, or whatever, to the most holy pres of that group, whomever she might happen to be or wherever she may be lurking."

He held some fingers aloft and wiggled them, hopefully telling Cindy that he was prepared to settle his account. She got the message and moments later brought over his check.

You have a fine establishment here, Cindy, and I expect we'll be seeing quite a bit of you over the next little while."

"Great, Michael. You'll always be welcome." She smiled and wiggled her tight behind sensuously as she returned to the long wooden bar.

Both men watched appreciatively. Alison grinned.

"Seeing that you have had such a strenuous first day in the trenches, Alison, how be you do a little quiet library research and see what you can dig up on our quarry. I'll give you a call on your cell—tonight okay? Fine. —and Pap, how about meeting me back here in an hour or so so we can plan our great strategic next moves?

"Cindy, sweetie, can you phone a cab for me? Yeah, whenever, I'm ready to go. It's a short trip but I'm a good tipper."

CHAPTER 3

"I'm Beatrice Brownsley, Mr. Shant. Among my other duties I am editor of 'The Word', the official newsletter publication for our church." She took his proffered hand and almost reduced it to a boneless organ.

She was almost 6 feet tall, and topped her imposing body with a bright red mass of hair or, most likely, a wig. Shant figured her to be in her early 50s.

"Nice to meet you, Miss Brownsley. And for the record, what is the correct name of your church?"

She reached behind her and grabbed the top copy from a large pile of printed sheets.

"Here's our latest newsletter. You may find it interesting. And as you can see, our church name is clearly printed right below the newsletter's title. We're proud of it."

Shant took the 2-page sheet.

"Yes, I can see that. 'World International Morals Protection Society'. Quite a mouthful."

She frowned and Shant saw that she was offended by his offhanded remark.

"Well, we had to include all the key words, to be accurate, and each of these 5 words is important."

Shant felt he would come out second if he challenged her to an arm-wrestling contest so he nodded instead.

"Sure, I can understand that, Miss Brownsley. When was the church started?"

"I think it's best that you get all those details from the Reverend Rambow. I'll show you into his study now. He has been meditating but I believe he's now ready for his interview."

She went across the small but scruffy room and tapped lightly on a door opposite them.

"Reverend? Are you ready to meet the press?" She smiled at Shant so he could acknowledge her clever greeting.

In the interests of staying healthy he smiled back.

Just then the door opened. The reverend stood there, one hand raised either to convey his blessing to the press or to accept a donation. He had barely had time to throw the Racing Form into a bottom desk drawer after BB had knocked.

He was tall, even taller than BB. Probably an inch or two over 6 feet. Black hair, and noticeable cheek bones, suggesting a touch of the exotic. Or the wild west.

"Mr. Shunt? Nice to meet you."

"Likewise, Mr. Rambow. And it's Shant, with an a."

"Do forgive me. And while we certainly do not stand on ceremony here at WIMPS, in the office I prefer to be addressed as reverend. Come in."

He stood back and beckoned like a friendly used car salesman greeting a yokel from the country.

"Okay, reverend is fine with me." (Actually he detested any and all religious nonsense but he had to keep cool, at least until he got into the real reason for his interest in Rambow.)

The office was furnished much better than the frowsy receiving area. Probably this was where the reverend put the finishing touches on his donation appeals to gullible members.

Rambow pointed towards a comfortable-looking leather sofa at right angles to his desk. On the desk were a leather box of pencils, a memo pad, and an old-fashioned telephone with several buttons. All of them were currently at rest.

Noticing Shant's appraisal, Rambow said, "I told Bertha to hold my calls so I could give you my uninterrupted attentions, Mr. Shant. I have great faith in the press of this wonderful country. And BB—oh, that's what I call my secretary Bertha, we try to keep things as friendly here at WIMPS as possible—agrees with that wholeheartedly. So, you have my complete attention, Mr. Shant."

You really do, you press scumbag. I know you and all your slimy associates would just love to find some way to injure my well-earned image in this city, Rambow's internal monologue carried on.

Shant nodded. "Good. Let's get underway then. When was WIMPS started?"

Rambow cleared his throat, obviously getting ready to unload a large pile of crap.

"The actual date was just several years ago. But our unique writings go back much further. In fact, we have had several experts tell us that they may be from a time similar to other authenticated materials like the scrolls, for example. But..."

"You're saying that they might be a couple of thousand years old?"

Rambow cleared his throat again.

"We don't make any specific claims about the exact number of years, but as I said some experts have theorized that that is possible, even probable."

This guy's as good as most politicians in saying nothing in a great many words, Shant thought. I'm going to have to watch that my personal disbelief in all things religious doesn't screw up this assignment.

"Most interesting. Could you elaborate?"

And elaborate he did, for the next 72 minutes. Shant made occasional entries in the notebook he carried to impress interviewees, and nodded a lot. He felt that he had convinced Rambow of his sincerity.

Rambow was wondering how really stupid and gullible this reporter was. Maybe he should hit him up for a church donation, or ask him to sponsor one of the church's fictitious "orphans abroad"; he might go for a pathetic child in Somalia or Haiti. Those orphans existed solely in giant scrapbooks he had BB cull from other churches' probably just-as-spurious appeal letters. But they worked really well with his "flock", especially the older females.

Shant was nervous he was going to nod off. He had rarely listened to such a monologue of self-adoration coupled with a touch of the old divine right of kings. He wasn't too sure exactly how much of the drivel Rambow actually believed, how much was purely titillating crumbs to get his members in the mood for contributing money.

Just as he felt his eyelids shutting down there was a welcome knock at the door. It was immediately opened and a man entered.

"Listen Gibbie...oh, sorry."

Rambow leapt to his feet, knocking over his box of pencils.

"Goddammi...Gee whiz, Clive. I have told you many times before not to interrupt when my sanctuary door is closed." Rambow forced an anemic smile.

"Well, since you've already violated one of my most important rules...." He turned. "This is Clive Clingingbotherton III. This is Mr. Shant, here from the west coast to do an article on me. And of course, WIMPS."

He threw a glance at the new man who was perhaps 5 feet and a few inches. "Clive's one of our, uh, scroll specialists."

Clive frowned. What?

Shant almost burst out laughing. A scroll specialist. He doubted that Clive could even spell that.

"Well, get on with it, Clive. Why did you come bursting in through my closed door?"

"It's just that Gertie, er, Miss Glein, said to let you know that she had found a new mass...uh, a new manuscript and that she wanted you to take a look at it as soon as possible."

"Okay, Clive. I have the message. Now you can leave me and this reporter to finish our interview."

Clive the scroll specialist scuttled out and carefully closed the sanctuary door.

"I'm terribly sorry, Mr. Shant. Do you have any more questions for today?"

"No, I think I have my fill for now." (Actually it was overflowing.) "But I will need to meet with you again."

"Of course."

"And any of your staffers who might have something to contribute. Perhaps the scroll specialist could add some important details?"

"Oh, no, I don't think so. He's kept far too busy deciphering new materials as we find it." (Or buy them from a friendly forger.) "But I will examine our employee rolls and see who else in this diverse organization you should meet with."

"Okay. After I've gone through the extensive notes I took during our first meeting, I'll have my secretary contact you for our second interview."

Rambow pressed the button which summoned BB, and she took charge of showing Shant out.

"How did the interview go, Reverend?" Few others in the 'organization' massaged Rambow's ego but she inserted the religious title into every conversation she could.

"Very well, BB. Although Tonto's unexpected— and unwanted entrance—almost threw a wrench into my superb handling of the esteemed Mr. Shunt, er, Shant."

BB wrung her hands. "I am so sorry about that, Reverend. If I had been at my desk, I would have stopped him. But I had just stepped temporarily out of the office, to the powder room"—she blushed—"when he showed up. I certainly hope he didn't cause irreparable damage, Reverend?"

"It was close. Whenever I think of all the problems Tonto had before his bosses had him defrocked officially..." Rambow shuddered as he recalled the litany of excuses Clive (known on his birth certificate as Clive Clingingbotherton III, but "Tonto" to almost all; fortunately he didn't know the word in Spanish meant stupid) had showered him with before Rambow agreed to employ him as a sort-of general go-fer and doer of odd and dirty jobs wanted by no one else.

"Oh, Reverend, all those problems they said I had with all the Catholic Boys' Clubs were just fabrications of those who wanted my job. I never, Reverend, never ever touched any of those boys they said I did, and if you hire me I promise right now that I will be your best and most trusted servant..."

In the end Rambow had hired him because he needed someone who would literally do anything and everything he was told to do. And ask no questions.

Since then Rambow's real reasons for employing the little man had been justified. He had performed so well that Rambow had even bestowed the largely symbolic "Assistant Manager" title of the massage enterprises.

Now Tonto seemed almost to enjoy those tasks others found disgusting and/or repugnant.

"Anyway, BB, try to make sure in future that my closed office door is secure against any unauthorized intrusions. Especially with this big shot west coast reporter sniffing around we can't be too careful."

Of practical necessity BB was privy to many of Rambow's secrets. She knew about his massage parlor ownership, but not the full extent to which he personally made use of its exotic facilities.

During her duties as editor of the church's "The Word" publication, she mentally eliminated Rambow's skin shop activities from her mind, concentrating instead on all the wonderful "causes" he espoused, as related by him directly to her. She was an editor, she reasoned, not a researcher.

"One for my father here, Cindy, and you can also top up mine, please."

"Father indeed. I'm barely old enough to be your slightly senior brother. Hi, Alison. Great to see you."

He turned back to Shant. "And how did your meet with the Rev go?"

Cindy delivered the drinks, smiled at Pap and inhaled enough so his roving hand just barely stroked her tight jeans-bound bottom, and threw a wink at Shant and Alison.

Shant took a healthy swallow then set his glass down.

"Pretty good, I think. He was pretty suspicious at first, but I think I eventually convinced him I was an overpaid, under-qualified reporter way out of his league up against the inscrutable Reverend Rambow."

"Sounds really good, Boss," Alison said.

"I agree," Pap added. "And so what's next?"

"It's still a little muddied. But I did get a small break.

"Doing our interview, a little man interrupted, called the Rev Gibbie, and got off a few unrehearsed comments before Rambow closed the tap. He started to say something about a Gertie Glein having a new mass. Then Rambow cut him off.

"But I got the impression that the word interrupted was massage or masseur or something like that, not the manuscript that Clive Clingingbotherton III, that's his name, believe it or not, tried to repair his abbreviated statement with."

"You said 'little man' before, Michael. Did you mean that literally?"

"Yeah, he was quite short, probably barely 5 feet."

"Well then, I know him," Alison said. "He's also known around town as Tonto—of course stupid in Spanish—and he's apparently a kind of do-everything guy for Rambow, especially stuff that no one else wants to touch.
"I don't think he hangs around the WIMPS office much, where you met Rambow.

"One of my sometime drinking pals has a boyfriend on the LVPD. She told me he said that good old Rev. Rambow had some kind of ownership interest in a massage joint on North LV Blvd. It's called "Happy Andings", and she broke up when she told me its slogan."

And Alison broke up herself, having to grab a handful of table napkins to stem the flow of tears as she laughed uncontrollably.

The two gentlemen waited patiently for the Niagara to subside. Eventually it did and Alison regained a little composure.

"Okay, so what's the slogan?" Pap couldn't wait any longer.

The laughing fit threatened again but Alison got it under control.
"Are you ready? The name, as I said, is Happy Andings, spelled like that, and the rest of its slogan is 'Relaxation Direct. Open Now.'

She tried but couldn't control the laughter. Several regulars at the bar looked over to see what was causing all the fun.

Pap frowned. "I don't get it. It's a little cornball but what's the joke?"

Shant had been jotting with a pencil on one of the few remaining napkins.

"Look at the initials, Pap. H, A, R, D, O, N."

Pap took a moment then he too started guffawing.

"Jesus Christ. Hard on!"

"Exactly," said Shant. "Rambow, or somebody, has a pretty sharp sense of humor. Just imagine the promotion possibilities: 'When you think of massages, just think Hard On'. Hard to beat that for suggestive advertising."

All three laughed, snickered, or guffawed, according to individual preference. Eventually normalcy returned.

"Did your buddy's cop friend know the extent of Shant's ownership interest?"

"I don't think so, Michael, although to be honest we were both laughing so hard that I can't clearly recollect. Would you like me to see if she, or he, knows?"

Shant pondered for a moment.

"It would be helpful, Alison, but only if our, more especially your, connection didn't become public knowledge. Would this cop keep mum?"

"I'm pretty sure, Michael, but I could confirm with Jennifer before she asked him any more questions. I do know that Jim, that's her friend, like apparently most or even all cops here, doesn't hold Rev. Rambow in very high esteem. Jenny said they all think he's a low-ball creep, and probably crooked as well."

"Okay. And we do have a name too, that Gertie Glein. She probably has something to do with that Happy Andings, so Alison, how be you get digging on that, see what you can find on both Gertie and HA.

"Pap, maybe increase the scope of your pix to include HA, Gertie, and Tonto. Don't at this point be obvious, just get background stuff."

"How be I sneak into HA with a mini camera and get some pix on the job, so to speak?"

"Sounds interesting, but they probably would have you strip completely. Where do you plan on hiding the mini?"

Alison grinned, Shant laughed, and Pap even blushed a very little bit.

"I'm going to go over my notes and get some more pointed questions lined up for my next meeting with Rambow. Whatever you can contribute from pal Jenny might be very helpful, Alison, although it may be a little premature to go right after his HARDON connection."

"That would be called premature ejaculation," Pap contributed. The other two ignored him.

"Incidentally, Alison, when querying her about Jim's sphinx-like willingness, you could maybe press Jennifer just a little to see exactly how much about the Rev the cops really know. We're not asking for confidential cop-only data, Alison, just stuff that any cop might know or find out normally from a buddy maybe doing more concentrated work on Rambow's activities."

"Gotcha, boss. Jenny's a good buddy so I'll get what I can, without making a public issue out of it. I know she's dependable and I think Jim is too, although I've only met him a couple of times."

"We all have our assignments, gang. If needed call and leave messages at my motel. I'll be in touch by cell as soon as I have things sorted out."

CHAPTER 4

"Nice to see you again, Reverend. I'll tell GG you're here."

The Happy Andings receptionist stood up, showing a skirt barely long enough to cover the extreme top of her thighs, and a peasant blouse designed to clearly show the goodies below.

Gertie Glein, who managed this pleasure palace for Rambow, was a strong believer in immediately getting customers into the right frame of body for the imminent delights awaiting in an individual massage room.

"It's been too long, Gibbie. C'mon in. She led the way to her private sanctum where no one was allowed to trespass without specific orders. She had too many secrets there, even from the Rev.

Gertie Glein was big. She was over 6 feet by 2 inches, and tipped—actually dented—the scales at well over 200; the actual reading was secret. Her hair was jet black, and only her hairdresser—a little gay guy who was terrified of GG—knew the truth of that. She had more muscles than many weightlifters and she drank beer with vodka chasers.

In her earlier days she had been a popular masseuse at a bikers' bar where she had practiced her various professions in a room at the back, and her gymnastics gave as much pleasure as did her capable hands and arms. A side benefit was the "Get up GG" she roared when the customer was at the moment of truth.

She knew what men wanted and made damn sure her girls gave exactly what she charged for, the fee which was about double what the quickie hand job joints further south on North Las Vegas Blvd. charged.

She also had her own little private enterprise. From the start she had convinced Gibbie, who was a real novice in the hands and mouth pleasure industry, that she had to maintain constant supervision and improvement of her girls, some of whom were graduates of sleazier massage joints.

The only way to do that, she convinced Rambow, was to periodically videotape a girl in an actual massage.

The camera was of course hidden from view and she shared some of the tapes with the boss. She also trained girls who needed training, without revealing where she had learned their shortcomings.

When she recruited a new girl, often from a completely different background, and who she was sure the boss would appreciate, she arranged for him to be one of, if not the first, customers serviced.

On these occasions she also made a videotape but didn't let Rambow in on the secret. These tapes were carefully separated and carefully hidden away from those featuring regular customers. They were her own future annuity program.

She hadn't really planned when she would use them, but she felt sure that she would fall from favor with Rambow at some point. She also felt that as his business and especially religious enterprises prospered an and became more numerous, the value of that annuity program would only increase.

GG had no intention of becoming an impecunious ward of the state. She fully planned to end her days in an oasis of luxury, somewhere in southern Arizona, surrounded by old farts who could only fantasize about the physical pleasures.

"I do wish you'd get those broads in the receiving area to stop referring to me as Reverend. What will the customers think? Have them address me as Mr. Rambow."

"Okay, Gibbie. I'll pass the word. And are you in for a treat."

GG paused to let his anticipation build. She knew him well.

"What have you got, GG?" He didn't quite lick his lips but only just.

"A sweet young thing, she's only 19. Never worked before, although she did give a little away."

"So why's she starting out now?"

"Like almost everyone else, she needs the bread. She lost her job as a sales person in a big department store chain and she has no other skills. But she's pretty, and very willing to learn. I've already done a couple of regulars with her, they both thought it was wonderful having two broads working on them. I showed her some of my special tricks and she picked them up real fast. So I think she's going to be a keeper for us. But she's still got a lot to learn and I'll tape her with you and we can discuss her together later. Okay?"

Ordinarily she didn't tell Gibbie she'd be taping him but she felt the allure of a real newbie, young, and pretty, would be enough to cover any modesty he might have. It was.

"Only this time, GG, and you'll erase the tape after we've seen and discussed it, right?"

"Of course." What a schmuck. "The instant we've seen it I'll punch the erase switch.

She knew that his anticipation was dangerously close to explosion time so she speeded up the conversation.

"She's available and waiting for you now, Gibbie. All she knows is that you're a special customer, and that she's to give you her very best efforts. Her work name here is Sheena. I've got her in the special soundproof room at the back so no prob with whatever." And it'll make for a better tape for my collection. "Let's go."

"Sheena, this is the special customer I told you about. You know what to do. And I've got you off the clock so there's no hurry. Enjoy, everybody."

She left quickly, the part about no time limit was merely to bolster Gibbie's confidence. She knew from experience that he wouldn't require even the quickie minimum 15-minute time.

As soon as she was back in her office she shut and locked the door, then opened the special locked cabinet hidden behind a picture of her in her prime wrestling one of the "toughest" bikers; she had knocked him out in 11 minutes.

She clicked the switch activating the camera hidden in the ceiling of the special soundproof room.

She checked to make sure the tape was running smoothly then closed and locked the cabinet.

"Get Tonto in here pronto." She slammed the house phone down, she didn't believe in wasting words on receptionists.

Less than four minutes later there was a knock on her door. She recognized the anemic rap of Tonto and unlocked and let him in.

Tonto was in fear of Rambow, who knew all too much about his problems with young boys. He almost wet his pants when summoned by GG. She not only knew about his activities with impressionable youth. She had pictures.

Where she had found them he had no idea, and certainly not the least inclination to quiz her. With those photos he knew she could have him very easily thrown in the slammer for a long, long time, and he knew that child molesters did not have enjoyable stays in places like jails and prisons.

While he did everything Rambow told him to, and to the best of his ability, he did everything that GG even thought about, even before she ordered him to do it. He was truly terrified of this woman who could pick him and throw him across the room. Across the block, probably.

She let him stand in front of her for what seemed to him like ten minutes. Finally, he broke first, as always.

"Yes, Miss Gertie? What can I do for you?"

She looked at him the same way a starved island castaway on an involuntary 30-day food-free diet would look at a hamburger.

At last she spoke. He listened as closely as he would have to a god-like wraith descending from the sky.

"The Rev is in the special room and will be occupied there for some time. In fact, I'll make sure that he's incommunicado for at least 45 minutes. Get your ass in gear, get to his apartment, find his secret files that he keeps taped to the top of his toilet tank—he thinks that's a secure place! —and go through and take pictures of anything with my name on it. Then get out and wait for my call on your cell.

"Clear?"

Like a sentence of death. He knew if Gibbie found him wrist deep in his toilet stash, he would be thrown from the balcony, and Gibbie lived on the 15th floor.

If he didn't get what Miss Gertie wanted he would have every bone in his body separately crushed."

"Don't stand there with your mouth open, Tonto. Go!"

He did.

He made the seven blocks to Rambow's apartment building in less time than possible, and was deep in Gibbie's bathroom soon after that.

As Miss Gertie had said—was she ever wrong? No! —he found a plastic wrapped package of papers securely taped to the bottom of the tank lid.

Once opened he found a motley assortment of letters, old paid bills, notes scrawled on bar napkins, and a few crumpled one- and five-dollar bills. Probably the start of Gibbie's pension fund.

After checking his cell phone for the time, the 20th since he had arrived, he did find a couple of envelopes with local Vegas postmarks. Inside were two sheets of paper, both addressed to Gertie Glein. He didn't read either, there was no time, probably no time to live, just took a couple of quick photos with his multi-purpose cell, replaced the sheets in the envelopes, replaced them in the plastic wrapped package, re-taped the package, replaced the lid, and got from there to outside the building in less time than it takes an athlete to do one pushup. He had probably lost 10 pounds, which he couldn't afford to lose, but he was alive.

Unless what he had wasn't what Miss Gertie wanted.

CHAPTER 5

"Welcome one, welcome all, to Casa Shant. Come in, remove your wraps, and get comfortable."

Both Alison and Pap did as ordered. At his direction, and his invitation, they were visiting Shant at his motel suite on South LV Blvd, not too far from Cindy's Bar.

"I have vodka, rum, and for the lower classes two kinds of imported Mexican beer. What're your pleasures?"

"A mild vodka, and ginger ale or something if you have it, for me, por favor," said the pretty one.

The more mature gent said he'd have a strong rum, mixed lightly with some ice and tap water.

"Good choices, all of them." And the host served each as ordered, then mixed another rum and water for himself.

"There are a few oddments on the table there if anyone needs nutrition. And once we're all set we can start earning our fees."

There was a round imitation-oak dining table in the kitchen part of the motel, and all three grabbed seats at it, placing their drinks carefully within easy reach.

"Probably the best way to get things started is to have each tell the others what if anything he or she has learned since last we met. Pap, you want to go first?"

He swallowed the mouthful he had been testing for quality. "Sure."

He straightened in his chair, placed his part empty glass within easy reach, and reached into an inside pocket and pulled out a small Kraft envelope. He upended it and dumped the contents on the table.

A dozen or so prints fell out.

"This is not a sample of my professional abilities," Pap smiled. "Those are a little better at least."

"At least. Actually quite a bit," Shant interjected.

Pap nodded his thanks.

"What they are are various shots of our target, in locales ranging from in his church HQ extolling his faithful, or gullible, to keep up their good works by keeping up their contributions, to a slightly sneaker entrance to a well-known local pleasure palace, the infamous Happy Endings."

He selected a couple of the prints and held them up.

"Perhaps not as sneaky as Bogart in some of his movie roles, but as you can see, he is checking the surroundings for nosy viewers. He has also replaced his normal churchy attire for a more inconspicuous brown jacket like that worn by hundreds of people."

Shant took the prints and examined them.

"Nice work, Pap. He obviously didn't see you and you also made sure his face was easily recognizable."

"I also have a couple inside. One shows Rambow paying very close attention to the necklace the very voluptuous receptionist was wearing. Except she wasn't wearing a necklace."

He handed the print to Alison who gave it a quick inspection, grinned, and passed it to Shant.

"How'd you get this one, Pap? Didn't they see you acting like Joe Scoop, the hotshot press photographer?"

"A good question, Alison, but if I told you my secrets, I'd have to kill you."

She laughed.

"Actually, all they saw was an old fart, probably waiting to work up his courage for his 'massage' treatment. People don't really see much."

"By any chance you didn't happen to get a close-up of the good rev getting his treatment, did you, Pap?"

"Sorry, boss, that one is on my to do list. But before we're all done, you'll have it, or one even better."

Alison looked skeptical. "Believe him, Ali. I've seen him perform miracles before. If you want, he'll show you pix of you in your private bathroom doing your morning ablutions."

"What! Do you mean that?" Alison looked both startled and indignant.

"Relax, my dear. The boss is just joking. He knows I'd never show him that one."

Now Alison was even more indignant, until finally she realized the men were pulling her leg. Or she hoped they were.

"Keep it up, Pap. All these shots will come in handy at the showdown."

"Alison, if you have managed to get your blood pressure under control, let's hear what you've been doing."

"I'll get even with both of you. Just wait and see. And as to my professional activities, I have followed up with my girlfriend's cop friend. Jim is proving to be a really good source, although of course nothing that he gives me can be attributed to him.

"He said that the cops, through their Special Investigations unit, have firm evidence that Rambow is the major owner of Happy Andings. A small number of shares in that corporation are owned by a Miss Gertie Glein, who also doubles as the joint's manager.

"She's a very large woman, over 6 feet, according to her arrest sheet. But all she's done, or even been questioned about, are roughhousing tactics at HA.

"She apparently serves as the prime bouncer there, and gets involved physically when a customer tries to get a little more involved with a masseuse than his fee permits.

"So basically no police record, the same as Rambow."

"That's about what I'd expect. Rambow sounds far too smooth to be on any police blotter. Con men rarely do, at least until the final act for them."

"A new wrinkle, Michael. Jim said that the SI unit has just recently gotten a lead on another possible Rambow enterprise. It's something in the publishing area but right now that's about all the cops have. But I have a friend who works in the Company Registrar's office in Carson City. They have pretty complete data on all companies incorporated in Nevada, so I could get on the blower to him and see what I can uncover. Are we interested?"

"Absolutely, Ali. Anything and everything about Rambow's activities. Get all you can. You know, if you find another company, what it was set up to do, who owns what, the full story."

"Gotcha, boss. Unless friend Sam is off work for any reason, I should have this info in a day or two."

"And Pap, keep up the great pix. Get some of the little guy, Tonto, or more accurately known as Clive Clingingbotherton III.

"Although at the moment it doesn't look like he is going to have much more than a walk-on part, I have a gut feeling his final role will be larger than that.

"He evidently works out of HA as a general dog's body there, so maybe catch him with Gertie the manager-bouncer or, if possible, with the rev himself."

"I'll try for both, Mike. Better to have too many shots rather than too few."

"My editor, and I, love you, you old fart. I almost feel honest when I submit your expense accounts."

"Honest? Abe Lincoln would be proud to review and okay my expenses."

"Great sums for 'massage research'? For 'liquid nourishment when stranded in the Nevada desert'? You've never even been out of Vegas."

"Slander! Defamation of character! My lawyer will be in touch with yours."

"Good, we can all have a drink together. On your account, of course, where it will turn up as 'entertainment for the men's church choir'."

"Not a bad idea, old pard. I'll file it for use sometime."

Alison shook her head as the childish goings-on of the two males.

"Back here on planet earth, gang, the program is much the same as before. Carry on with what we've discussed. If any new avenues open up, follow them. Expenses be damned, full speed ahead."

As he ushered the two colleagues out into the clear, desert night, Shant smiled. As with his previous Vegas assignment, he was fortunate to have two such dedicated—and talented—people to help him.

He had a good feeling for the current assignment. Although there was a long way to go before

the rev Rambow could be featured on 'It's Your Money'
cover, he felt that would happen. And soon.

CHAPTER 6

"GG, there's a man in reception. Says his name is Big Bobbie Klassen—he's actually very short—and he insists on speaking with you. Personally. What should I do?"

"Two things. Use my name when you talk to me, not initials, and don't comment on customers who come in here. What they call themselves is their business. Ours is getting money for the services we provide. Understand?"

The abashed receptionist blushed and nodded. She didn't want to lose her job here, she was thinking of writing a juicy book about it. Some day. Far in the future, in fact, when people like that weasel Tonto wouldn't worry her.

"Show Mr. Klassen in, and close the door on the way out."

The receptionist returned with the bald short customer. He had a western movie gunfighter moustache which almost obscured the lower half of his face. As she turned to close the door and leave, he gave her ass a good feel, then smiled at her and looked at GG. "Nice stuff you have working here nowadays, Gertie."

The receptionist was used to such mauling, many of HA's customers were short of polite manners. More material for her book.

"Well, Bobbie, what brings you to the Happy Andings?"

"What do you think, Gertie. I'm here for my massage. This is Tuesday, ain't it?"

"No, it's Friday, not that that makes any difference."

"You told me about a new broad you had hired, Gertie, the last time you and me were, what do you call it? oh yeah, screwing. You said she was a cheerleader just out of school."

"Well, maybe a year or two, Bobbie. But I expect she'll meet your strict requirements. She is young, has big boobs, nice ass, and is dumb enough to do almost anything you say."

He started towards the service rooms.

"And I'm free tomorrow after six, and I'll be here after the day employees have gone home.

"You'd better be here too, Bobbie, or your cheerleader supply will dry up. Fast."

GG had a problem. Partly because of her size, and partly because of her unwillingness to settle for men like Tonto—who would happily and willingly try to climb her frame and service her—she ended up with other somewhat defective men like Big Bobby.

He serviced her in secret in return for substantial "discounts" on HA services, and for access to new masseuses who would agree to wear cheerleader costumes so BB could relive his high school days when his shortness and other defects hadn't precluded an occasional quickie with a second—or third—string cheerleader.

Now she was doubting her choice in taking BB over Tonto. Neither of the shorties was much in the sack, but at least Tonto was deathly afraid of her, and would do literally whatever she told him to do. Big Bobbie still had to be jollied along with rehashes of his fabled and imaginary school days exploits.

CHAPTER 7

"Hiya, Polly. Wanna cracker?"

"Oh, Gibbie, you always use that joke. But you know the only cracker I want is the one between your legs."

"Is that any way for an employee to talk to the boss? Haven't you heard about respect for the man who pays your salary?"

Polly straightened up in her chair behind the desk in the front office.

"Of course, master. I welcome you on one of your too-rare visits to the offices of Concise Urbane Manual Publishers. We are known far and wide as publishers of quality hard and paperback editions of material designed to titillate and stimulate the senses, causing even highly refined personages to get short of breath."

Rambow laughed. "Well done, Pretty Pussy. Can I interpret that little monologue to mean that CUM Publishers provides manuals of hard core and deviant sex for readers who want to whack off as they broaden their educations?"

"That sums it up, my wonderful employer. And as the infrequent recipient of your talented tongue, fingers, and a strong dick, I can only say thank you, for my paycheck, all the wonderful employee benefits I have yet to receive, and, most importantly, that lovely dick."

Polly Peters, known to her many friends as PP—anointed that by Gibbie who had a thing for matching initials--was in her mid 30s, about 5 inches over 5 feet, thin, but with huge boobs that measured a full 3 feet 6 inches around, flaunted green hair, and smoked cigars. Perhaps needless to add, she enjoyed all types of sexual activity, from extreme deviant to ye olde missionary.

Rambow had a taste for big breasts, and being able to utilize PP's when the need arose, along with her real ability to find and develop authors who could make weird and wild sex interesting, made her position in

CUM Publishers logical, handy, and even tax-deductible.

"How are sales coming, PP?" Even when aroused physically Rambow kept a close eye on the financial sector.

And he needed more money to cover his unfortunate losses on the sport of kings, along with the current slowdown in donations from his religious flock, due to the recession or depression, whatever the government called it when they also denied its existence, stating that 10% unemployment was merely a temporary glitch, even though that particular statistic had been present for over 4 years, a longer time than the present resident of the white house had been claiming he was going to solve that problem.

As always, Rambow thought, cheat, steal, even murder at the national level, and the moronic voting public cheered you as a hero. Do the same on a far smaller local scale and they tried to put an entrepreneur in jail. PP took a deep breath and Gibbie forgot all about the crooked political scene.

"Sales are really good, Gibbie. We had a real run last week on our latest lesby title, 'A carrot a day will keep your juices flowing'.

"We sold 85 copies to a group of girls who have a club in San Francisco. And another bunch of guys in Palm Springs ordered an even 100 copies of 'Simple exercises to keep your tongue limber'."

"No straight stuff selling?"

"Sure. Just today I shipped an order to a bookseller in Chicago. They ordered five dozen each of 'Girls: How to know when your climax is approaching', and '1 is good, 2 are great, and 3 at a time are fabulous'.

"We're also continuing to get good orders for our 6-week internet courses in 'Easy & Effective cunnilingus for beginners' and 'Creating really memorable orgies on a budget'.

"Overall, Gibbie, sales are fine. The accountant phoned me yesterday and said he'd have the quarterly P&L statement for us by Monday."

Rambow nodded. At least one of his enterprises was doing well.

"You don't mind being out here on East Fremont, PP? You thought when we first moved that you'd be too lonely, away from the Strip and Old Town action.

"No, I sorta like it now, Gibbie. Parking right in front of the office is great. You know that we don't have many drop-in customers, I guess some of them are a little embarrassed to be seen. So they order by phone or on the web. Actually, I would like to meet with you more in person, so we could discuss stuff better, but as long as I know I'll see you sometimes I don't mind. And I have lots to do. Nope, I sorta like where this office is now."

Rambow had dropped in mainly to see how sales were going. There were several big races this weekend and his bookie had put a tight limit on the amount of credit he'd extend.

As the bookie told him when Rambow had protested that he was a top quality, long term customer who had never stiffed him, and deserved unlimited credit, the prick said the recession/depression had affected him too, and his bankers—of the leg breaker variety if payments were even tardy—had screwed down his float.

He needed cash to get some healthy bets down on horses he was positive would go off at reasonable odds and trounce their fields.

He told PP to write him a check for five big ones.

"For $500, Gibbie?"

What a dumb broad. But great tits.

"No, my pet, $5,000."

It took just a few minutes and she gave him the check. "That only leaves a little over a thousand in that account, Gibbie."

"No problem, PP. I'll transfer some bread from the WIMPS account if you need it."

Besides GG at the Happy Andings enterprise, PP was the only woman he trusted to know about more than one business.

"And now, with that grubby stuff out of the way, my pet, let's get down to the good stuff. I have an hour before my next appointment (with a new girl at HA) so put the closed notice on the door and get your panties off."

PP looked shocked. "Oh, Gibbie. I didn't know you were going to be horny. When you phoned all you said was about how much money we had in the bank."

"So, I got horny watching those tremendous tits of yours, Polly. Now get cracking, so that I can get cracking." He laughed loudly at his pathetic pun.

"But I can't, Gibbie. I have one of our bestselling authors coming in with a new manuscript. He said the working title is, 'How to Use the Back Door for Fun, Variety, & Surprises'. We'll sell loads of it. His appointment is for," she looked at her watch, "about 4 minutes from now, and he always comes promptly."

"I'm sure glad to hear that, PP." He hesitated before continuing.

"Well, what I had in mind will take far more than 4 minutes. It would take that long at least just to get you ready."

"Oh, Gibbie, it sounds like so much fun! Can I have a rain check on it?"

"The kind of rain I have in mind would still take too long."

There was a buzzer sound. All businesses here on Fremont tended to keep outside doors locked until a visual inspection showed that the ringer at least was clothed and not obviously armed with an automatic weapon.

"Okay, PP. Go and make some money for CUM Publishers. I'll fuck off and give you a call later."

"I'm so sorry, Gibbie. But next time I'll give you half and half for at least an hour."

Christ, that would wear it down to the nub. "Okay, sweetness. I'll be seeing you. All of you."

Making money was all well and good, but right now he had a more pressing matter.

What's the point of owning a massage parlor if you couldn't make use of its services when needed? And they were needed now.

Besides, Gertie had told him she had a new, young girl just in off the farm. It was time he got involved in some healthy back to the land stuff.

CHAPTER 8

"Nice to see you again, Gertie. You look like a breath of spring." The hornier Rambow got, the more poetic he got.

"Sure, Gibbie, and my dress size is 4. What can I do for you?"

The day had been crappy. First that idiot, and now probably ex-sex provider, Bobbie Klassen. Tonto now looked an easier and more malleable partner.

Klassen had screwed around with the new girl, insisting she change into the cheerleader costume he carried around for all his massage 'dates'.

Finally, she had objected to the gymnastics he wanted her to perform, and she had threatened to quit and go to some other whack parlor where customers got down to business quickly and without a lot of costume changes.

GG had finally settled the girl down and personally handled Klassen, an unpleasant job.

Now the boss was here, and he probably had a personal request, considering the size of whatever he had in his pants. Possibly it was a gun and he'd go on a shooting rampage of a different kind. At least it might be interesting.

He soon cleared up that possibility.

"You said you had a new girl just in off the farm, Gertie. What's she look like?"

GG knew he meant 'all over'.

"I suppose you mean does she have a sweet face?"

"You know exactly what I mean, Gertie."

GG groaned.

"Okay. From the top down. Nice blonde hair. Big blue eyes. Nice firm chin..."

"Get to the good stuff, Gertie. Does she have good firm tits?"

"Any firmer and you'd swear they were implants."

She groaned internally. Didn't these yahoos ever get beyond the skin, didn't they realize these girls might have minds, personalities...Of course not, why waste time dreaming.

"She has a nice flat stomach and pretty good legs. And of course, standard female equipment."

"Sounds good, Gertie. What are the negatives?"

She hesitated. She knew that stressing any minor blemish would just encourage Rambow to try his luck at putting pressure on that point to see if he could force her to change.

"Well, Gibbie, as I said, she is just off the farm, she comes from some flyspeck in Kansas or one of those farming states. So she is pretty inexperienced. When she applied for a job, I had to ask her if she knew what a hand job was.

"Oh sure", she said. "I had a boyfriend who regularly wanted either that or a blow job, so I learned to be convincing in the hand department."

"I thought she had had some real experience, but when I asked what half and half was, she looked blank. Then I asked her what her reaction would be if one of our good customers reached up and grabbed her ass during the concluding moments of her massage, and she said she'd slap his face.

"So then I had to sit her down and give her a quick but colorful description of what a Las Vegas masseuse's job description was.

"As I detailed it her face went from normal to completely white. I thought she might pass out on me. But she finally pulled through. She said she was flat broke, she had been looking for an office job—in Vegas! —for over three months, and now she simply had to make some money.

"She finally said she could tolerate what I had described. If the customer kept his hands strictly on her ass and stayed away from her pussy. I assured her that most customers were not likely to extend their activities beyond her firm cheeks, and if anyone got really rambunctious, she could ring the bell to summon Tonto or me.

"But she was still a little spooked by the thoughts of some guy fondling her ass while she stroked his dick. She understood the tool massage because of her boyfriend (probably the only one she'd ever had), but the friendly caressing of her behind was a new aspect of massaging. I'm going to try and keep the real apes away from her for awhile, at least until she gets used to normal male depravity."

"Depravity? I've never heard you use that word before, GG. I'm surprised you even know what it means."

Gertie frowned.

"I do, Gibbie, and I am asking you nicely to go easy with your hands if you use her.

"She's a nice girl, better looking than most we get, and in time I know she'll bring in a lot of lucrative hand job business.

"But if the other areas fondling gets too rough, she'll split and try to find a parlor where the customers are at least a little housebroken."

"What a sad story. Well, I'll see what I can do to tame her spirit a little, GG. I think she just needs a firm hand. And probably on that precious pussy of hers as well.

"You don't really believe that famous boyfriend of hers wasn't in there feeling around? Farm girls may be slow, GG, but they're not stupid.

"They know what brings the honey bees. Honey."

Oh fuck, GG thought. He's going to go in there and immediately grab her pussy in one hand, her boobs and/or ass in the other, and demand that she starts inhaling on his dick at the same time. She'll be screaming and out the door within 5 minutes.

But he was the boss. All she could do was cover her ears and wait.

Rambow strode into the special room.

"I'm the owner of Happy Andings, my dear, and I'm here to officially welcome you. And to see how well you do as our newest masseuse."

Gertie sat frozen at her desk for a moment, then realized she hadn't pressed the start button on the hidden camera in the special room. She did so immediately.

She knew Rambow would replace her with some younger cunt sooner or later, and she wanted to have enough hard video evidence that she'd be able to negotiate a fair pension settlement.

Her outside line rang. It was Bobbie Klassen, confirming their appointment.

"And make sure you got the whipping cream and rope, Gertie."

If he wasn't such a dependable degenerate she'd switch to Tonto, who she knew would fulfill her every fantasy. Except he was such a weasel. She'd see how it went with Klassen. If he didn't come up with a few new moves she might drop him in favor of Tonto.

Her forehead was damp when she hung up. How ironic, she was in charge of a place where sex in some form went on 24 hours a day—this was Vegas—and still she had to put up with runts like Klassen or Tonto. Certainly no justice in this rotten world.

She checked her watch. Strange. Rambow had been in there over 10 minutes, almost 15, and not a scream or shout of maidenly outrage.

Maybe he had listened to her and settled with the new girl just for an acceptable hand job; she knew his staying power wasn't all that great.

She had tipped the newbie that often the best way to diffuse unwanted attentions was to quickly get hold of the guy's dick and get it to the point where he couldn't stop nature's progress.

The girl had agreed. That technique had been a favorite of her best friend back home, she said. That friend had more variety in her small-town romantic life than she had with her steady.

The best friend had often encountered the problem in a pickup truck, the favorite necking spot for wayward farm boys, and she had found that simply unzipping and grabbing the current boy's cock, then strenuously stroking it to climax, solved otherwise difficult advanced-petting problems.

And the newbie agreed with Gertie that this time-proven technique could be useful in situations where roving hands were becoming a nuisance.

At the 20-minute mark GG felt she should check. She was sure that a horny Rambow, as he obviously had been, wouldn't be capable of holding out for 20 minutes. Maybe he was just talking to the newbie, giving her the benefit of his experience in the massage industry.

Sure, and pigs could fly backwards.

She left her office and quietly moved past the regular massage rooms to the special room at the end of the corridor.

She checked to make sure no one was going or coming—funny! —behind her, and reached up to slide aside the boilerplate notice from the city about washing hands frequently. Behind it was the tiny slit opening that with the aid of a built-in magnifying glass gave her almost a full room view.

At first everything looked somewhat normal, at least for an HA massage room. But the new girl was sprawled out on the massage table. Maybe she did have a few new tricks after all.

But then she saw Rambow. He was sitting on the end of the table, his pants below his knees. He was bent over, his hands covering his face.

That certainly wasn't any position Gertie had ever seen before.

The girl looked very quiet. Maybe Rambow had decked her. But he didn't seem to be the fisticuffs type.

She'd better check.

She replaced the "Wash your hands often"—a rather unnecessary piece of advice in a massage parlor—and moved back to the special room door. She knocked fairly gently.

No response.

She knocked again, harder and longer.

A muttered sound.

She opened the door a crack.

"Gibbie, everything okay?"

He looked up. He was crying. Christ, had he found true religion with a hand job?

"Gertie, that you? Get in here and close the door."

She did.

When she looked closer she could see that the girl was really out, not moving a bit. Then she looked really closely. She didn't seem to be breathing.

The new girl, on her first massage with the boss, had died. Shock at what he proposed?

"I killed her, Gertie. It was an accident..."

"An accident?" Gertie's brain was in neutral. What the hell was happening here?

"What happened?" Not a brilliant opening but she had to say something.

Rambow reached up and wiped his left hand across his eyes.

"I just told her I wanted to see her, her full body, you know, like I was the boss and I was entitled to have a look to see what she had for our customers...you know, my standard interview.

"But she objected, then started to shout and scream and I just held her down and put my hand over her mouth to shut her up, so the other customers wouldn't get all excited, you know, and she did shut up and when I took my hand away she didn't even move and then I saw that she wasn't breathing...and, Gertie, she's dead.

"It was an accident, though, Gertie, not my fault, she shouldn't have started to act so uppity, I never would have hurt her, I just wanted to see her, just like I was going to be undressed, you know, and thought it was only fair she showed me what she had.

"But it was just an accident, GG, so all we have to do is call the cops and clear it up. I didn't really do anything wrong."

Gertie looked at her employer. What a fucking moron.

"Listen, boss, you call the cops and you will be inside the slammer before you can even pull your pants up.

"You own this joint, and most Vegas cops know that, and that you're also a masseuse molester, whatever that is.

"Your story about an accident will be laughed at by the cops all the way to city jail. Even that sleaze ball you call your lawyer will puke when he hears your 'defense'.

"A new girl, brand new on the job, and you snuff her on your first trial? An accident? Not even a judge in Vegas would keep a straight face over that."

"But what can I do, Gertie? I can't risk all I've worked for, to lose it over some country bumpkin who didn't even know when to keep her mouth closed.

"I mean I didn't demand a blow job or anything heavy, I just wanted a look at her bod. There's nothing wrong with that, is there? I mean, I'm, or I was, her boss.

"I should be entitled to at least see her boobs and pussy. I wasn't going to do anything with them, just look. Gertie, it was an accident."

Gertie sat down on the other end of the massage table. These rooms didn't have chairs, there didn't seem to be any call or need for them.

She considered her options. She appeared to be in the clear on what would obviously be at least a manslaughter charge for Rambow, maybe even a murder charge if the DA really wanted to make re-election points. No one except current customers liked massage parlor owners.

But if she helped him out of this cesspool, think of the points she'd make. Far more potent than even her secret special-room filmings would be her knowledge of the girl's death, whatever the legal term for it was.

And the longer the time between the event and when she would need to use it against Rambow—and she knew with absolute certainty that that time would come—the more potent that weapon would be.

After even a few months Rambow's claim of an accident would be ignored as the DA filed murder charges. And of course she might be involved at that point. But Rambow wouldn't be likely to 'fess up.

Now, how best to handle it. She knew that Rambow would be useless. If he didn't actually go to pieces like a maiden aunt, on his own he'd screw up even the most elementary cover-up. She would have to take charge.

"Here's the situation, Gibbie. We call the cops and you're looking at a long time worrying about bending over. Or we get rid of the bo...evidence, and you may be able to scrape through in one piece.

"What's your choice?"

Rambow, the straight-talking preacher, the honest massage parlor operator, and the porn peddler, looked up at Gertie now standing over him, his pants still at half mast.

"Gertie, if you help me, I'll never forget it."

Truer words were never spoken, boss.

"Get dressed, go into my office without talking to anybody. Shut and lock the door. Use the blue button on my inside line phone and get Tonto here—in the special room—ASAP. Stay locked in until I knock and identify myself.

"Clear?"

In answer Rambow got to his feet, pulled up his pants, and looked at Gertie much like a homeless dog looks at the first young boy who pats him on the head and appears to be a soft touch.

"I'll never forget..."

"Yeah, I know, Gibbie. Get going."

She sat down again and waited for Tonto. He knocked on the door within 2 minutes.

As he came in, smiling at what he thought was some afternoon delight with his supervisor, he saw the girl on the table.

"Oh boy, a threesome? Great, GG, I love them."

"Shut up, Tonto, and pay close attention. This is important and if you screw up you will be very, very sorry."

Gertie got up and pointed at the girl.

"She's not sleeping. She's dead. Snuffed by our exalted leader."

"Snuffed? Like you mean dead? Did she have a heart attack or ..."?

"Or, Tonto. Rambow was trying to stifle a scream and he kept his hand over her mouth a little too long."

There was no point in not filling Tonto in on what actually happened. He was needed to help in the disposal, and she didn't want him thinking he had something on Gertie. Much better he knew the facts.

"It might qualify as an accident, Tonto. Or maybe not. So the boss wants to play it safe and not worry about filing an official report. Understand?"

Tonto might be short, sleazy, and basically stupid. But he wasn't dumb. Immediately he realized that if Rambow was arrested, even if later freed, the Happy Andings would likely disappear, and with it his lucrative and enjoyable job.

"Yeah, I get the picture, GG. We're going to help the boss make the evidence go away."

"That's more or less what the situation is. Now, do you have any ideas on how to do that?

"And remember, Tonto, that if word one of any of this leaks out, not only will you also be in a legal jackpot, but the glory days of Happy Andings—and all the nice innocent girls you get to feel up—will be nothing but a wet memory. Clear?"

Tonto realized that Gertie was excluding herself from any 'legal jackpots', implying that only he would be in the spotlight. But he knew better. If things went bad, they'd both be accomplices or accessories or something. And he intended to keep some kind of proof to show that GG had been right in there up to her big tits.

"Yeah, it's clear, Gertie. Let me think a minute."

Gertie felt that was something of an oxymoron or something—grammar wasn't her strong suit—but she waited while the little guy considered what options, if any, they had.

"Well, here's one possible answer, GG. I got a pretty good buddy who has a 3-ton truck. He uses it sometimes to move things for money. It's got a canvas-type cover on top so you can't see inside."

"You plan on us going into the moving business?"

"Not exactly. But he'd rent it to me for a few hours if I told him I had a little job. Maybe to move some stuff from the boss's preachin place, like to here for storage. Or something like that. My pal Wayne isn't that sharp, and if I gave him some bucks in advance, I don't think he'd really care about what I was going to use the truck for."

GG thought for a moment.

"Okay, Tonto that gives us a way to get the girl"—she didn't like to say body, that implied a finality that she wanted to avoid— "out of here, maybe after dark. But what then?"

Tonto stroked his chin. He'd probably seen some actor do that on TV to indicate thinking.

"Well, how be we take the body"—Tonto was realistic— "from here to, say, a disposal dump, you know, where the garbage guys dump all the crap?"

"So, we drive in there in your nice covered truck, and hope nobody sees us unloading a dead girl? Brilliant."

"We'd have to do it in some place where there won't be other people. Do you think people just stand around and shoot the breeze in garbage dumps?"

"How the fuck do I know? But there's always a chance some bum might be there, rummaging around for supper or breakfast, right?

"And all it takes is for one eagle-eyed prick to decide he's going to make a little extra white lightning money by calling in a tip to the boys in blue, and our grand plan is dust. No, you can't take that chance."

Tonto caught the shift from "our plan" to "you". Time to get this bitch cleared up about who was doing what.

"Let's get it straight, Gertie. I am willing to help you, and help our boss, by doing this. But I sure ain't doing it solo. It's not 'me' taking that chance, it's 'us'. If not, then I'm bailing right now."

GG felt like grabbing the shortie by his balls, giving him a few loops overhead, and then throwing him through the cheap plywood wall.

Common sense prevailed. At least for now.

"Sure, it's us, Tonto. Don't worry about it. But getting back to the problem—and our boss is sweating his nuts off in my office right now, let's get some action on it—where can we go with a reasonable chance of being somewhat invisible?"

"I been thinking. One a the broads I was dating"—GG knew that meant one he was paying for head— "a month or so ago liked to go to that park. You know, the one just before you get to the state road to Pahrump. Any time we was there, and that was about 4 or 5 times, there was nobody else anywhere. Like it was completely empty. And there was even a public can, where she went after, our uh... date, to clean up a little, so that'd be an excuse if we was even stopped by some prick cop or something."

Gertie knew the park he mentioned.

In fact, in her earlier days, while working on the street, if a john wanted complete privacy for his half and half, and was willing to pay for the time in getting to it, she would take him there.

Once the sun went down everyone disappeared. She thought it was because the park had a sort of haunted-house look or feel to it. Her marks hadn't been bothered but most normal people would be. Could be the answer.

"Could you, ah, we, drive that truck in without a problem?"

Tonto laughed.

"Sure, that truck has been in a lot tighter spots than that. In fact, if I remember right, the road in the park is wide enough for even bigger trucks, probably bulldozer-carriers for when there are forest fires. Yeah, no prob, GG."

He felt this might be a good time to discuss his rewards for his help.

"Incidentally, GG, I wanna help the boss, of course, and you too. Especially you. It sorta seems to me that you and me might sort of talk about what's in it for me. You know, like something special, just between you and me."

Gertie knew exactly what the runt was leading up to. From the moment she had decided to use him in this rescue effort she knew he'd be whining around for some pussy, in whatever form it took.

"Look, Tonto, this is not the time to be discussing that. I will say that if you help out, and do things right, I will give you such a night of fucking bliss that you'll think you're in sex heaven.

"And you know I can do that. I'll get your dick in places you never even knew existed.

"So don't worry, Tonto. Just dream about it for now. When the time is right, we'll have to find another park so your screams of delight won't be misconstrued. Misunderstood," she added, in case he was unfamiliar with the term.

Tonto leered. "Yeah, that's what I wanted to hear, GG. I know I can give you a great time, too. I may be a little short but my dick is plenty big enough..."

"Yeah, enough, Tonto. Put a clam on it until later." She'd probably exhaust the midget in 10 minutes. One of her nips in his mouth and he'd probably blow without any further action needed.

"You get on the blower to your buddy. I'll get $100 from petty cash in my office. Is that enough for his truck?"

Tonto started to say it was way too much, his friend would immediately know something smelly was up, and would demand a bigger slice. Screw it, he'd give him $50, still plenty for a couple of hours, and pocket the rest.

His thoughts drifted to GG's delights, all of which would be his. At least for one night, but maybe he'd be able to perform enough to bring her back for more. Maybe not too likely—she was pretty experienced—but possible. A longshot, like most of the boss's horserace picks.

"I'm going to see the boss and explain what I'm, ah, we're up to. And get the bread for the truck. I'll be back in 10 or 15 minutes. You have your buddy lined up by then.

"Tell him you need the truck here within a couple of hours, we can keep the girl locked in the special room for that long. Offer him another $10 to cab it from here, we don't want him hanging around. And after we've finished in the park, you can drop me off here then deliver the truck back to him."

Now she was putting herself smack into the picture, so his little sharing lecture had worked.

He nodded and grabbed the phone, punching an outside line button.

On the way to her office she thought about what she, and Tonto, she added somewhat unwillingly, had accomplished.

If things worked out okay, they had just saved Rambow from at very least a business-crippling exposure with the cops. At most, an immediate arrest on a charge of manslaughter or even second-degree murder.

How much was it worth?

She'd have to have some firm numbers to give him when he was in a very appreciative and still-numbed state.

Think big, she said. You've progressed from a street pro to the manager of a very successful massage business. Now you've got the owner's balls in your hot hands.

What was an excessive, yet reasonable to a panicked Rambow, amount to demand? And remember, she'd have to allow some minuscule percentage for her midget helper.

She was sure her physical charms, and her intimidation of him would carry much of the obligation burden, but he might also demand some kind of monetary payoff.

She used her key to unlock her office door.

"Where the fuck have you been? I thought you'd split or something."

Rambow's face was red and he was sweating profusely. He looked on the brink of a massive heart attack.

"Slow down, you're about ready to keel over, Gibbie. Relax, if you can, I've already taken care of the more pressing problems."

Rambow looked at her in a daze.

"What do you mean?"

He was obviously incapable of uttering more than a few words.

This wreck was the silver-tongued beseecher of his brain-dead gullible flock? Shit, what a disappointment he was. Her demands just went up 20%.

"Sit down and listen. We don't have all the time in the world, Gibbie. And pay attention. Your future depends on it."

Get the jerk scared and defenseless, practices she had learned during her street days with johns who thought they could wheedle a free blow job out of her.

Obediently he sat down, just barely catching the edge of the armless chair. He looked like a kindergarten kid on his first day away from mama.

"When you were sitting in here relaxing"—she was deliberately taunting him— "I was busting my ass getting your problem cleared up."

"Cleared up?"

Hopeful yet unsure. Good.

"Well, a start on clearing it up anyway. The girl you killed"—drive the dagger in again! — "is safely, for the moment, locked up in the special room.

"I've got Tonto scrounging around trying to get a vehicle so she can be moved." No need to give the shortie credit for that idea. "I'll need some petty cash and won't be putting in any documentation so expect the weekly total to be short."

No reason to just take a hundred or so, might as well make it 5 or 6 bills, he's not going to be doing any checking.

"If I"—fuck the we— "can arrange it, I'll get Tonto to load her in, and after dark I'll"—she liked that pronoun— "have him take the body to a deserted park I know about."

He barely nodded.

"Before she goes, I'll strip her of all I.D. so that she'll be just another Jane Doe when somebody stumbles on her. No connection with here, and I don't think she had any friends in Vegas.

"If somehow someone should make a connection, 'Sure, she worked here for a day, wasn't any good, so we paid her off in cash, and that's the last we saw her'.

"What do you think?"

He nodded again, as if too much movement of any part of his body might cause that part to fall off.

"Any comment on this carefully constructed scheme to save your ass?"

He cleared his throat. "It sounds great, Gertie. If you can pull it off you'll have my eternal thanks."

Does he think a pat on the head is going to work?

"Well, now, Gibbie, we have some serious talking to do. We won't even have a vehicle, a truck of some kind, for over an hour, so there's no hurry." She paused for effect.

"Yes, of course I am, GG. What do you want to talk about? I'd feel a lot easier if we had her, that girl, out of here."

"I'm sure you would but that's not possible right now, like I told you." She paused again, knowing they added to his discomfort and fear.

"Now, onto the main subject.

"Gibbie, I'm putting my neck literally on the line for you. If things go wrong, I'll be in a pile of shit almost as deep as you."

Again, he barely nodded.

Well, now it was time to stop screwing around.

"What we have to determine, Gibbie, and pretty fucking fast, is what my neck is worth to you."

He started to understand where this conversation was going.

"It's worth a great deal, Gertie. As I said, you'd have my eternal gratitude..."

"And that buys zip at the store. Look, Gibbie, we're going to have to come to an agreement very quickly, or my neck gets pulled back in like a turtle does."

"So. Your friendship has a price?"

"That's news to you? You honestly think I'm going to risk a possible long stretch in the barred hotel because of 'your eternal gratitude'?"

"In the same kind of situation, Gibbie, how far would you stick out your neck for me?"

He started to say something but she plowed on.

"Not anywhere as far out as I already have. I like you, Gibbie, and you've treated me well since you got me off the street.

"But I have repaid you for that, building Happy Andings into a profitable operation from a sleazy hand-job store. Without me you'd have had to rely on the pennies you squeeze out of those gullible jerks you preach to.

"No, don't interrupt. I have made you a lot of money, let you keep on making those crappy horse losing bets, and let you even get into the publishing business.

"Oh yeah, I know all about CUM Publishing, Gibbie. That's part of the reason I'm so successful running HA, because I really know what's going on in this town.

"So now here we are at the 'show your cards' place. Without me your HA business is kaput, and quite probably your other ventures as well; not too many preachers can live down the killing of a masseuse in his own whack parlor.

"And there's a pretty good chance the cops and the DA would not believe your story of an accident. You weigh 175 or so. She tipped the scale at maybe 90 or 100. You're almost a foot taller than she is, or was. Who is going to believe that you 'accidentally' stumbled and fell onto her face for long enough to smother her? No one."

She stood up and pointed a finger with a tiger-like nail at his face.

"The truth, pure and simple, Rambow, is that you're in the palm of my hand"—she showed it to him in case he wasn't following— "and I want to be a full partner in HA. As of right now."

"Holy fuck! Are you out of your mind? Do you know the market value of HA? It's a lot..."

"Yes, and I have almost singlehandedly created that value. Horneys now know they can come to HA, day or night, 7 days a week, and get a reasonable firm price on whatever type of massage they want. No hassles, no holdups on prices because the customer is super horny and it's obvious. Just good old-fashioned hand and mouth treatments as quoted. All that is my doing. When I came here there were two broads, both with saggy boobs, and almost toothless. They might or might not give what the customer had ordered and paid for. Few customers returned, and most of them had to wash up with antiseptic after their 'massages' because they were afraid of what they might have been exposed to.

"Now the marks come in. They tell me specifically what they want. I quote a firm price. They agree and they go into a nice private, clean room where a young girl or woman greets them and services them. No hassle. And they come back the next time they get horny.

"Me, I did all that. So no more 'holy shit!' I want a full partnership, Rambow. In writing. In this room and witnessed by a notary. I know one around the corner who's a regular, he'll be glad to come over now in return for an 'on the house' trick.

"Object, and you're on your own. I'll give you a phone number so you can arrange a truck for you to rent but that's it.

"I'm going to be busy here in my private office, with the door locked, doing bookkeeping chores. If the cops come, I say 'What's going on? I've been inside my office since, oh, about noon I guess.'

"You can tell any story you want. If I'm questioned, yes, the new girl was in the special room, someone had phoned and asked if she would be available in 15 minutes or so. I said she would, sent her there, and never left my office."

Rambow had listened, his face registering increasing disbelief in what he was hearing.

"I can't believe you'd turn on me this way, Gertie. After all I've done..."

"Shove it, Rambow. That's the way it is. My offer is a good one." She faced him directly, meeting his eyes.

"Rather than a paid employee, who might at any time depart for greener pastures, you'll have a partner who is vitally interested in keeping Happy Andings at the top of the Vegas massage parlor pile.

"And I'll even make a point of hiring a young farm girl now and then, so that you can dazzle them with your oral and physical charms. Just so long as you don't try shutting them up the permanent way if they object to your approach."

She sat down and waited. She knew that from here on the first one to speak would be the loser.

Rambow sat silently also but his nerve fractured first.

"If, and I stress if, Gertie, I agree, do I have your solemn word that you would never divulge a word of what accidentally happened earlier today? I mean your absolute promise?"

She had won.

"Of course you do, Gibbie. How could I say anything without jeopardizing my own situation?"

He made no move to get up.

"But this offer is time limited, Gibbie. It expires in 60 seconds flat."

She made a point of looking at her watch. A digital, it had no seconds' indicator but he didn't know that.

Time passed. No one moved or said anything.

Then, at what she guessed was about a minute or so later, he cleared his throat.

"It seems I have no choice. Partner." He attempted to add a smile to that concession but ended with a snarl halfway obliterated.

"Great, Gibbie. Let's shake on that."

He reluctantly took her hand and gave it a weak touch.

"So now that we have agreed, in the best fashion of true partners, I guess we should get busy on that truck and stuff."

She smiled internally. The old fraud was still trying to postpone the actual consummation, much like a shy virgin on her first date.

"Of course, that's right after I phone Joel, the notary, to draw up a partnership agreement and get it over here."

He looked defeated.

"Whatever you want, GG. But let's do it as fast as possible. I think it would be best to have her, the girl, out of here ASAP."

There was no need for words.

GG nodded, reached across her desk, and punched an outside line. She opened her top drawer, flipped open her directory, found the number, and punched it in.

"Joel, this is Gertie from Happy Andings. I have a little favor to ask, and also a favor to give.

"Here's what we need, Joel."

She spelled out clearly what she wanted, and what he would receive in lieu of a monetary fee.

He seemed satisfied.

Down the hall Tonto had accomplished the first of his tasks. He had arranged for his friend to deliver the truck at the alley entrance of HA.

He was to come in, give the key to Tonto, and receive his $50— "That's great, Tonto, I can really use the bread; 3 hours is fine."—plus an unexpected bonus of $10 for cab fare. Tonto had been planning on stiffing him for the cab fare but his inherent sense of fair play prevented that. He also sort of felt his $50 profit on the transaction was sufficient, with even more physical rewards to come, so there was no need to be greedy.

The second task, not part of GG's instructions, took a little longer.

But he was finally able to track down Bob, a known and talented thief, who owed him a favor for a freebie blowjob when Gertie had been away doing banking, and the masseuse Tonto supplied was definitely a second stringer, and pleased to be able to help HA's "assistant manager" with 'an important out-of-town client'.

He also had warned her the whole matter was confidential and made a zipping motion on his lips.

She had nodded and repeated the motion. Since then he had used her several times for his own needs and she still hadn't unzipped her lips, except to do necessary chores.

From Bob he was able to borrow one of the newer pencil-sized cameras based on the Bond-type movies.

He was assured by Bob that he had stolen it from a prosperous lawyer, who Bob felt sure wouldn't be using inferior cameras.

Bob said it would take up to 150 photos in light so low you could hardly see your hand in front of you.

Tonto thought Bob was laying it on pretty thick, but he knew that Bob had his eye, or more accurately his dick, on more free blowjobs, so Tonto felt confident that the tiny camera would serve his needs.

He planned to document the entire disposal operation, with plenty of shots of Gertie, the dead body, the dump location, and whatever else struck his fancy and would shoot at least recognizable —up to 150— pictures he felt would be useful at some time in the future for assuring his own pension plan.

A fellow had to always plan for the future.

Unfortunately, he had no pictures of the principal character in this melodrama, but he could think of no way to get Rambow to pose, other than walking up to him and saying, "Gee, boss, how be I take a few pictures of you around the dead broad's body?"

He thought that might be pushing the employer-employee relationship a little too far, so he decided to just settle on Gertie and the other disposal activities for the time being.

CHAPTER 9

"Are you interested in masseuses employed by a", the lieutenant looked down at the sheet he was holding, "Happy Andings massage parlor here in Vegas, Mr. Shant?"

As Shant started to answer, Pap intervened.

"Don't answer that, Mike." He looked at the cop, considerably larger than he was.

"Why do you want to know? He has rights, you know.

The lieutenant sighed. His tour was over in 16 minutes. Why hadn't he left early?

He looked at Shant, then at Pap.

"Sure he does. But I don't think I'm putting any of those rights in jeopardy, Mr...."

"Just Pap is fine, officer. I didn't really say you were, I was just making an announcement so all you guys in blue would know that we, my good friend and employer and renowned magazine writer Michael Shant, and me, were very aware of our rights, and would defend those rights to our last breath."

Shant moved forward slightly and rested on the chest high counter.

"Everything's okay, Pap." He looked at the cop. "You just asked a simple question, but I guess I also would like to know why."

"It's no secret, Mr. Shant. Our grapevine has turned up what appears to be a healthy interest in massage givers, especially those at the Happy Andings shop. All I was asking was why the interest, especially by someone from out of town."

"You haven't really answered my question, Lieutenant, but in the interests of getting this show on the road today, not next month, I'll answer your original query."

He turned to Pap, threw his arm around his shoulder, then looked at the cop behind the counter.

"Nothing very mysterious, although I hope you'll keep something of a lid on what I tell you." He asked the question with his eyes.

"If it's not anything that is or could be official police business, I'll certainly try to keep whatever you tell me confidential."

"Good enough. I'm a writer for a pretty big magazine published in Vancouver. BC, not Washington. My assignment is to do a story on one of Vegas's citizens, who apparently has interests in more than field.

"On the one hand he appears to be a fairly normal TV preacher. But my researchers, including Pap here, have uncovered what appears to be a solid connection from the TV pulpit to a fairly active massage parlor, and that of course affects my story."

The cop nodded.

"Okay, that sounds straightforward. I assume you can verify the magazine and your assignment from it?"

"Sure. Since I do a lot of work for this magazine I've noted it on my business card."

He pulled out a small black leather card holder and withdrew a card. "It has the mag name and address, including phone number, on it."

The cop took the card, looked at it, and nodded.

"Great. Could I ask the name of our wonderful citizen who is soon to enjoy magazine fame?"

Shant thought about that request.

"At this point I'm trying to keep our profile guy convinced that I'm doing a straight 'gee whiz' article on him. If he thinks I'm looking into some of his more interesting activities, it'll make my job, and those of both of my researchers, a lot more difficult."

He frowned.

"How about this? You give me a clue as to why the LVPD is interested in my innocuous interest in the Happy Andings, and I'll tell you who my lead character is."

Pap, until now dormant after his protection of their rights, piped up.

"Sounds like a deal to me, officer."

The cop looked at him, was about to say something, but changed his mind and looked back at Shant.

"I see no reason why we can't do that. In fact, if you were to check the noon local news, you'd probably understand our reasons anyway.

"A young woman's nude body was found earlier today in one of our local parks. The autopsy hasn't been completed yet, but it looks like she was murdered.

"Her body is in much better shape, no drug marks, no tattoos or any other gang stuff, than most Jane Does found. A little initial tracking shows she may recently have been employed at Happy Andings, although we haven't yet had any confirmation from the company.

"So when we started sniffing around, your name—mostly your activities—surfaced and I thought it might be useful to talk with you. Nothing more."

He looked at Pap.

"And I can promise no rubber hoses or any other infringements of your rights."

Pap grinned. He had won the legal battle.

"Now, how about your subject's name?"

"Fair enough," Shant said. "He's Gilbert Rambow, although evidently his surname is a contraction of the original French name."

The lieutenant frowned.

"Your subject is well known to some of us here at LVPD.

"Nothing illegal," he added hurriedly. "Just that his 'activities', as you described them, have attracted some attention.

"We know he's got probably a big slice of Happy Andings, and of course you know about his preaching stuff.

"He may even have interests beyond those, but we can't confirm. How about you, anything else turned up by your researchers"—he looked suspiciously at Pap as though doubting his ability to research anything— "or yourself?"

"Not yet. But we're all looking. My other researcher, her name's Alison Adams, and like Pap she lives here in Vegas, thinks she has a hint of something he may be into in the publishing field. Like you said, Lieutenant, nothing illegal in that, although my personal view is that a lot of publishers should be charged with grand theft against the poor freelancers like me who work long and hard for pittances."

The cop's smile increased as Shant's mock tirade continued.

"Strange. That's almost exactly what I feel towards politicians and bureaucrats."

"Don't forget bartenders who pour with their fingers, hell, their whole hands, in your drink," Pap added.

The cop paused, then looked at Shant.

"It seems that you, or at least your magazine, and the LVPD have a little in common regarding Mr. Rambow. My partner, he's off today, has been sort of keeping an open file on Rambow for quite a while.

"His mother—my partner's, not Rambow's—was talked into making a pretty big—for her— 'donation' to Rambow's church. It's got a weird name, and Steve, my partner, is pretty sure she was conned into it, but she claims it was voluntary and what she wanted to do."

"Not so voluntary?"

"Well, the old dear gets Social Security. Period. How can an older woman on a small pension afford to give some shouting preacher $1,000?

"Simple answer, she can't. But she won't say a bad word against Rambow or his 'church', so there's nothing we can do. But Steve is keeping a pretty close eye on Rambow.

"If you or your team" --he again gave a dead eye look at Pap— "should come up with anything, I know Steve would love to talk with you. Me too."

"How about a little sharing here, officer?"

Pap was eager to get back in the fray.

"If you guys uncover any info, not classified cop stuff, but of a more general nature, about Rambow's activities, maybe you could give me or Mike or Alison a call.

"After all, we came down here pretty quickly after you phoned and asked Mike if he could stop around. He didn't ask a lot of time-wasting questions, he—and me—headed down here pronto.

"That's good citizenship, isn't it? Yes, of course it is," he continued on without waiting for an answer. "So as a taxpayer and a citizen here in Las Vegas I think we should be able to expect at least some co-operation from the LVPD."

He looked directly at the cop.

"Shouldn't we?"

The cop laughed.

"If you had stopped talking half an hour ago, and given me a chance to answer, I would have said yes."

"What? You mean yes?"

Shant and the cop grinned at each other.

"Yes, I meant yes."

The cop pulled out his badge holder. On one side of it he had put a small card holder and he pulled one out.

"My name's Dan Southfield, Mr. Shant." He offered the card.

"Thanks. Mine's Michael Shant. Nice to meet you Dan. And I believe you have met my researcher Pap?"

Again the cop laughed.

"Yes, yes I have. And a pleasure all around.

"I'll tell my partner about your article, Mr., ah, Michael. If either of us trips over some good Rambow stuff, stuff which isn't actual cop stuff, maybe we could all"—he looked at Pap as though he was reconsidering the breadth of that offer— "get together for a drink and compare notes."

"That would be great, Dan. My cell number's on my card. Let me have it for a sec and I'll give you my motel number. There's a 24-hour receptionist so I should get any message pretty quickly."

The two men left the station and walked over to Pap's car.

"There, just like I told you, Mike. Nothing to it. A snap." He grinned widely,

"When you're with me in Vegas, amigo, you have nothing to worry about."

Shant laughed loudly. "Except you."

CHAPTER 10

"This place looks familiar. I think I've patronized it before," Pap said seriously.

"Considering that we're in Cindy's Bar, for what is probably the 97th time, I'm not surprised." Shant settled into the comfortable booth just back of the row of tables.

"Alison said she'd be here shortly," Shant said. "She was checking up on some gossip about our target."

Cindy herself was behind the bar, filling five drinks for a barmaid's order. She waved happily as she saw them, caught the barmaid's attention just as she turned to leave, and whispered something to her.

After delivering the drink order herself, and adroitly fending off two of the drinkers who made half-hearted grabs at her attractive behind, she came to their booth and smiled.

"Nice to see you two again. "The first round's on the house."

Just then Alison walked in, saw the men, and headed over.

"And I meant all three of you," Cindy smiled. "What can I get you all?"

Pap ordered a glass of beer with a tequila chaser, Shant said dark rum over ice and tap water, and Alison, a little flustered from arranging her chair, said she'd have a martini.

The three settled down, and after their drinks were delivered, took a moment to gather their thoughts.

"Okay, gang, who's going to jump in first?"

"Maybe I should bring Alison up to date on our little meeting with the LVPD?"

"Good idea, Pap. And I'll be here in case your sometimes-faulty memory should slip."

"It never slips. It may need a little oil, or more precisely some of that delicious Mexican lubricant better known as tequila, but that's the only maintenance it requires."

Shant smiled, took a drink, and leaned back into the comfortable cushions. With just a little more comfort he'd fall asleep.

Pap covered the meeting with Lt. Southfield, slightly embellishing the tale when he was describing his valiant and heroic battle to keep Shant's rights inviolate.

But on the whole Pap adequately summed up their experience with the cops, and Alison expressed appropriate approbation for Pap's exploits.

"With our past taken care, Alison, now you can have the floor to let us know what you've been doing. In a strictly research sense, of course."

She smiled.

"Sure. Not too much hard info, I'm afraid, but a couple of rumors and bits of gossip that may have some value." She took a quick drink.

"Probably the most interesting scrap I got, from a sort of sleazy bookstore way up on Paradise, a friend had given me the lead to it, might be about Rambow.

"The store owner or manager, whatever, was very willing to talk about both his clientele, who from what he said were one step above perversion, and his suppliers, who might even be on a lower step.

"As you've both figured out, the store specializes in hard core porno.

"Not just the usual girlie mags and posters, although they were also on view, but what in my limited experience I'd call manuals for grad porno students."

She paused in her monologue to take a drink.

"Anyway, the owner said that one of his better suppliers of that crap was a local publishing firm. He showed me one of their masterpieces. Not badly produced although the pictures looked a little amateurish.

"The company was Concise Urbane Manuals. Or CUM, for god's sake."

Both Shant and Pap laughed aloud.

"You both should be ashamed of yourselves.

"Anyway, the bookstore guy wasn't at all sure, but he sort of thought that CUM might be owned or operated, or both, by a local man who was also involved in other aspects of the 'adult entertainment' business, his words.

"Later I got thinking about it. We already have a neat slogan on another shop, that 'Happy Andings Relaxation Direct- Open Now', or 'Hardon' on the massage parlor.

"And you're going to love this. Besides that cute slogan, there's another one they use on giveaway matches and memo pads. It's 'Cum On In To Us'."

Alison paused and looked at both men.

They both looked uncertain, then Pap literally jumped up from his chair and shouted "I've got it!"

Shant shook his head. "I don't. What are you two yahoos so worked up about?"

"COITUS, my boy. Coitus," Pap smiled.

Shant looked chagrined, then smiled. "Sure, of course."

"And who likes those crappy suggestive slogans, you guys? None other than our pal Rambow."

Shant pondered for a moment.

"It's pretty thin, Alison, but I think you may be on to something. The two slogans at the massage parlor could just be the masterpieces of a somewhat addled sense of male humor.

"But when you add in the publishing name, it hangs together."

Shant reached into his jacket pocket and pulled out a small ruled notepad.

"So, let's see what we have.

"At the top is our target. That's GR.

"First line below is his religious operation, World International Moral Protection Society. WIMPS.

"Next we have the Happy Andings whack parlor. HARDON.

"Possibly next, a publishing enterprise that at least dips its toes into hard core porn. CUM."

Shant sat back and regarded his notes.

"The common denominator is obviously someone's liking for company names that are at least descriptive, or suggestive."

"Could just indicate a crazed copywriter lose in Las Vegas, and paying off big loans to knee breakers by writing slogans for as many companies as he can corral," Pap said.

Shant looked at him.

"Yes, it could. What do you think are the odds of that?"

Pap ruminated for a moment.

"Well, to be honest, I'd have to say about 6,000 to 1. Against, of course."

"And I agree with those odds." Alison chimed in. "While I agree it could just be a wonky copywriter, I think it's more reasonable to attribute them to one common owner. And I use the word common in its lowest meaning."

"Does that mean, dear Alison, that your fondness for friend Rambow is waning?"

"Fondness, shit. Excuse my French, but whatever pleasant feeling I may have felt because of his so-called religious efforts has totally, irretrievably, and irrevocably disappeared."

"Well spoken, Alison. I agree," said Pap. He nodded his head.

"And now there's another factor involved," he continued. "Although we certainly can't charge him with anything—yet—involving that massage girl's possible murder, there is a link to Happy Andings, and we all know who ramrods that outfit."

"By ramrod, old pard, I assume you mean boss? My cowboy idioms may be a little weak," Shant said.

"That's exactly what I meant, boss. Where do we go from here?"

Shant nursed his half-full drink, rotating it as he checked that the glass had no leaks. Evaporation in Cindy's Bar was apparently a real problem. He'd have to mention it to her.

"I think it's time for another powwow with Rambow.

"How be you and me try him out, Pap? Alison, maybe you could slip into your exec secretary role again for a few minutes, and make an appointment with him, ASAP. Then you could 'carry on', just like the hilarious

English comedy series, and see if you can uncover anything more specific on Rambow's activities that we should know about, or anything new that crops up. You're doing a fine job, young lady."

"Thanks, Michael. This is really interesting research, far better than working in some hushed library where the old maid librarian shushes you if you breathe too hard.

"I'll see if Cindy will let me use her office phone again. It probably doesn't help your serious writer image if in the background someone's shouting 'Give us another round of drinks, and have that great looking broad with the beautiful ass serve us'."

She went to the bar and spoke to Cindy, who nodded her head immediately.

"This time, Pap, I want to start playing hardball. Not end game yet, but certainly trying to have Rambow feel a little heat. I've found sometimes that when I turn up the heat on a subject, it brings things to a boil faster."

"Great. I love that idea, boss."

"Just remember, Pap, that we're not yet far enough along to make hard accusations. That might blow up the whole article.

"Try to restrain yourself, partner. Follow my lead. If you see an opening, go for it, as long as you're not closing any doors completely. In short, a modified version of what our new friend Lt. Southfield would easily recognize as 'good cop, bad cop'. Clear?"

"As the bottom of my empty glass. It's my round, let me order."

Pap stood up and shouted, "Another round here, barkeep, and if possible, have that great looking broad with the beautiful ass serve us." Pap smiled at Cindy to show it was a joke.

"Christ, Pap, you'll get us cut off."

But Cindy herself served them, and smiling, said to Pap, "Does my ass meet your requirements?"

Shant and she laughed, and Pap had the grace to blush.

CHAPTER 11

"I thought maybe you had given up on my article, Mr. Shant. Haven't heard from you for a couple of days so thought you might have returned to the coast."

"Not a chance, Mr. Rambow. I needed some additional research and my researchers have been gathering that."

"More research? I don't understand. I sort of thought that you had enough information after our first interview?"

"Oh, hardly. For a cover story in 'It's Your Money', read by literally hundreds of thousands of readers of average high incomes, we have to have an article researched in depth. Far more than just an hour or so casually talking, Mr. Rambow."

Shant felt that a little grease might make Rambow's wheels slide easier. What a ridiculous metaphor!

"Well, if you feel it's really necessary, Mr. Shunt."

"I do, and it's Shant. Let's pick up on the subject of your extensive business enterprises here in Las Vegas." Shant acted like he was referring to his pocket notebook.

"What exactly are they?"

"Business enterprises? Perhaps you are referring to the World International Moral Protection Society, our religious association, as a business? But it's not really. It's a church, and even acknowledged as such by the good old I.R.S. And you know how carefully they check into that kind of thing."

"Not really, but I'm glad to see that those bureaucraps are really doing something.

"But it wasn't WIMPS so much, Mr. Rambow. But don't you have other interests, or however you want to define them?"

Rambow acted confused by the question.

"I am still confused by what enterprises or activities you're talking about, Mr. Shant. I may have small interests in a couple of local shops, those designed to help lower income people buy clothes and such, and even a food bank shop, but aside from a small—and I do mean small, half the size it was before those feds allowed lunatics to be in charge of finances—brokerage account I'm at a loss to know what you're referring to."

"I certainly agree with your description of the bandits put into high places formerly by a man whose sole occupation was teaching other lawyers how to prosper. As though what was needed was more ambulance chasers.

"Who was it said, 'First thing to do, kill all the lawyers?"

"I know the quotation, and agree with it completely, but the author escapes me, Mr. Shant. But back to these other businesses, of which I'm sorry to say I haven't a clue."

To hell with it. This was more than enough pussyfooting around the subject.

"Well, for one example, how about your interest in Happy Andings, the well-known massage parlor?"

There was a full minute of silence. Rambow looked shocked. Finally, he regained some control.

"Massage parlor? While I completely agree that each individual should be free to pursue any interest which is not illegal, immoral, or fattening"—he smiled broadly to show that even as a WIMPS preacher he could enjoy being something of a man of the world—and folded his hands in front of him.

Probably praying for a sudden typhoon or hurricane to end this meeting. Well, Mr. Rambow, not quite yet.

"Are you saying, Mr. Rambow, that you do not own a large portion of Happy Andings. Maybe if I recited a couple of their slogans it might refresh your memory.

"Here's one: Happy Andings-Relaxation Direct, Open Now. Or more simply perhaps, HARDON. A very creative copywriter created a very cute, and memorable, slogan.

"Does that ring your memory bell?"

"Certainly not, Mr. Shunt. And I object most strongly to this type of interview, more designed for lowlifes than church officials like me."

"I had no intention of causing you embarrassment, Mr. Rambow. Or alarm. And it's still Shant, with an A. But my researchers have found that legally the ownership of Happy Andings is listed in the Nevada State documents as Gilbert Rambow. Not you?"

Rambow pressed the blue button on his phone. It was apparently answered immediately as he put the receiver to his ear.

"BB, ah, Beatrice? What time was my appointment with the mayor?

"What mayor? What the fu..., ah, the mayor of Las Vegas, of course." How stupid can she be? "No, not here, I was to meet him somewhere else. The Pickwick Club, I think it was."

BB or Beatrice was evidently having a problem with her appointment book.

Rambow looked at Rambow, shook his head, mouthed the words "It's hard to find good help". He jiggled the phone button.

"Can you hurry up and get me that information, BB. I have Mr. Shunt, Shant, here in the office and I know that I'm now overdue with the Police Chief for my appointment. What? No, damnit, not the Police Chief, I said the Mayor. The mayor, for christ's sake! Well, BB, stup, er, call me back as soon as you find that appointment time."

He slammed the receiver down.

"Sometimes I wonder why I do it all. I hire poorly trained women, try to give them whatever help I can"— and lots of head, I expect, Shant thought— "and look at how they repay me.

"I've had that appointment with the Police...the Mayor, for at least two weeks, and now BB, Beatrice, my secretary, can't even locate what time it's for.

"Like I said, it's very difficult" (Shant noticed he didn't use the word hard again; Freudian correction?) "to find and keep good employees. Do you have that problem up, where you come from, Mr. Shunt?"

Shant decided to ignore his rantings. And his use of an incorrect name.

"What about the Happy Andings massage parlor? Do you want me to quote you as saying 'I have absolutely no financial interest in it'? Should one of us contact the Nevada department concerned and tell them their official records are in error?"

"Must you keep harping on that insignificant little business? Sometimes my business manager makes little investments on my behalf and fails to notify me of what he's done. Actually, that's his job, I guess, to do investments without bothering me..."

"What your business manager's name? And his address? One of my researchers can get this cleared up in a flash. Maybe I should get that name and address from BB, or Beatrice, and let you get off to your appointment with the Police Chief, or the mayor, or whomever. How does that sound?"

Rambow slammed his right fist onto the desk so hard that he flinched in pain.

"Bullshit! Let's just drop this whole fucking interview, Mr. Shunt. You can find somebody else to feature on the cover of whatever your magazine's called."

"I can certainly understand your reluctance to pursue this interview at this extremely busy time, Mr. Rambuw." Childish, but see how he likes his name mangled.

"But I must say that this project has proceeded too far already to just scrap it.

"If you do want to postpone our interviews, I can certainly understand that, what with all your civic meetings your secretary has lost track of.

"If you are saying that you don't want to participate any further, I can also understand that the glare of publicity might be a little too strong for a dedicated churchman.

"But regardless, Mr. Rambow, this project will continue, with or without any further active participation by you. That would just mean that the final published article would depend greatly on information my researchers could dig up."

Had Rambow flinched a bit on that last phrase? Why? Maybe it was just Shant's imagination.

"Let's let the interviews rest for awhile."

"Interviews? You actually mean plural, Shant? There's absolutely no way I'd even dream of meeting with you more than once more, and that would be just a cleanup interview, answering relevant questions about WIMPS. Nothing more. That is my main activity, saving souls."

And releasing pent-up hardons, according to your Happy Andings ads, Shant smiled to himself.

"So, if you want to schedule one final interview, perhaps you could phone my personal secretary, Beatrice Brownsley, and make an appointment. I may have my lawyer present, just to ensure you don't accidentally misquote me in your article."

"Okay, Mr. Rambow. That would be great, the more the merrier. I expect to be doing research myself, along with my two colleagues, so I'll be tied up for the rest of the week. But early next week I'll get in touch with BB and see what we can set up. Let's hope she handles my meeting time a little better than she did today with your civic officials.

"Oh, incidentally, I have a meeting scheduled tomorrow with a lieutenant at LVPD. Would you like me to pass on your regards to his chief, the one you may have had an appointment with today?"

If Rambow had been armed, Shant would have ducked for cover. He was incapable of intelligent speech but it was obvious that any warm feelings for the magazine writer who would help him to be even better known locally had completely evaporated.

On the way out Shant made a point of saying hello, and goodbye, to the secretary stationed at a large desk in front of Rambow's office.

"My, what a lovely pair of earrings you're wearing. Are they a family heirloom?"

The woman, who looked to be in her late 40s or early 50s, was quite tall, probably close to 6 feet, and had very bright red hair, or a wig. But with Shant's genuine compliment she lit up like a birthday cake.

"Yes, they were my grandmother's. They are nice, aren't they?"

"My name is Shant, Michael Shant, and I am to be phoning you next week for another appointment with Mr. Rambow."

"I do hope you won't wait that long, Michael. I know you're from out of town. If you'd like a long time local to help you get, ah, acclimatized, call me anytime. I live alone and it wouldn't matter what time it was."

She pulled a business card out of a plastic container on her desk.

"Here. Michael.' She drawled out the pronunciation into three syllables. "I'll just put my home cell number on the back. Do call me. Whenever."

"Thanks, Beatrice. I may."

"Make it BB, Mikey. Everyone does."

Shant figured that if he stood around any longer, she'd be curled up in his lap and purring.

"Beatrice! Are you talking to him? Get your as...get in here. Now!"

Apparently, BB wasn't fazed by the boss's anger. She smiled at Shant, threw him a four-fingered 'see you later' goodbye wave, and vibrated into Rambow's inner sanctum.

Outside, Shant stopped to get a paper at a newsstand.

The newsie was an older man, and looked like he knew where some if not all of the bodies were buried. (Probably including Jimmy Hoffa.)

"How's business?"

"Like always, amigo, enough to keep me out of a soup kitchen, not enough to buy me some pussy on a cold night."

Shant laughed.

"Been in this spot long?"

"Only about 16 years. Much longer and the city will owe me a pension for being a tourist attraction."

"See much of the reverend from inside?"

"You mean Rambow? Only when I'm at the Diamond Horseshoe down on Fremont. I go there to make my $2 show bets because the waitresses always seem to be friendly, even when I can only tip them every second week. Some of the Fremont joints have broads who act like you're real dirt if you don't give them a fin tip for each free drink. Fuck them."

"Rambow?"

"Oh yeah, forgetting what the fuck I was talking about, it's a sign of getting old, I guess. Shouldn't complain though, a lot of the guys I grew up with around here didn't have to worry about old age, most never made it past their 20s before they were gunned down or ended up buried alive in desert sand graves. I drive my old lady out into the desert sometimes, just to shut her up, and it's like I'm visiting a big open cemetery for the wise guys I once knew.

"But yeah, Rambow. He's there as often as I am, checking the active races. But for some reason he's always used a bookie, even the DH has a big race book with plenty of tellers. Probably because a bookie will let him run a tab a lot longer and a lot bigger than the casino would.

"The only diff is that I'm betting 2 bucks, and Rambow's often putting 5 centuries, sometimes a lot more, on horses that should be pulling rickshaws, not racing."

"Does he ever win?"

"You couldn't prove it by me. Lately I've seen his bookie, a big SOB named Klassen, keeping an eye on him pretty close. That treatment usually means one of two things: the bookie wonders where his client is getting all the good tips. Or he's starting to be a little nervous about how much the client owes him." He paused to relight his cigar stub.

"With the reverend, as you jokingly call him, I think it's the second thing."

"Jokingly?"

"Everyone, except his 'flock', I guess, knows he the bread behind Happy Andings, that's a whack parlor downtown. Guaranteed to please, if you know what I mean. And the word on the street is that if he didn't own it Rambow would be one of its best customers.

"Trouble is, according to some of the girls who work there, or did, is that he gets into real bad rages, you know the kind, where he does things he prob'ly wouldn't do ordinarily. It's like some drunks, nice as pie one minute, grade double-A pricks the next."

"Yeah. Is that all he has, I mean owns or at least runs.?" This guy was like a fountain of information. Shant wondered if he should hire him full time.

"Not what the street guys and broads say. He has some piece, maybe a big one, of a whack-off publisher in the east end. You know, they put out that hard porno stuff, everything from one guy on three broads to three guys on one broad. A lot of girl-on-girl porno too."

"Seems a little strange for a so-called preacher."

"Ain't it just? But he don't waste time preaching at me, and that's all I care about."

A car pulled in to the curb. The driver leaned over and shouted through the open passenger window. "Hey, Sid, put the usual in a bag for me, willya?"

Sid moved to fill whatever the usual was. Shant pulled out a ten, gave it to Sid, who looked at it. "You want change?"

"Nope, it's yours, Sid. Nice meeting you, hope to see you again."

"Anytime. Thanks. I'll put it on a sure winner." He laughed and grabbed a bag.

So the rumor that Rambow had more interests than preaching to a bunch of superstitious 'believers' appeared on the money.

Massage parlor owner, and heavy user, porno publisher, big but losing hors races gambler. Almost a classic story of how to be a 'bad guy'. In Rambow's case, in sheep's clothing, assuming his flock qualified for the sheep label, and at the moment that was about a 50/1 bet.

CHAPTER 12

"I've got some news. Hope everybody else does too. Everybody get seated.

Shant dropped into his seat in the back booth, now automatically reserved by Cindy as some of or all the gang was there almost every night.

"Me too," Alison responded.

"Sort of, for me," Pap said, a little despondently as it looked like he was the only one without a red-hot news flash.

"Sure, boss." Alison slipped off her sweater and hung it loosely on the back of the booth. As there were no clear separations between the seats it immediately slid down and lay in a heap.

She looked at it, smiled, ignored it, and moved in closer to the table, empty at the moment. Shant had just caught Cindy's attention and held up three fingers. She had nodded and started preparing their first round.

"I've found a great contact at the Diamond Horseshoe Casino. He bets there, small time compared to what he said Rambow does, and moves around a lot in and at the race and sports betting books. He knows our great friend the Rev Rambow—by sight—quite well.

"He told me that Rambow makes nearly all his big horseracing bets through a bookie, a guy name Big Bobbie Klassen, although he's pretty short, not much over 5 feet. But he's solid, looks like one of those football guys whose job it is to eliminate the opposition players.

"Even though the racing books at the DH are right there, for some reason Rambow goes the bookie route."

"It might be because a bookie will usually run a tab, whereas most casinos require cash on the line for any bets."

Pap was happy to contribute a little inside info to the group, today he didn't really have that much 'scoop' information to share.

"Yeah, that's what Sid my contact said," Shant added. "And normally a bookie will back up a large bet, betting through the book as insurance. If they didn't, a 100/1 longshot might wipe them out."

The drinks had arrived and Alison paused to take a taste.

"Mmm, good. Okay, back to work.

"Sid said that while Klassen extends the credit, it certainly isn't his money. The bookies arrange a credit line, just like a respectable businessman would, with a mob-run bank.

"Sid said the current bookie rates are between 10 and 15 percent."

"Not bad. Maybe I could get one of those loans," Pap said.

"That rate is a week, Pap."

"A week! How do those bookies handle that? That's about, ah, 50, no 500, percent a year. Jesus christ!"

"Sid told me they manage to pay that—or disappear from earthly view—by charging their clients, the bettors like Rambow, even more. He wasn't sure but he thought that Rambow, because of his notoriety with his several business enterprises, not likely including the WIMPS stuff, might qualify for a 'preferred' rate. He figures that would be about 7 for 5. He explained that to me.

"A client, like Rambow, would have to pay back 7 bucks for every 5 of credit. Or, and he figured it out for me, about 40 percent a week."

Pap's mouth literally dropped open.

"You mean he would be paying a rate of," he closed his eyes in thought, "about 2,000 percent? Incredible."

Shant looked surprised. "That is a helluva lot of interest. But Sid seemed pretty sure of those figures."

Alison chipped in. "I asked my contact the same question, Michael. He said that most bookie-client deals are made orally, very few bookies have legal loan documents that they carry around. So Joe, my contact, in his travels—his job is 'floating security', he's not anchored in any one department or area—gets to overhear a lot of deals being negotiated and transacted. He's confident of the data he gave me."

Both men sat back and each took a healthy slug from their glasses.

"That's great info, Alison and Pap. Really good." He patted her gently on the shoulder. She wished he'd explore a little more 'woman', a little less 'uncle' territory. But time for those thoughts later.

"Thanks, boss. And I have to give credit where's it due. Pap was responsible for introducing me to Joe. Without that I likely wouldn't have gotten any hard info from him."

Pap smiled, and he too patted Alison, although somewhat lower than her shoulder. She just smiled.

"Okay, now some news from me," Shant said.

"Oh, Michael, I did have a little more. Do you want it now or later?"

"Now, now. Carry on, secret agent 007."

"This is actually the most interesting to us part. Joe said he knows this for sure, thanks to a one-sided shouting match conducted in hushed tones by Klassen to Rambow just outside the men's bathroom.

"As near as he can remember, here's the key part: 'Look, sport, as of the last race you owe me just under sixty big ones. That means I owe my bank the same amount. Way too much.

'You'd better get that amount reduced to fucking near zero, and by next Monday when my loan's due. Clear?'

"Joe said Rambow just nodded, said he had a bunch of cash coming in this weekend, and he'd get Klassen straightened out long before Monday. Klassen just nodded, said 'You'd better, Rambow, this is the only notice you'll get'."

"Not too much in the way of good customer relations there. Did Joe feel Klassen had made a definite 'my way or the highway' threat? Or more of a gentle 'past due' notice?" Shant looked at Alison but Pap replied first.

"Based on my experiences, I'd say that a bookie like Klassen, with something in the neighborhood of sixty grand owing him, would not be passing the time of day. That was a definite threat."

Alison nodded. "Just what Joe said."

All three sat back and refreshed with a drink from their rapidly-emptying glasses. Shant turned his head, couldn't see Cindy but did catch the eye of their short-skirted waitress and circled his hand over their glasses.

The blonde smiled and mouthed "You got it."

"The plot thickens," said Shant. "Our hero is deeply in hock to a guy who probably issues threats only when he intends to carry them out. But Rambow says he'll have a bundle of cash within just a few days. Where's he getting it? Was that just a stall tactic? Or is his world coming apart?"

Conversation paused while the waitress served their drinks. Pap watched appreciatively as she had to lean a little forward to put Alison's drink in front of her. But in his new self-awarded role as elder gentleman, he confined his thoughts and actions to the mental. Both Shant and Alison were impressed.

As soon as the waitress left, however, his role dissipated. "Wow. Did you see those legs? Must have been 5 feet long. Each of them! Beautiful."

Shant grinned. "Didn't notice." The other two rolled their eyes, indicating they didn't for one second believe him.

"Anyway, moving on, I also have a new tidbit for us.

"From Sid, my news vendor source, we now have pretty solid confirmation that Rambow is involved in a porn publishing operation. It does the whole gamut, everything that's fit to print. If you **really** believe in freedom of the press.

"But even allowing for a lucrative market for porno products, it's hard to imagine Las Vegans spending a hundred grand or more by this coming weekend on pictures of a nurse-doctor photo fest.

"Where would Rambow be able raise that kind of money so quickly?"

No one spoke. All three tried to imagine a Rambow fund-raiser of that magnitude.

"Not from the whack parlor," Pap said. "A nice steady profit, maybe, but no sudden surges like that."

The other two looked at him closely but apparently he wasn't trying for a labored pun.

"The only possible place would be his church activities. But it would have to be something planned ahead, you'd think." Alison sat back, her money raising ideas exhausted.

"But I agree the church is the logical answer," Shant said. "It's the only possible source. Maybe he's been running an appeal for poor orphans somewhere and he figures the money will pour in over the next few days."

"But he never mentioned anything like that in the two interviews we've had," Pap said, "and knowing the creep I think it's a sure thing he would have been blabbing about anything like that, showing us what a wonderful benefactor he was. Don't you, Mike?"

Shant slowly nodded his head. "Yeah, I do, Pap."

There was only the sound of the jukebox at the far end of the bar. Someone had jammed it with coins and it continued to roll out sad songs about a cowboy and his horse, or his lost love, or his dear dead mother. Didn't cowboys ever laugh?

Alison sat forward.

"I've never had any contact with that church thing, the WIMPS. Maybe I could go there, looking like a prospective new member, one with lots of bucks but not too many brains, and see if I can get someone talking about their very worthy charity events."

Shant looked at her, then shook his head.

"A good idea, but no. I don't want you involved at the church, we may need you later for something else where your little miss innocent but really rich act would be useful."

He sat for a moment.

"But you could do something by phone. How be you try that same scheme but just on the phone? If there is a big harvesting of the church flock scheduled soon you should be able to get some dope on it. Up for that?"

"Absolutely. If Cindy will let me use her private office again, away from weeping cowboys, maybe I can find something out right now."

She got to her feet and quickly walked over to where Cindy was totalling some figures on a ledger sheet. The two women talked briefly, then Cindy laughed and pointed to her closed office door. Alison was through it quickly.

The men nursed their drinks, Shant lost in thought, Pap keeping a close eye on the miniskirted waitress, especially when a multiple order had her bending over a table.

A few minutes later Alison returned, looking dejected. She slumped into her seat.

"Nothing. I spoke to a very friendly and talkative woman named Beatrice. She went into incredible detail on all the good WIMPS did, righting so many wrongs that there can't be many left.

"But after all the BS the results were zero.

"While the church always welcomes new members, and especially new contributions, noting special is underway right now. But she assured me that next month I'd have several opportunities to get rid of some cash.

"Sadly, I had to tell her that Prudence Right— me—was just leaving for a South African leper colony, and would check in on my return."

Shant said, "Thanks, Alison. For now, we know that Rambow needs a lot of money, and he has assured his main creditor that all will be taken care of before next Monday.

"As the fortune tellers often say, time will tell."

CHAPTER 13

Rambow hoped that Klassen would be elsewhere. But he had to get a bet down on the 5th at Aqueduct, he knew he had the winner in the 11-horse field.

He had made it through most of the casino, was almost into the race book, where bookies rarely hung around except to make covering bets, but his luck ran out.

"Got my money, Rambow?"

"Oh, hello, Klassen. It's only Friday. We agreed on Monday, did you forget?"

"Forget that some deadbeat asshole owes me over sixty-plus grand? How dumb you think I am, Rambow, like some of your whack-off broads at the Happy Andings?"

Rambow was tempted to honestly answer that question but common sense prevailed. He said nothing.

"Well, I ain't, preacher. I expect your tab cleared up first thing Monday. In full. Or you know the 'or else'. One of Goldie's special masseurs will give you a real massage, one you won't ever forget."

Rambow swallowed. He had seen a couple of Goldie's enforcers. They looked like someone had planted a ponderosa pine 25 years ago, and it had grown into the mob enforcer.

"No, I haven't forgotten. I'll have it in full first thing Monday. What's the exact amount?"

"You ain't thinking of something fancy like writing me a check, are you?"

Rambow shook his head vigorously.

"Well, don't. I operate the same as your whackers do, cash before the happy endings."

Klassen laughed at his joke, then slapped Rambow firmly on the shoulder. Although quite short Klassen was built like a fire plug. Small head, no neck, just a squat heavyset body.

The slap just about keeled Rambow over but he regained his composure and his upright position by grabbing onto the nearest table where sports bettors could toss a coin and then make their intelligent bets.

"What was the exact amount again, BB?"

Klassen reached into the inside pocket of his size 52 sports jacket and pulled out a dog-eared sheet of notepaper.

"What's your name again? Oh yeah, you're the preacher man who also gives sinners those great whack jobs. Rambow, isn't it?"

Klassen guffawed loudly as he appreciated his humor, humor that only he laughed at.

He straightened out the sheet, then had to reverse it. He pulled it in closer. He needed glasses but of course his vanity prevented them, so anything he read—not very much—had to be held no more than 2 inches from his eyes.

After mumbling a few incoherent words, and again reversing the sheet, he found what he was looking for. No name, just the initials HA, apparently in honor of the massage parlor where he enjoyed cheapie hand jobs because of his banking relationship with Rambow. Even the amount had been lined through several times and new figures entered, so it took him a few moments to get the current number.

"Looks like 214700."

"What! Impossible. The total is just over 100, you know that."

Klassen laughed and looked up.

"Oh yeah, I musta added in a tip for Susie at your place, she's got great hands. Tell her I said so. She'll be glad to hear from a satisfied customer."

He used a very dirty fingernail to trace a line or two down on the sheet.

"Here we are, sport. 122500."

"That can't be, BB. When we talked a couple of days ago it was just 115 grand."

"So what cave you been living in, Rambow? Never heard of interest? Or late payment penalties? Just think of friendly Klassen like your local bank, where those pricks are always ripping people off every chance they get."

"Shit, if you keep adding stuff on, I'll never get it cleared off."

Klassen chortled. "So? How you think I'm going to stay in operation if I can't grow my business? Again, just like those suits in your local bank. Their motto: 'Screw them once. Then screw them again.' You want me to act different than those crooks?"

Rambow pulled out a classy notebook and withdrew what looked like a solid silver pen.

"I'm going to jot those figs down, Klassen. I assume they'll be still valid on Monday?"

"Valid? You mean good? It's against our bankers' union rules, Rambow, but I'll make an exception for you because of your lovely ladies and their super soft hands.

"Yeah, okay, that's the number, but only till noon on Monday. One minute past and that figure will jump like a fly on a hot stove.

"Even if we hafta collect from your estate."

He laughed loudly again and left to pay his respects to a tall brunette cocktail waitress he thought was intrigued by his boyish charm.

She thought he was asshole number 1.

Rambow moved into the race book area. He looked up at the TV screens showing tracks around the country where there was racing today.

The 4th at Aqueduct had finished and the official payouts for the various wagers were shown. Beside it a timer showed the minutes to the next race: 12. Plenty of time to check his figures and get that winning bet down.

He slid into a corner where no one else was standing. Furtively he plucked some bills from a side pocket, then pulled several more from his pants pocket, ending by reaching deep into an inside pocket for a few more.

If Klassen saw the mother lode he'd grab them in a flash.

The bills were wadded and scrunched up. He started to straighten them, counting as he went.

"Five, six, seven, eight, nine, ten, plus about three and a half in my hidden wallet. I'd better keep 10, no 20, out for tips and the car valet. Just in case, although I'm positive that Classy Dreamer has a lock on it."

He folded the bills into a relatively neat bunch.

He looked up at the odds shown behind each horse's number. Still 4 minutes to go. And number 9, Classy Dreamer, showed 16. That meant his four grand and a bit would return somewhere about $60,000. That would come in very handy until he got the phones busy back at the WIMPS office.

Rambow normally didn't like longshots, and anything that went off at more than 8 or 10 to 1 he considered a longshot.

But he had been talking yesterday via Skype with a fellow preacher who had his church in NYC, fairly close to Aqueduct, and thus captured the occasional trainer or jock who was so desperate that he sought financial salvation any place.

The NYC preacher had formed a sort of friendship, insofar as a 'bible believing' preacher—at least to his flock—could ever be friends with an atheist trainer whose vocabulary consisted about 95% of the popular 4 letter words.

The trainer, needing some spiritual support, had let slip that he knew about a boat race the next day at the track.

Even though Rambow wasn't much of a sportsman he knew that a boat race was a fixed race, where either the favorite would lose, or a longshot would win, due to skullduggery on the part of at least two—probably several—trainers and/or jocks. Now days such fixes were rare indeed. Better regulation, and more on-track cameras, served to limit them to trainers and jocks who had literally nothing left to lose, even if the race was discovered and they were banned from racing for a long time, perhaps even a lifetime suspension.

In return for a modified 'blessing', the trainer had given up the race number and the supposed winner. But only when the preacher had promised to share it only with friends far from the track, using only satellite betting so the local bookie odds wouldn't take a big hit.

The satellite bets would affect the track odds, but local bookies normally used the last-shown odds before the start of the race. (And of course the NYC preacher couldn't be seen standing in a betting line at a racetrack. His flock might be shocked.) Sometimes that worked against them, but often they used the odds to their advantage when they had decreased dramatically with heavy after post last minute big bets.

And in consideration of Rambow agreeing to sharing with him a really responsive sucker list of charity contributors, he had cut him in on the apparent windfall.

The board showed less than 1 minute. He hurried to the "Big Bets" line where apparently no one else had the winner in their pocket. It was empty.

He counted out his bills.

"Gimme 4,250- no, 4 grand even—screw the valet if he lost--on number 9 in the 5th at Aqueduct."

The cashier, thinking of the easy cutie he had lined up for later due to his wife's absence up state at her mother's--he hoped she'd decide to stay there for good—smoothly counted the bills, punched in the ticket, and when it popped up gave it Rambow.

The odds board now showed 18. Great, he'd cash in well over 70 big ones.

Ordinarily he'd stay to watch the race but he had urgent business back at the office. He'd get the result later on his computer.

CHAPTER 14

"Bertha, is the email list for 'The Word' right up to date?"

Big Bertha, lover of fine convoluted editorials in the WIMPS newsletter, especially those about chastity, virtue, and other misnamed feminine traits, also loved giving head to her hero, Gibbie Rambow.

And occasionally, when the preacher was able to convince her of the necessity for pleasuring a big potential convert and contributor, she allowed that she could make exceptions to her unwritten—and usually unfollowed—rule of sticking to one penis at a time.

But BB had to be careful. And fast. Not in the performance of her extra-curricular duties, but merely getting there first.

The WIMPS receptionist was a hot competitor.

Susie was a real shortie, and at 28 'just a kid', but she had learned fast. She was chubby with stringy blonde hair, and because of her awkward lisp she had few male friends.

None, in fact, so when given the opportunity to try out her female skills on the big boss she lost no time in practicing, she got right into the main event.

She had quickly learned that her sloppy typing efforts, coupled with multiple accidents with computers—"I didn't know you had to unplug the damn things before you moved them"—were a detriment to job advancement.

But a little physical activity on the job more than compensated for those problems.

And like a striking hawk, she was always ready to do battle with BB, even though outweighed and out-heighted by the large woman.

She weighed the situation at the moment. While the boss looked distraught, and definitely in need of some succor, he didn't even glance at her when he entered the office. So she bided her time, checking her Facebook page to see if anyone had yet responded to her "young, attractive, lonely blonde" blog.

BB straightened up from shoving a bunch of "payment overdue" notices into the bottom drawer of her desk. She had firm instructions to "file them", and that meant getting out of sight.

She knew better than putting them in the garbage. Rambow had once seen a split garbage bag on the curb, and displayed prominently were several large red-print "Past Due" letters.

Since that loud reprimand she had simply stuffed them into some handy empty drawer.

"Yes, Gibbie, I updated it yesterday. Do you need it?"

"Most urgently, BB. We need to get out a special "Your church is in desperate need of funds to maintain our overseas missions.""

And angry bookies.

"How much do we need, Gibbie?" She was unaware of any missions, either overseas or domestic, but didn't feel it was her job to question the boss.

"A lot, BB. A whole lot. And faster than a teenager comes when he's stroked."

BB loved it when Gibbie was able to introduce some raunchy sex talk but clothed in nice respectable language. She liked the images but didn't want to be clobbered with vulgarity. She had her standards.

She adjusted her bra to best display her ample breasts. That was something that bitch Susie couldn't do. She had almost nothing to display. What Gibbie saw in her....

He looked pretty impatient so she felt she should stick to business.

"Could you at least give me a very rough idea of what we need, Gibbie?"

"Look, BB, I don't have the time for a discussion. Get on it, raise as much as you can, and as quickly as possible.

"Suggest to the members that they send in money orders. Charging to a credit card is okay but we get stuck with the fucking extortionate charges those pricks levy."

She knew that he was really in some kind of jam. He rarely used such rough language with her. Maybe with that slut Susie, but never, well, maybe when he was approaching the final moments of his physical pleasure with BB, but hardly ever at any other time.

She went out to her desk, and caught Susie peeking into Gibbie's office.

"What are you doing there?"

BB was technically in charge of the office, although Susie, since she had started 'doing things' with the boss, had ignored protocol and acted pretty damned independent.

BB would love to find some excuse to get her fired but knew it would have to be something really major.

Susie had been having rather frequent 'meetings' with Gibbie, and even though his office door was always closed tight during these meetings, from the sounds she could hear she knew that the miserable slut was doing something indecent with him.

Now Susie just looked at her and turned her back to walk to her own desk, which as always looked like a tornado had blown through; papers, pens, pencils, used Kleenexes, bits of yesterday's lunch, all littered the desk.

When Susie actually used her computer, without mistakenly dumping it on to the floor, she simply brushed her hand and swept away most of the debris.

If challenged about this gross behavior: "That's why we have janitors. They need jobs too, you know."

Now BB was too busy to worry about what the bitch was doing.

The mailing list was separated into three categories: New members who haven't yet contributed over $100; older members who have contributed at least several times the $100 minimum, and the jackpot, members who had contributed several times at least over $500. The A List.

BB knew this A List was what was needed. It had only been used a couple of times in the history of WIMPS, all when Gibbie faced real emergencies for fast cash. Twice for bookie calls, once for a red-hot investment opportunity, which unfortunately turned out to be far more smoke and mirrors than a genuine chance at legitimate profits.

(How many street hookers were actually interested in purchasing a portable stool which could be collapsed quickly to fit into their usually large purses? As it turned out, not too many. Actually zero.)

With the A List she summoned Susie to her desk.

"Mr. Rambow has ordered me to prepare immediately a special mailing to this list. He said to have you run off the envelopes. Now do it."

Susie wasn't happy but was somewhat impressed by BB's use of the "Mr." Title. That normally meant BB actually had the authority to get Susie to do some work.

She frowned but took the list. She did know how to run the printer, sometimes with not more than 20 percent spoilage. For Suzie that was nearly perfect.

"And what are you going to be doing while I do all the work?"

The bitch was really pushing it but because this project was really important to Gibbie she decided to overlook the impudence. What did Gibbie see in her, she was just a cheap slut.

"I am going to be creating the contribution letter that will be mailed to whatever names get through your mangling."

Susie wasn't sure what mangling meant so she ignored what might be an insult.

Actually, the contribution letter was already written. There were three of them, ranked "Funds Needed", "Funds Essential", and the A List A Letter, "WIMPS may have to close some operations".

It had been used only once and brought in a barrage of money.

"That letter alone was worth what the kit cost," Gibbie had confided in her.

When he first started his church, he had been contacted by a flimflam artist he had known some years ago.

"Look, Gibbie, if you jump into this church stuff, you're going to need top quality materials. The industry is getting crowded with newbies, and ever since that former hack writer started his own church, something to do with science I think, every con man around thinks it's an easy field.

"But it isn't. I have available, only to friends, Gibbie, a special kit of materials that will put you on the profit path right from the start."

The kit had the three contribution letters, several form "thank you" letters which also tried to get contributors to increase their amounts, and a bunch of other forms for keeping mailing lists updated, getting members to each sign up two new members—sort of a party plan variation—and a couple of forms for recording bequests in members' wills, in favor of the church of course.

Although the fee asked had been high, and Gibbie's handicapping then was as bad it is was now, he realized the value of the kit. He'd had to hit up a couple of new masseuses for short term loans.

Even including the pawn-shop interest they had demanded, Gibbie said it was the best $1,500 he'd ever spent.

BB went to the office safe. Only she and BB had the combination so she checked carefully to make sure the slut was out of visual range.

She dug out the kit, found the A Letter she wanted, and made a typed copy of it at her desk. Gibbie's instructions had been clear: "No one is to see the original. Each time we use any letter from the kit, immediately type a copy to make it look like I've dictated it to you."

After doing that she returned the letter to the safe and spun the dial.

She sniffed in Susie's direction. Gibbie may use you for a few gross physical duties, that he doesn't want to soil me with, but only I have the safe combination. She stuck out her tongue at the slut although Susie's back was turned.

A few minutes later Gibbie called her in.

"What's happening on those contri letters?"

"Just as you wanted, Gibbie. I have the slu...Susie, doing the mailing list now, and assuming she doesn't spoil too many I should have it within the hour.

"I have already typed a copy of Letter A. Here, you can sign it, and I'll have the instant printer next door run off some quality letters which will look like individually typed."

"As always, BB, good work." He signed the master copy.

"In a few minutes you can run this next door. Seeing that you have a little free time, and I'm definitely in the mood for some stress-relaxing action, how be you shut and lock my door, then come over and get down on your knees."

BB knew he wasn't suggesting a spiritual session.

Just goes to show, she thought, that when the boss needs really expert attention, who does he choose? That cheap slut, or me, who knows exactly how to relieve his stress.

She entered and locked the door, found the foam pad she used to protect her knees, and enthusiastically took the position.

Later that day the A List envelopes were stuffed with the "original" A List letters, put through the postage machine, placed into the mailing bag, and carried by Susie to the postal depot around the corner on Paradise.

Rambow was so pleased with how things had worked out that during Susie's absence he had a repeat stress-relaxation session with BB.

She loved it. Score: BB-2, Susie the slut-0.

CHAPTER 15

In spite of his two therapeutic stress-relaxation sessions, Rambow still felt tense and uneasy.

His appointment with Klassen was fast approaching. Even with 'special delivery" postage on the A Letters, he knew that contributions from even the most dedicated of his flock wouldn't arrive for two days. That put the earliest possible time for some cash dangerously close to Klassen's threat of "noon at the latest".

He knew that Klassen was a notorious bullshitter, but he also knew that Klassen's business activities—his bookie activities—were handled on a firm basis.

Mostly because Klassen's bankers, the individuals who thought nothing of treating a reluctant debtor to "break both his legs" bill collecting techniques, were extremely businesslike when it came to money.

Over a hundred grand owing to that prick. It was going to take a miracle to come up with that.

Was his faithful WIMPS flock capable of that?

Realistically that was a stretch. Even when the previous "$ needed" letter had gone out, there'd been a few rumblings of discontent. Several old-timers— anyone who stayed in Rambow's flock for more than one year was considered an old-timer—had even returned their letters, with critical comments scrawled on them.

"What do you want this money for?"

"It's only been a few months since WIMPS last 'desperate appeal'. Where's all this money going?"

"I lost my job in this recession. I can't send any more money, even though I deeply admire what WIMPS is doing. In fact, how's about a small loan for a month or two?"

That final comment had bothered Rambow. When the faithful started to question what the church— never officially recognized as such by any known accrediting body, including and perhaps especially the various leech tax collecting agencies—was doing, it was a bad omen. To compensate for the absent but perhaps simply belated recognition by some verifying religious group, Rambow had several official looking certificates printed and hung in the office.

"The World Counsel (Rambow wasn't a great speller) of Religious Bodies" had a particularly colorful document. In four colors. It had cost 45 bucks but Rambow thought the end result was worth it. It was also signed by four "trusties", a term that Rambow had seen in use at a local jailhouse and which sounded nice and official. Another imposing placard was issued by "World Churches Association", headquartered in Haiti, although in only two colors, and signed by one "Chairman". He'd had it printed in French, the print shop owner said he knew that idiom perfectly from visiting Montreal from Boston several times to get some exotic frog pussy.

The pussy had been expensive and not really exotic.

Well, there wasn't much he could do at the moment. Just wait until BB was able to give him some specific figures on incoming contributions.

And thinking of BB, he did enjoy her therapeutic sessions. But the office was too stark for his tastes. He wanted to see what was going on and he couldn't do much of that trying to look into a desk's leg space.

No, he needed a place with something like a bed. Privacy. And mirrors.

The Happy Andings special room was called for.

He phoned GG at the massage parlor.

"Got anybody new, Glory?" He rarely used her name, usually just the GG initials. When he did it often meant he wanted something special.

She hesitated. After the last catastrophe with that new girl she was hesitant to tell him that she had indeed just hired a new girl. Just in LV for the first time.

Not actually inexperienced in the whack parlor industry but capable of portraying an innocent 18-year-old maiden with her first, or fifty-first, massage trick.

She'd get a premium price for at least the first month, until most of the regulars had tried out her soft but very firm hands.

GG knew that if she failed to tell Rambow about the new girl, he'd find out anyway—massage customers are notorious boasters of their exaggerated physical talents, especially with a newbie who wouldn't do anything to contradict them because it probably increased her fees, certainly tips—and he'd be royally pissed off.

Even with her full partnership in HA she was still in a subordinate position. To become a full partner in every sense she'd have to use her blackmail. And once used it might prove worthless. It also might prove deadly.

She groaned.

"Yeah, I have a sort of new girl, Gibbie. Just started here but not inexperienced. But new here in Vegas, so we should get good prices on her for awhile. How're things with you?"

She knew it was a vain attempt to distract him. A new girl would be all he heard.

"What's she like, GG? Describe her."

Even though she was sorely tempted to describe her as a short, chubby broad with no boobs, she knew better.

"She's not bad. She's about average, black hair. Not bad looking."

"Boobs?"

"Two of them, partner." Maybe throw him off the pussy trail a little with thoughts of how she had become a partner.

It didn't work.

"Size?"

"I think she said about 32, or maybe 34." The girl had 36's and they looked very firm.

GG had the new girls go topless for a quick look, just so she could be sure they weren't transvestites. In Vegas it wasn't unusual for one of them, or even a full homo, to try and get a job being paid for fondling men.

"Is she working today? Now?"

Oh, shit, he was obviously on the pussy trail. She knew that to try to deter him more would likely be anti-productive.

"Yes, she started today on the early shift, and so she'll likely take off a little early, she said she still has to make arrangements for electric and gas at her new apartment."

"You know that I like to meet new girls, GG. I think it's the best way for them to start, meeting the boss in a friendly atmosphere."

GG knew that meant with Rambow lying naked on a massage table and the new girl's hands caressing his worries away.

She didn't say anything.

"So listen, GG, keep her free in about half an hour. If she objects to missing a paid trick just tell her this is a new employee requirement.

"And keep the special room available too. I don't want to have to interview her in a regular room with those paper-thin walls."

No of course not. Someone might hear your probably obscene and indecent suggestions to the new girl, all in the interests of good management relations with new employees, of course.

If she didn't make as much bread as she did, she'd tell him to stuff it. Including even the hard-earned partnership.

But at her age she knew all too well there was no place in Vegas she could make the nine or ten grand a month—most of it tax free—that she did at Happy Andings.

In the sex industry here, every year past 30, hell, even 25, caused a reduction in earning power. Even if she switched to straight hooking, she'd be lucky to earn one-third of what she netted now.

She muttered an okay and disconnected, then pressed the internal call button and pressed the room number where Tammy was working—as likely to be the girl's real name as Glory was hers. She had earned hers in the early days when doing actual tricks was half the business of massage parlors. Several times in the fake enthusiasm for the client's climax she had shouted a former joking expression that some hookers used at that critical moment, Glory Glory, and it had stuck with her, now often abbreviated to simply GG.

After a few moments Tammy answered. Obviously she had been involved at a turning point in her massage. GG imagined her drying her hands on a paper towel.

"Come in for a moment when you're free, Tammy."

Should she tell the girl the truth, that Rambow, HA's apparent owner, wanted to give her a trial run, meaning the full massage package. He'd also likely want her to be wearing as close to her skin as possible.

Tammy wasn't a newbie, and she'd probably experienced a fair amount of "special boss privileges". GG hoped so, she was getting tired of having to recruit and break in girls after Rambow had caused problems.

But some girls objected to these privileges, so maybe she should gloss over them a little.

A few minutes later there was a knock at her door. She shouted "come in", and Tammy did.

She was actually quite attractive, and GG knew that if she stayed, she would do well at Happy Andings. Some of the customers were regulars and once they found a compatible masseuse they often would stick with her for some time.

GG got right to the problem; Rambow might show up anytime.

"Tammy, the owner of HA is a guy named Gilbert—Gibbie—Rambow. "GG thought it best for now to omit her partnership interest. If Rambow fucked up as she expected she didn't want her name dragged down with him again.

"He's not a bad guy but he likes to sort of try out new girls. Normally just a regular massage. Any problem with that?"

Tammy frowned. "He wants a freebie, right? Well, the fee split deal you offered me, GG, is a little better than most shops here in the North End. So, providing 'Gibbie' doesn't go crazy I should be able to relieve his stress. When do I meet him?"

GG felt better. Tammy was as cool as she'd hoped she'd be. Maybe this time Rambow would settle for just a hand job and go one his merry way.

"Pretty soon. He phoned a little earlier and said he'd be dropping by in a while."

"Okay, GG. Am I expected to curtsy for the big boss?"

GG laughed. "No. Just be as polite and friendly as I already have heard you are with regular customers. Incidentally, Tammy, I am pleased with how quickly you have fit in here at HA, and I'm sure you'll soon be one of our top earners."

"Hope so." She turned and started out.

"Oh, Tammy, Rambow likes his first meeting with a new girl to be private, so you can wait for him in the special room."

The girl looked at her sceptically. "Okay. Private? Well, let's get on with it." She didn't look all that thrilled about the location but went out and closed the door.

GG did a little bookwork, trying not to think about Rambow and his predilection for nude masseuses.

"Knock, knock. Can the boss come in?" Rambow entered without waiting for a reply. GG could tell by his eyes that he was definitely in the mood for some interesting physical pleasure.

"Did you get the new girl lined up, GG?"

"How about saying hello or something? Yes, I did talk with Tammy"— "Oh, I like that name", Rambow said—and GG knew that if the name was Mary or Gertrude his reaction would have been the same.

"Did you explain what I wanted, I mean how I interviewed all new girls, and expected to have a trial performance so I could rate them for our customers?"

"I told her you wanted to talk with her. In the special room. The rest is up to you."

"Well, that's not much of an explanation for a new employee, GG, but I guess it'll have to do. Is Tammy in there now?"

"I think so, a few minutes ago she said she was going there."

"Goodie!" Rambow clapped his hands like a little boy at his birthday party.

"Okay, GG, I'll see you later. We can maybe talk about the books or something."

Rambow's interest in the books was restricted solely to how much money he could take out for his stupid racing bets.

He entered the special room, heavily soundproofed and with no outside windows, without knocking. He was the boss, and didn't need to worry about those kinds of formalities.

"Hi, you're Tammy? I'm Gilbert, Gibbie to friends and good employees, Rambow.

"As GG should have explained, with a new girl I like to have her treat me just as a regular customer, so that I can make suggestions for how she might improve her performance. I have been in this business for quite a while, and one is never too old or experienced to learn, is one?"

Tammy smiled. Oh fuck, she thought, a real asshole. Well, he is the boss, although GG seems to actually run things, so I'll give him a good whack job and hope he's satisfied. If not, there's lot of other parlors here in Vegas.

GG noted the time that Rambow had entered the special room. She gave it a few minutes, then went to the secret spot and pressed the video record button. Although she already had plenty on Rambow to ensure that her full partnership survived, it never hurt to get a little extra insurance.

And she was just a little curious about how Rambow would handle things. She only had the one previous video of him, with the then new girl, but he hadn't gotten far into his act before he had...she didn't like to use the word, but nothing else really fit, killed her, whether an accident, or otherwise.

CHAPTER 16

Tonto knocked, then entered on her shouted "come in".

"Hi, babe, you look really hot today."

If he weren't such a shrimp GG thought she might take him on, show him what a real woman could do. He always made her laugh, and in a massage parlor that was a rare event. In fact, masseuses who laughed when with clients ordinarily didn't last long.

"I bought all the stuff you had on that list, they promised to deliver in later today. What does HA do with five gallons of baby oil?"

"Caress a lot of dicks, shorty. Maybe someday I'll rub you down from head to toe, make you so slippery no broad will be able to hold you down."

"Promises, promises. Just let me know where and when."

He turned to leave, then stopped.

"Oh yeah, I gotta have a word with Rambow, I see his car's outside. A guy named Klassen, I know he comes here quite a bit, came up to me in Sammy's Coffee Shop. Said to tell Rambow that Monday was just a day or two away. Don't know what he meant but he said to make sure I passed the message to Rambow. Is he busy?"

GG laughed. "I guess it depends on what you mean by busy. He's with Tammy, that new girl, in the special room."

"Lucky prick." Tonto grinned. "Literally."

GG smiled.

"What do you think I should do about that message from Klassen?"

"I guess you have three choices, Tonto." GG held up one finger.

"You could go and just walk into the special room and tell Rambow you had a message for him."

Tonto's eyes widened.

"Sure. Why don't I just take poison, that'd be faster."

"Two. You can write out your important message, put it into an envelope, seal it, and put it somewhere here in the office where he'll probably see it when he's done...finished what he's doing."

"I ain't much at writing stuff, GG. You know that. What's three?"

"You go to the lounge, pour us both nice cups of coffee—two sugars, no milk in mine—bring them back, find a chair and a copy of Playboy or something of similar educational value, and relax quietly until Rambow makes an appearance."

"Have any idea on how long that might be, GG?"

"It's hard to say, Tonto, but based on past experience I doubt it will be more than half an hour, quite probably less."

"Then I guess that's what I'll do, GG. I'll be back with the coffee ASAP."

Tonto actually was a pretty good guy, GG thought. A little slow in the brain department, maybe, but not really a prick.

He returned, set her coffee down— "2 lumps, no white" --and grabbed a chair in the corner near the curtained window. She saw that he had picked up a copy of a racing paper undoubtedly left by Rambow.

He noticed her glance. "Thought I might learn something about this crazy stuff that Rambow seems so hot on."

GG returned to her books. If HA business kept up as good as it had been the last few months, they'd have to think about hiring at least a part time bookkeeper.

Now that GG was a full partner, even if a very silent one, she'd be keeping a close eye on expenses. But her own time was limited so a part timer might be a good idea. Seemed to be a lot more guys wanting the relaxing joys of a full body massage. Or maybe it was just the better quality of girls she was hiring.

When she had first started with Rambow, working herself as a masseuse, she had been surprised at most of the other girls.

Several were street hookers who had even lost their abilities to charge a sawbuck for a quickie in a dark corner.

A couple of newbies had been hired basically under false premises. Rambow had convinced them their jobs would be pure massaging, even though none had any formal practical training.

When they found out the job involved the store name—a happy ending—they either quit or turned their massages into full press fucks, hoping to bump up the tip they were able to get from the customer.

Sanitation was minimal. Often a masseuse would take on another trick without even changing the sheets on her table.

After putting in her time, GG had gone to Rambow. "Look, let me run this shop. You're not here all that much anyway. I'll get rid of the outright whores and replace them with more attractive, younger girls who know what the score really is: a happy ending but no screwing."

Rambow had finally said okay, and within just a few weeks she had made some major changes.

All girls now wore a standard uniform, short skirts and revealing but full blouses, and high heels when they had a trick. Most girls switched immediately to loafers between jobs.

GG had trained the girls on how to use their fingers to build anticipation, so that her final strokes came as a real pleasure and relief.

She had insisted on cleaned up rooms, and made sheet changes and hand washing between tricks compulsory.

Really, she realized, it was her good managerial talents, and the ability to spot and recruit girls who would enjoy the limited pleasures of massaging, as opposed to hooking, and who knew the benefits of much more safe income opportunities.

Now, even the regular customers were far more satisfied, more relaxed, and when GG had inadvertently walked into a room where the girl had forgotten to light the "occupied" sign, the man, regardless of the stage he was in, had not seemed nervous or embarrassed. All that was happening was they were getting a full body massage from an attractive female, with the store name assured as an anticipated and promised pleasure.

Idly she wondered how many rapes Happy Andings girls had prevented. Unlike many of the massage parlors, where customers slunk in through semi-hidden doorways, men freely entered HA, knowing that for the quoted fee they would get a quality, half or full hour body massage that definitely relaxed their tensions.

She finished her coffee. She looked at the large clock over the door, she sometimes had to remind new girls that a half hour session was 30 minutes, not 35 or even 40.

The new girls frequently got so involved in their new, interesting, and totally safe physical pleasures, that they ignored the time.

Time. Shit, well over half an hour had passed since Rambow entered the special room.

She took a quick peek at the hidden video camera timer, she looked first to make sure Tonto was deeply engrossed in the racing paper, and saw the camera was still running.

She sat down. Memories of the previous Rambow session with a new girl flashed through her mind. No, it wasn't possible. That idiot had done some damage to Tammy?

Even Rambow, prone to sex-induced fits of unnatural excitement, couldn't be that stupid. Could he?

She knew the answer to that. She went to the hidden video camera and pressed the off button. By now she's have more than enough of Rambow. And she didn't want any of her if she had to go into the special room.

"Tonto".

He looked up. "Yeah?"

"You'd better go down and knock on the special room door. I'm pretty sure Rambow said he had an appointment later down at the WIMPS office, and we don't want a hand job to interfere with the boss's business appointments."

"Are you sure it's okay, GG? Maybe he'll be mad for being disturbed."

"If he says anything, just tell him I said we had to remind him of the time. He won't be mad at you, Tonto."

The short man got to his feet, dropping the paper on the chair seat.

"Okay, GG. I just hope you know what you're doing. I do know if Rambow is at the point of coming he ain't go to welcome a cheery 'hello' from me at the door."

"Go. There won't be a problem."

She crossed fingers on both hands. She really hoped not.

A few minutes later Tonto returned.

"Like you said, GG, I knocked lightly on the door. Zilch. So I knocked again louder. I could hear the boss mumbling something, so I put my ear to the door.

"It sounded like 'get GG'. Does that make any sense to you?"

Fuck. She knew instinctively that HA had another Rambow-created disaster on its hands.

She hoped fervently that it was something she could smooth over, maybe give Tammy a little payoff and promise her a really good recommendation at the next place she tried.

But her instincts tingled, and she knew that this problem wouldn't be resolved that easily.

Did she want a witness with her when she entered the special room?

Yes, it would probably be better to have someone dependable with her. Someone she could control, and trust as far as needed.

She looked at Tonto. He had resumed his seat and was again paging through the racing paper.

He was ideal. He was already involved in the previous Rambow disaster, and GG could control him totally. She knew that he was totally afraid of her, even though in his wildest erotic dreams he pictured her submitting to his charms.

Besides, he had actively participated in every part of the previous Rambow cover-up, so forcing him into more undoubtedly dangerous and illegal activities shouldn't be a problem.

"Tonto. Come with me."

She headed out of her office. He immediately fell in behind.

At the special room she knocked authoritatively on the door, then listened. There was no sound.

She knocked again, louder.

This time, by straining forward almost touching the door, she heard what appeared to be moaning, or crying.

She turned the handle but the door had been locked from inside. "Tonto, zip back and get this room key from my desk. Top drawer on the right side. It's a big key with a red emblem on top. Hurry."

He did, and within a few moments was back, holding the key out as a prize.

GG inserted the key and turned it. The lock disengaged but the door was still stuck. She pressed against it more strongly. It gave slightly then stopped.

It felt like something was wedged against the door. Something big. Like a....No. She thought, not that.

She tried to move the door again but it still resisted.

"Rambow. Can you hear me?" She listened with her ear literally against the door.

She could hear some kind of mumbling but could not make out words.

"Tonto, get over here. When I say shove, put all your weight against the door. We have to get it open, at least enough to get in."

He moved beside her, put his shoulders against the door, and looked at her.

GG got into position, almost overlapping the smaller man, then nodded. "Now."

They both pushed, and slowly the door gave way. They stopped for a breath and GG tried to wedge in to the slightly larger opening.

Not yet.

She looked at Tonto and motioned with her head. He brought his shoulders back into position.

She nodded, they pushed, and this time the door unwillingly opened another few inches.

She knew it was still too small for her but she motioned to Tonto, and he slipped into the opening, inhaling to decrease his width, and with some pushing by him, and shoving by her, he popped into the room.

For a few moments there was silence.

Then "Oh fuck".

She was very afraid she knew what that meant.

"Get it open, Tonto."

She could hear something being dragged away from the door, and soon there was room enough for her large frame.

She stumbled through the door. The overhead light was on and the first thing she saw was Rambow, lying in a fetal position on the huge bed. He had his head buried in a couple of the large deluxe special room pillows, more like sleeping bags actually.

He was still mumbling into it, and now that she was closer she could make out a few words: "laughed at..., she said..., too small."

She turned around. Tonto had been down on his knees, looked liked he'd checked the pulse. He got to his feet, dusted off his knees, looked at GG.

"It was Tammy. Looks to me like a busted neck." He pointed across the room where a shattered hardwood chair, one of only two in the room, lay against the wall. One of the solid arms was broken almost off, and the leather straps which served as a back were torn almost in two.

GG hesitated. "Is she...?"

"If you mean dead, yeah. No pulse, no chest movement. And she had lovely chests."

GG shuddered. Tonto had a very morbid fascination with death; she wanted nothing to do with it. A reminder of her own mortality perhaps. Who gave a shit, she didn't like dead things. Even sparrows splattered on a glass reflecting door upset her.

Behind her she heard movements. She turned to the bed as Rambow sat up groggily, rubbing his head.

"What happened?"

She reached the bedside in a jump.

"What happened? What happened, you fucking moron, is that you've killed another girl. Getting to like this killing business, are you?"

Rambow got slowly to his feet. He looked at the body, then at the broken chair against the wall.

"It was an accident, GG. I didn't mean to even hurt her. If she had just stopped laughing..."

He noticed Tonto.

"What he's doing in here. Get out, you little prick."

"Watch what you're saying, Rambow. I needed Tonto to help me get into this room. It was blocked, you may remember, by a young girl's body.

"And we'll likely need his help once again with that." She gestured at the body.

He covered his eyes with both hands.

"Jesus, it was just an accident. We were just talking, you know, sitting here on the bed, she even had nearly all her clothes on, there was no problem with that, GG, and then I said I wanted to give her a trial run as a new employee.

"And she said okay, and stood up, and I thought she was getting undressed, you know, GG, the way I like a massage, and so I started to get naked too.

"But she was just taking off a sweater she was wearing, and when she came back to the bed, just standing beside it, I was already undressed.

"And that didn't bother her, because all HA customers get naked, GG, but then I said I wanted her the same way and she started to laugh. Said she did a better job with some clothes on.

"Then I guess I sort of, you know, held up my, ah, dick, and maybe said something about I thought a newbie would want to at least kiss the boss's dick, you know, like sort of a joke.

"But she started to laugh, almost hysterically, you know, and even when I said forget it, let's just do the regular massage, she kept laughing.

"Then the bitch said something about how it was so small she'd need a flashlight to find it, and once in her mouth she might mistake it for a tiny little french fry and swallow it.

"Then she started laughing even more. I tried to get her to stop, but she kept laughing more. And louder.

"Then I grabbed the chair which she had moved beside the bed when she hung her goddamned sweater on it.

"I was just going to push it across and bump her legs from behind, you know, GG, so she'd have to sit down for a minute, but before I could do that she was at the door and starting to turn the inside lock. And laughing louder, and more, all the time."

He paused for a breath.

"That fucking laughing! It was like one of those crappy sideshows in a circus where there's an artificial clown with his mouth wide open and all these phony laughs pouring out.

"I thought if the cunt didn't stop, I'd go crazy, so I shouted at her to stop turning the lock. And then she turned her head, looked right at my.... dick, and started laughing even louder. And louder.

"So I lunged from the bed and swung the chair. I was just aiming for her legs, GG, but I guess I wasn't very accurate and sort of smacked her higher up.

"As soon as that happened, she just fell, her neck still sort of turned around to stare at me."

"Sort of smacked her higher? How could you mistake her neck for her legs? Fuck, Gibbie, you can't be trusted alone in a room with any broad. She laughs at a joke and you'll snuff her."

GG grabbed the remaining chair and plopped down in it. How could anybody be as completely stupid, as useless, as Rambow?

She'd have to think carefully about her own snuffing venture. Not by herself, of course, but maybe Tonto could be titillated enough with her body, or threatened with mayhem if that failed. Whatever.

But now was not the time for her long-range financial planning. They had to get rid of Tammy's body damned quick, before someone stumbled in on them.

"Tonto, lock the door with my key." She tossed it to him.

He turned and did that, then tossed it back to her.

At least one member of her immediate male group did as he was told without argument. Maybe he was more infatuated with rubbing his dick between GG's obviously generous boobs than she had thought.

She had to check the application Tammy had filled out when GG interviewed, and hired, her. As best she could remember the girl had no local friends or relatives. Not even emergency contacts, if she recalled correctly.

It would have to be something very similar to the other girl Rambow had murd.... hurt.

Any incriminating paper work would have to be destroyed.

Tammy was just a possible masseuse who had come in for an interview, but she didn't match up to HA's standards. What standards? Well, Tammy just didn't seem to be the wholesome type that HA wanted.

She implied in her interview that she wasn't averse to a little hooking on the job, provided the fee, and the split, was favorable to her. GG wasn't against the concept, that in fact was how she had started her massage career.

However now as a full member of the manager class she had found more customers could be processed in a shorter time with straight massages; even at a lower per-body fee the gross income was higher.

But sure, that BS would do. Of course, any cop or detective who had been on LVPD for more that 15 minutes would burst out laughing at that "HA's standards". So what?

GG thought for a minute.

Why should she put herself in the spotlight over what Rambow had done?

Sure, say that Rambow had done the interview, and "As you know, officer, as a nationally advertised television preacher his standards are of the highest".

Make him the interviewer, and thus one of the last few people to even see Tammy in the HA shop. Even after GG had seen her. Great!

If he caused any trouble over this slight re-arrangement of the facts, threaten to walk away.

Of course with her full partnership now secured that wasn't about to happen, but with Rambow still in a state of shock, and hopefully even a little remorseful, although the latter was barely probable, she doubted he would be critical of anything less than a full written confession for both girls.

GG hadn't really introduced Tammy around. The girls worked when at HA and they didn't view kindly to having their earning day interfered with, especially for someone who could be a new competitor and thus after the same johns.

The one or two who might have met or even seen her at HA could be brushed off. Girls in whack parlors came, and went, even oftener that their horny johns.

Tammy would be just another girl who had tried out for a job but didn't make it.

Because she laughed too much and too loud. A jury would love that excuse for a homicide.

(That word sounded better than the m word; she'd remember to use it in the future.)

Well, she'd obviously have to take control of this situation. Tonto was an order-taker, and Rambow was.... what? Besides an asshole, not much.

"Tonto, from here on this will be sort of a replay of our earlier cleaning up of Rambow's error. Right?"

He looked fully at GG's munificent chest and cleared his throat.

The girl's death didn't really affect him, he hadn't even known her.

But GG appeared to be offering some exciting times for him, in addition, of course, to the interesting money rewards.

He was sure, well, almost positive, that he'd be able to handle any and all of GG's physical requests, when the time came for her payoffs.

He expected they might be quite exotic, or was the word erotic? Whatever, he knew she'd really been around, and he was more than willing to try anything she suggested. Anything.

He looked up at her face. "Understood, GG. I assume the same, ah, financial gifts are involved?"

No need to draw her attention to her body contributions. He was sure she understood exactly what those involved. And pretty soon, he hoped. And expected.

GG nodded. She had him.

He desperately wanted to spend some 'quality' time her, and she grinned to herself as she imagined how he would try to cope with some of the really interesting maneuvers she had learned in her years of practice.

She actually looked forward in some strange way to granting the little man his turn at bat. She almost laughed out loud at the corny pun.

"Okay. Tonto, get the wheelbarrow from the basement, and a big sheet of tarp or something. Get Tammie's body into it, cover it completely, and leave it here in the special room.

"Here's my own key to the special, no one else has on. Lock the door from the outside and give me the key.

"Once it's fully dark make arrangements to move the body just like the other one. Then do it, and return the barrow and tarp to the basement with no, ah, you know, marks on them."

She hoped he understood she meant blood; he sort of nodded to indicate he did.

"Both of you listen up. Here's the official story." She outlined in bare detail her earlier failed-interview plan.

Tonto nodded at the end of it.

"Got it, GG. I'll get all that done."

She was really going to make his turn at bat spectacular. Too bad Rambow wasn't more like him.

As for Rambow, he lolled in the chair, his dick still hanging outside his pants.

"Jesus, Gibbie, stick that thing back inside. Did you hear everything I said? Do you understand and agree to that plan?"

He took a deep breath, then nodded.

"Yes, Glory, I do. And you know how much I appreciate your help with this, ah, accident."

Yes, she did.

And before the day was out, certainly before the body had been moved, she planned on Rambow 'voluntarily' increasing her 50% partnership share to, say, 60. Or even a little higher. Because of her outstanding management abilities, of course.

In any event, enough to give her for the first time a controlling interest in Happy Andings.

That was something she had wanted and schemed for ever since the first day she had met Rambow, and he had pulled exactly the same shabby trick with her that he had tried with Tammie.

The only difference was that GG had gone along with it. She could see right then that Rambow was a long-term mark, just like the HA customers, and she planned to get a big slice of HA.

And now she had.

"Stay here all afternoon, Gibbie. If you have to cancel any WIMPS appointments use this phone. This button gives you a private outside line.

"Later after Tonto has been able to cover the body, I'll come and get you.

And take you to my office where the partnership percentage change will be quickly worked out, agreed to, signed, and witnessed.

She left the special room and went to her office. She unlocked that door and went to the small file cabinet where employee records and payrolls were kept before she shipped them to the accountant for permanent storage.

First, though, she did something she should have done earlier. She went to the secret video camera, shut it off and took the current tape to her office.

She locked the door, turned off the overhead light, and then she replayed the tape until the time marker showed about when Tammy had left for the special room.

With her office darkened the video pictures showed up clearly. She watched as the girl entered, and the first minutes until Rambow has flaunted his 'weapon' and Tammy had begun laughing. The tape ran and she watched in horror as the events she knew about played out before her eyes. Finally, she pressed the stop button and took a large breath.

Rambow was an animal. Period. If he wasn't necessary for a while, until she could ease him out completely from HA, she'd throw him to the wolves right now. She knew that Tonto would corroborate anything she told him to.

Tonto, meanwhile, was making the preparations that GG had ordered. She really had great tits, he thought, not for the first time.

And along with GG's requirements he was also arranging to borrow again the miniature camera he had used on the previous girl's death.

A man had to look out for himself.

CHAPTER 17

Tonto knocked on the office door, identified himself, then entered when GG shouted okay.

"I've done everything you asked me to. The girl's body is in the special room, and completely covered by an old tarpaulin.

"When it gets dark I'll have my buddy drive his truck into the alley and we'll load it up. Then we'll take it into that deserted state park and dump it.

"Unless we bury it way deep it'll be found, probably by some hiker or druggie, but we'll take all her clothes, and anything else like a watch or whatever, so her ID will take a while. Okay?"

"Okay, Tonto. Do as thorough a job as last time and both your financial and physical rewards will be just the same."

He smiled.

"But I'll still need some bread to cover my buddy. He's not greedy, likely settle for a hundred or so all told for everything, time and truck included. Maybe a little more, though, GG, so you better give me say 150. If I get it cheaper, I'll return the diff."

Sure you will, Tonto. And you'll become the only honest man in LV. Make that Nevada.

She reached into her big right-hand bottom drawer and pulled out the petty cash box.

She peeled off $150.

"I'll just enter this as, let me see, entertaining a really good client."

Tonto took the bills and stuck them into his shirt pocket. For his own payoff he was thinking far more of the physical part. GG sure had great tits, and soon he'd be enjoying every nipple of them.

"Speaking of clients, what's Rambow up to in the special?"

"He was still lying all scrunched up in the bed, mumbling something about laughing. I don't think he even realized I was in there with the wheel barrow with the body in it.

"Has he gone loopy?"

GG paused, thought about it.

"Probably a good question, Tonto. I don't honestly know.

"But I do know that we're going to keep him away from all our girls. At the rate he's going he'd have most of them knocked off— 'accidentally' of course— within a week or so.

"When you leave here, please go and get Rambow on his feet. Tell him it's important, no, vital, that he gets his ass in here immediately."

GG stood up, signalling the meeting was over.

"If he gives you any trouble, Tonto, come back and report. If he does manage to stumble to his feet, wait till he's outside the room, then use my key to lock it from the outside.

"You can keep the key until your buddy gets here and the body is loaded, then bring it to me. I'll have the maid go in there then and clean things up once you're gone. Those maids are used to wild things happening here at HA, especially in the special room, so they won't even notice anything unusual.

"And don't you ever make even a joke of it with them or any of the other girls, Tonto. What we want is just for everybody to carry on as usual.

"If any cops come by, not likely but you never can tell where those jerkoffs will wander in their detecting modes, remember you never met Tammy, have no idea of any girl they describe, assuming by that time that they may have photos of her body. Are you sure that your trucking buddy will keep quiet?"

"Hell, GG, he's already got a sheet with half a dozen misdeams, even one felony, on it. He wouldn't say 'hello' to any boys in blue unless they hung him on a stake and tortured him."

GG shuddered. "Let's hope, and assume, it won't come to that. Keep that special room key safe, Tonto. It's the only one that overrides all room locks."

Good info to know, he thought. Never can tell when it might be useful.

He sort of saluted her and left.

She continued to pile up mental points for the little man.

Almost 10 minutes passed, GG was just about ready to go down and physically pull Rambow out of the special room, when there were scuffling sounds in the hall.

She went to her door, opened it. There stood, or more accurately slumped against the wall, the big HA chief and famed TV preacher for the WIMPS organization.

He looked like he'd been demoted several levels. Quite a few, in fact.

She grabbed his left arm and hustled him in before any of the girls saw him. She closed the door, then moved him to a chair right beside her desk, and he immediately fell down into it.

She wanted him close for her next business transaction, something she had wanted ever since she began as a hooker in a very low-class whack parlor in extreme north LV.

CHAPTER 18

She waited until he got his eyes open and reasonably focused.

"Listen carefully, Gibbie. This is very important. You could be charged with murder for Tammy. And also, probably for that other girl."

Rambow's eyes widened. He tried to affect an innocent, 'just a preacher', look but failed miserably.

"Murder? What do you mean murder?"

His voice was so low it was almost inaudible.

"I believe that would be the charge, Gibbie, if the law ever found out. Murder, I believe, is taking someone's life."

"But it was an accident, GG. They both were. You know that. All you have to do is tell exactly what happened. That's all."

"Okay, Gibbie." She smiled but didn't mean it.

"With the first girl, we had to almost break into the room where there was only you and her.

"When Tonto and me got inside, the girl was dead, and you were moaning what appeared to be a confession."

Rambow held up both hands as if to stop her.

GG kept on.

"Now, on the second event, Tonto and me had to again almost break the door down. Inside we found the girl sprawled right at the door, and it looked like someone had broken a wooden chair over her neck.

"There were only two people in that room also. You and the girl.

"Her neck looked broken.

"It was.

"Now, do I have the facts right, Gibbie? Is there anything I've missed? Any points that might incline a DA to say, 'Sure, Gibbie, I can see what you mean. They were both accidents. Why not just leave the station and carry on with your regular business?'

"I don't know, Gibbie, I'm not a lawyer. Maybe a sharp one could make that interpretation stick. Whaddya think?"

Rambow's head was lowered, almost resting on GG's desk. He was either crying or doing deep breathing exercises.

He looked up. He was crying.

"What do you think I should do, GG?"

GG sat back and thought for a few minutes.

"Concerning the girls' deaths, I can't suggest anything. Tonto and I have tried to cover up the first one, and we're working on doing the same for the second.

"But a lot is up to you. If you keep your mouth firmly shut you may be able to ride it out. And stay completely away from HA and its girls."

Rambow looked up, surprised at this condition. He started to smirk but Glory cut him off.

"I'm serious, Gibbie. You've become a walking disaster area. Two dead is enough, far more than enough.

"You need some female companionship, take a quick flight to Reno. Or anyplace away from Vegas."

Rambow still was smirking. GG reached over and gave him a generous smack on the shoulder.

"I mean that absolutely. If you come sniffing around HA then I'm out of here, and you can handle your personal affairs on your own."

Rambow looked more contrite, almost as if he understood and agreed to what GG was spelling out

"As far as here at HA, I need a new agreement. I'm risking my neck, covering up for you. I also need more money from petty cash. Getting rid of dead bodies is expensive, you know. There are truckers, helpers, park deadbeats: they all need some green.

"And I'll leave it to you, or your accounting whizzes at WIMPS, to create and turn in appropriate vouchers as cover.

"Unless you insist I do it, then I'll turn in some dandies for 'transporting and hiding dead bodies.'"

Rambow appeared to be slipping into a sort of daze. Maybe that's how he managed to get through his church sermons.

"Let's get the business out of the way first.

"For my own protection, and of course yours too, Gibbie, I need more control of HA."

She paused to let that sink in.

He started to bluster.

"I just gave you a full 50% partnership, just a few weeks ago...."

"You didn't 'give' me anything, Rambow." She deliberately switched from the friendly Gibbie. She wanted him clearly on the defensive.

"I earned it. In fact, I should have had it long ago.

"And now I've earned it even more. 70%"

He objected with his arms and eyes, although with all his crying it was really difficult to see what they were doing. But he didn't shout or scream; a good sign.

GG reached into the middle right drawer of her desk and pulled out a single page document prepared on a computer; margins were nice and even everywhere.

"This is a simple revised agreement. My lawyer friend said it would meet any legal demands.

"As of today, you award me 20% of your ownership. That gives me 70%, you 30%."

"Read it. When you're doing that I'll have Nancy come in to witness your signature.

"She knows nothing about it, all she'll do is sign as a witness after you've signed.

GG pushed the document across. Slowly Rambow picked it up. He put on his reading glasses and appeared to read it carefully.

GG doubted if even one sentence had registered with him.

I shoulda increased it 80, even 90%. But then what's the difference. I now have control of Happy Andings. Even if he tried to use his 30%, there's not a damned thing he could do.

Success!

She picked up the internal phone and dialed the room where Nancy was waiting. Her next appointment as almost an hour away, and from sheer boredom the girl was happy to do a favor for GG.

Like most of girls she had no idea of the ownership shares of HA, but she thought of GG as the boss anyway.

Rambow was at HA infrequently; one of the older girls had said it was because of his WIMPS activities: "He probably doesn't want to associate with us low lifes".

Nancy knocked and entered, Rambow scrawled his sig on the paper, Nancy certified its authenticity, then left.

Rambow had gone into one of rarely-used rooms to lie down. He likely really needed it.

With her office now empty GG held up her both hands like a winning boxer.

Success. A long time coming. She hoped Rambow didn't do anything stupid—was that reasonable? Or possible? —to jeopardize it.

CHAPTER 19

Pap had gone over to the liquor store across the street to replenish a much-depleted liquor cabinet.

The two researchers had been contacted by Shant and a meeting requested.

He felt that the end game was now in sight. Certainly not all the open questions had been answered but he had a good feel for how the final article would shape up.

Often his initial mental plan for an article changed completely by the time he started hitting the computer keys. That was obviously the case with Rambow. What had started as a simple semi-humorous profile of a small city preacher had morphed into what could easily be a major expose, if what Alison had hinted on her late evening phone call was accurate.

There was a short solid knock on the outside door. Pap must have his hands full, he usually announced his presence with a modified 'shave and a haircut' tattoo.

Shant didn't bother looking through the small eye hole but just swung the door open.

"That was fast, Pap, you must be thirsty...."

It wasn't Pap.

The face was familiar but it took Shant a moment to connect the dots.

"Lieutenant Southfield. Good to see you again. Didn't recognize you without the uniform. C'mon in."

"Hi, Michael. Okay with your first name?"

"Sure. And yours is Dan? If you want to, grab a chair, they're nice and comfortable."

"Did I get you at a bad time, Michael? I should have phoned you first, but I was just cruising—plain clothes today—and realized I was only a couple of blocks from your motel."

"No problem, Dan. Pap was here and left to get a little more booze, and my other researcher, Alison, is due to clock in anytime.

"But it's just a regular 'catch-up' meeting, and I'd like you to meet Alison. She's turned out to be a great researcher and a fine person."

He smiled.

"Just like Pap, who you've already had the pleasure of meeting."

Southfield smiled as well. "Yeah. He's a feisty old guy, isn't he?"

"And for the second time I've used him a lot on a story, he's also doing some fine work."

There was the now familiar tattoo on the door and then it was pushed open.

"That damned store was packed. Well, three customers ahead of me, and I consider that packed...."

Pap dumped a large heavy-duty plastic bag on the counter and turned, spotting Southfield for the first time.

"No, don't tell me, I know, you're, ah, that cop."

"You mean the cop who rides roughshod over innocent people's rights," laughed the cop.

Pap even reddened a little.

"This is Lt. Dan Southfield. He's not here to bust anyone, at least at the moment"—Shant threw a warning glance at his senior researcher— "and his name is Dan.

"Dan, Pap's suspenseful shopping expedition was to get booze, and we are anticipating that event. You're more than welcome to join us.

"I know there's good Mexican dark rum, vodka, even a few beers around somewhere."

Dan took a quick look at his cell phone clock.

"Sure, rum would be fine. Thanks. My tour is over in just a few minutes so I'm not"—he threw a look at Pap— "screwing Vegas taxpayers too badly."

"Pap, could you do the honors? When Pap pours, there are no fingers in the glass. In fact, most of his pours don't really need the glass."

A firm knock on the room door. Pap, on his way to the small kitchenette, started sliding in the door's direction but Shant quickly headed him off. He'd prefer to make the introductions himself, just in case Pap got started on some rights lecture.

She came in looking so great that even Pap was momentarily speechless.

"Hi, Michael. And you too Pap. And?" She smiled and looked at the cop.

"You look great, Alison. Really great. This is Dan Southfield, he's a lieutenant with LVPD. Pap and I met him, as we told you, in connection with that girl's death."

She stuck out her hand and he took it gladly.

"Nice to meet you. Lieutenant or Dan?"

"Dan, please. But I should warn you, before Pap interrupts, that he thinks I'm abusive of people's rights, so beware of what you tell me." He was smiling broadly.

Pap, in the midst of preparing the drinks, muttered something to himself. Both men smiled.

Pap finished the drinks, put them all on a tin serving tray, and doled them out. Each settled into chairs—enough but none left over—and small talk circulated for a few minutes.

With a pause, Dan spoke.

"I did have sort of a reason for this visit, Michael."

Pap muttered something.

"It's in a way tied in to that massage parlor we discussed last time."

"Good old Happy Andings. What's happening with the slogan place?"

"Well, as is too often the case, nothing specific. But another girl's body has been found. In the same deserted park area as the other girl.

"Same as before: no ID, nothing. No clothes and nothing in our files."

There was silence for a few seconds.

"But this girl's neck was broken, and the coroner has already found some minute wood splinters that may be identifiable if we find the chair or whatever they came from."

"How much chance of that?" Alison asked.

"Not much, I'm afraid. Chair or whatever would be easy to get rid of, and we don't have the manpower to check every Sally Ann store or dump site. If we had a perp, that piece of furniture could be very helpful in making a solid case, but until then...."

"Does she have any connection with HA?" Pap asked.

"Nothing direct, no employment record or anything. We haven't found Rambow yet, I had men watching that church of his, and of course HA itself. I did have a little talk with Glory, or GG, the woman who manages it, but she said she'd never seen the girl, based on coroner's photos.

"Frankly, we're nowhere on either girl."

Alison cleared her throat. She looked at Michael.

"Like I mentioned on the phone last evening, Michael, I do have some possible info, at least on the first dead girl."

"Let's hear it, Alison."

"Well, I have sort of a contact who is a firm patron of the massage arts."

All four smiled at the unintended pun.

"He moves his business around, but does have favorites that he returns to.

"One of these works at Happy Andings, so he spends a fair amount of time there. He has become friendly, or at least acquainted, with a man who seems to work there, maybe just doing odd jobs.

"My contact, I'll call him Bill, said that normally the guy, whose nickname is Tonto—which means stupid in Spanish—is very closemouthed about HA. But in just the last few days, whenever Bill and Tonto would meet for a beer, Tonto acted like a cat after the canary went missing.

"You know, almost on the verge of spilling some interesting beans, then at the last minute completely freezing up."

"That's it? Not really too much, Alison."

"That's what I thought too, Michael. But yesterday, just before I phoned you, I ran into Bill when I stopped in to have a coffee break.

"He saw me and waved me over so I took my cup and joined him.

"I have a loose agreement with him. I pay him $5 for a loose tip, $10, even more, if it's something that sounds hot. You'll see from my expense sheet that on your assignment I've never paid him more than ten.

"As soon as I sat down, he leaned forward and in a stage whisper told me he 'had a $20 hot tip'.

"I tried to beat him down but he held tight, said his tip was 'huge'.

"Knowing Bill as I do, I discounted that huge down to something a little better than usual but he wouldn't budge from the twenty.

"So, I blinked. If you think I went crazy, Michael, I'll eat this one myself. But I have the feeling you'll think it was well spent."

By now she had her audience in her pretty little hands.

Pap was leaning so far forward that he was defying gravity. The cop looked poised to make an arrest, and Shant's blue eyes sparkled.

"The 'hot tip' turned out to be actually two separate tips.

"First, Bill said that his favorite girl at HA had told him on his last visit, early that afternoon, that she had seen 'the girl the cops found in the park'.

"She said that she'd seen her in the hall, near the special room. It's a well soundproofed room reserved for big customers, and rarely used by the regular masseuses, and only then with special permission of GG, the manager.

"That was all, his favorite said she hadn't seen any more, but Bill got the feeling she was holding something back, like maybe, just maybe, who was with the first dead girl."

She paused to sip her drink. The other three were spellbound and silent.

Alison looked around, measuring her audience like an experienced actress.

"Christ, Alison, is this a serial? You want me to wet my drawers?" Pap wanted more, and now.

Shant and Alison both laughed and shouted "NO!" at the same time.

"Okay, Pap, I'll speed it up a little.

"I thought Bill my contact had come to the end of his tip, but he hadn't.

"Actually, the second part was even better than the first."

Pap shook his fist at her.

She grinned and plunged on.

"Bill's favorite must have expected a larger than normal tip, because when his massage was finished, and she was cleaning up, Bill said she said that although GG was the manager, all new girls were now being first 'tested' by the HA owner. And when I checked a week or so ago that was our religious friend Rambow."

"What did Bill's favorite mean by 'tested'?" Shant and the cop and Pap were apparently interested in the answer.

"Bill said just what it sounded like, that every new girl, or even prospect I guess, was given a personal test by Rambow. His favorite laughed when he asked her about it, just as you men are doing, and said the other girls were sure he expected a full massage, in the special room. And maybe a little more, she added."

"So Rambow comes down from the religious clouds to experience a little human pleasure. Did Bill give you his favorite's name?" Shant asked.

Southfield sat forward for the answer.

"He said she wouldn't repeat what she'd told him to anyone else. I imagine she thought it would be safe with Bill, he doesn't come on as a man about town, in fact he's usually dressed a little seedy. Not a bum, you know, just not much of a swinger."

Shant looked at the cop.

"Well, Dan, that info changes things for me. How about you?"

Southfield stroked his chin.

"I'm actually a little embarrassed. I can't believe that my guys didn't get this info before now. Yes, Michael, it does change things. A helluva lot."

Shant stood up to relieve the tension.

"If this knowledge is good, Alison, the next time you see him give him a twenty as a bonus. From the LAPD, although that's confidential.

"As I see it, the first murdered girl might quite possibly have applied at HA, been required to have

Rambow "instruct" her, and either refused or made it obvious she would resist any such condition."

"And maybe for the second girl as well, Michael, if she objected to the same conditions."

Southfield also stood up and shook his shoulders a bit. Dan lifted one finger.

"A couple of key points are missing. First, as described by Bill's fav, did these conditions occur?"

"Second", and his second finger responded, "can we prove that Rambow insisted on these conditions? If so, the case against him, on a possible murder one, is starting to look pretty good.

"In all of this, we have no substantial evidence. It's all circumstantial. So we need hard evidence before we even fondle the cuffs.

"Getting that will be difficult. I have a couple of reasonably attractive policewomen in my department but I know they're all married, and it would be worth my life to ask their husbands to approve this kind of duty." He frowned to show what he thought of the odds.

The three men sat, all of them now frowning. Alison wasn't. It was apparent that she was thinking.

Smithfield picked up his glass and emptied it.

"I've got to get back downtown and make some changes. I sort of hate to ask you, Alison, as this was really an unofficial meeting, but now that it's turning into a murder case, could you let me have Bill's name or somehow to get hold of him.

"Don't worry, I'll treat him with kid gloves, and not mention your name. I'm used to handling snitches and I'll be able to get his story from him again, without him realizing that it has anything to do with you.

"In fact, if you'd prefer, I could have him and several other street guys pulled in on a so-called sweep. I could get the story and he'd be back on the street—no rubber hoses, Pap", who actually responded to the cop's smile with a grin of his own "within an hour or so."

Alison looked at Shant, who thought for a moment, then nodded.

"Of course, if you think it's possibly a murder case, I'll give you Bill's real ID. I would appreciate it if you could keep my name out of it, Dan. I've used him for several years and he's been dependable."

"Sure, count on it, Alison."

She grabbed her purse, no bigger than a trunk for a family of 12 on a month's vacation, surprisingly found his name, and wrote it out, then handed the slip to the cop.

"Thanks, Alison, and of course you, Michael." He caught a frown from the senior member and amended his statement, "And Pap, of course."

"I'd sure like to confirm that story before going too much further. I'll think about it and maybe lightning will strike."

He paused at the door.

"I really do thank you all. I'm in your debt. Just holler if you need anything."

After he left Pap finished his drink and put it into the sink.

"Sorry to cut and run just when things are getting exciting. But I have a sure winner at Belmont, and they're running nights now.

"I'll phone you here as soon as I have my high finance taken care of. And I'm going to check with a guy I know. He claims to be something of a buddy to that GG at HA."

At the door he looked at Michael.

"Don't worry, boss. I won't blow anything. I'll just sneak up on the subject of hand jobs, sorry Alison, and work it around to HA."

"Okay, Pap. Good luck at the races. Talk to you later."

Pap threw a wet kiss at Alison, bowed, and left.

CHAPTER 20

"I could use another belt, Alison. How about you?"

"Absolutely. I've never been involved in a murder before. I'll get the drinks."

She got up and floated to the small refrigerator. Shant noticed that her hips moved in two separate sections. Lovely.

She returned with the two glasses.

"Here you are, sir. Is there anything else you'd like?"

He looked at her eyes. She was smiling.

Could she have meant the invitation? No, she had never made any come-on play at all. Was she just a sweet little virgin, on her first big assignment with the writer from the big city?

He almost laughed aloud. Virgin? The last virgin had been spotted in Vegas in October 1957. Since then the species had been officially declared extinct by the Greater Las Vegas & Area Sworn Bachelors Club.

He decided it would be best to just ignore the probably unintended inference.

Alison sat down on a chair opposite him, then crossed her legs.

Her tight skirt had seemed short before, now it disappeared before his eyes. Her legs stretched from the floor to, ah, quite high, and her skirt, built with more than enough material to completely cover and make invisible from human sight the full, untrimmed area of a regular, not airmail, postage stamp.

Rather than gaze, as he truly wished, at the tops of her nylons, where he could almost make out the manufacturer's name, he decided to concentrate on the stunning scenic vista outside the room's magnificent picture window. It must measure at least six square feet. And where else could you feast your view on such a dramatic car parking lot?

He started pacing, thinking of the problem he, and his article, faced.

"To make this assignment hang together I only have two choices, Alison.

"One, turn it into a normal 'Gee whiz, ma, ain't that preacher man something?'

"Or we finish it with a slam bang ending with Pap's pix illustrating Rambow being led handcuffed and leg chained away to durance vile.

"What's your pick, Alison?"

"Most certainly, pa, the one about the magik preacher man." She clapped her hands together and let her mouth droop open like the stereotype of an Alabama hillbilly.

He laughed aloud.

"That's what's needed here, young miss. More serious discussion of the issues of the day."

"What are the chances of our lieutenant being able to nail Rambow, and maybe even some of his crew if they're involved?"

"They'd have to be involved at least a bit. There's no way Rambow himself could have physically handled all the necessary moves.

"As to your question, I just don't know. At the moment, even with your snitch Bill's outstanding contribution, it doesn't seem that the forces of law n'order have too much solid evidence that would prompt a jury to shout 'Guilty!

"It's going to be damned difficult to put Rambow at the scene of either killing. His staff at Happy Andings, including that manager GG and that odd jobs guy Tonto, will obviously be somewhat reluctant to turn on their meal ticket boss. No other witnesses have surfaced.

"One or two of the masseuses might break under pressure, but even that's doubtful. Like any basically one-industry town, working again in a Vegas whack parlor would probably prove long odds against."

They both had short pulls at demon rum.

"I know it may be slightly off the affairs of the day, Michael, but could you tell me a little more about these somewhat mysterious whack parlors?"

She smiled innocently.

Shant, although totally without the need of a religious security blanket, thought that the storybook Eve had probably smiled just like that as she had presented fictitious Adam with his delicious apple.

"Well, I shouldn't be referring to all massage parlors as whack parlors, Alison. That's just a crudity used by men."

"But what exactly is a whack parlor, Michael?" That innocent look again.

He cleared his throat. He had already mentally cleared her of any childish virgin charge, so she must have at least an elementary knowledge of male anatomy. Quite possibly a better firsthand knowledge than he did.

So why was he acting like some pimpled teenager on his first date?

Consideration for the younger woman? Consideration for an employee? Consideration for her sensual sensibilities because actually he'd love to screw the pants off her? (Unless, like several he had known, she didn't wear any. In that case, he'd gladly settle for just screwing.)

Maybe she was merely joshing him, seeing how raddled he became just because she was young, female, and reasonably attractive.

No, he didn't think so.

"It's very simple, my young protégé. Massage parlors first existed solely to slake men's ugly unromantic physical needs. The modern-day version, with all kinds of healthy family activities for young and old, is sometimes a completely different kettle of worms.

"Some MPs—massage parlors—offer their men customers a Happy Anding, just like Rambow's MP.

"At the end of a regular massage, when the male customer has often seen and felt his body reacting to the sensitive ministrations and titillations of a female masseuse, in order for him to easily get dressed and walk gracefully from the premises, he requires something to ease the pressure.

"In short," he concluded, "he needs a whack job to get rid of, what is spectacular at least to him, his monstrous hard on."

Alison laughed and again clapped her hands.

"You mean a hand job! Why didn't you just say that at the start?"

He made a fake swipe at her bottom.

"You were just having me on, young miss. That's very naughty to take advantage of your elders that way."

She smiled. "Elders? Yes, you must be at least eight, maybe even nine! years my elder."

She got up, set her drink on the kitchenette table, and walked to his chair and sat down on his lap, almost capsizing the pair of them and the already defective chair.

She looked at him full in the face. A serious expression.

"I have had too much booze to drive home. This time of day is when the cops make their quota of traffic tickets for the week in just an hour or so.

"I can check with the front desk of this establishment and see if they have a spare room. But I don't want to be alone tonight, with all those details of two murdered girls so fresh.

"I know you're a traveling man, Mr. Shant, and I'm not a cowgirl, I'm not trying to lasso you. I like you, maybe a lot, and before you toddle off to the Wild West coast, I'd like to share a night with you.

"If you have other business plans, I'll understand. If they involve a female in any shape or form, cancel them.

"This night of adult pleasures will not in any way affect our business-contractor relationship. I will not expect birthday, Halloween or, heaven forbid, Mother's Day cards.

"If you ever return to sin city, and want to do a little more of our good stuff, I do hope you'll give me a call. That's the only obligation either of us has.

"Now, instead of sitting here having an earnest discussion of how some men get their rocks off, why don't we have one more drink, and then adjourn to the small but private bedroom?"

The evening passed pleasantly. No one came knocking, and only Pap phoned later, to say he had won his bet, and had talked briefly to the guy who knew GG at Happy Andings, and would check in for breakfast with them about nine in the ayem.

"Sounds good, Pap....say, what do you mean 'with them'?"

"Would you prefer that I say you and Alison? I thought them was shorter."

Shant paused. "But how did you know Alison would be here?"

"I been handling broads since long before you realized they had funny mounds on their chests. I knew what would happen. The only question was when. And now that puzzle has been solved.

He laughed. "Sleep well you two. See you both manana."

Alison was an early riser, and even with a night of fun filled debauchery she was up and making instant coffee long before 9.

Shant crept up behind her and hugged her. She hugged back, then looked over her shoulder.

"You know, boss, it's customary to greet a key employee with at least shorts on.

"But," she giggled, "that feels a lot better than doing exercises to keep in shape." She rubbed her bum hard against him and his body responded.

"Hmm. Maybe a quick little nap before a shower and coffee?"

He nodded and she also felt his more direct answer.

Later they sipped instant coffee and gazed at that spectacular landscape outside their window.

"You know, Michael, I've been thinking about our dilemma, not having any solid evidence against Rambow.

"What is needed is not some married policewoman whose husband would probably come looking for our friendly lieutenant.

"What is needed is to find some hard"—she looked at Shant and grinned in the direction of the family jewels— "evidence of his atrocious behavior. A female who is single, knows quite a bit about this case already, and who is so brave and true of heart that Rambow doesn't frighten her too much. Someone who knows Vegas, areas to avoid, and stuff like that. Finally, someone who has a good idea of the kind of evidence probably needed by the cops to throw a pretty crooked TV preacher far back into the slammer."

She took a sip of coffee and looked directly at Shant.

He nodded absently. "Right. Now if we only had three magic wishes...." He looked up. Alison was still staring at him.

He shook his head.

"No. No way, babe. Absolutely no way. Positively no way...."

She smiled.

"I want to do it, Mike. I promise to be super careful. I won't go anywhere with Rambo alone."

He looked at her seriously.

"If I ever agreed, brave and true of heart, how could you get next to that prick?"

"Easy. I'd go in to good old Happy Andings looking for a job, but I'm in a hurry right then, could I talk to someone later, maybe in a couple of hours?"

"But what if Rambow himself shows up, says you look promising, but he'll have to give you a short test to see if you're HA material?"

"You mean, dad, what if he wants to get a freebie hand job from this fresh young girl just in from, say, Kansas City?"

Shant nodded.

"Look, contrary to the image that men have of younger females, Michael, there're probably not more than four females in the entire country who haven't given some creep a hand job, either as a my way or the highway routine—it still happens, and few want to hoof it ten miles to the nearest phone—or just as a simple and proven way of getting out of a difficult situation with some once-and-only-time date.

"Relax. Most girls by their teens know quite a bit about that monster men think they have tucked away in their pants. Grabbing a dick for a couple of minutes is easier than walking a long way at night, and sort of easier than carrying a pistol and banging away at some creep on a first date.

"So, in the interests of justice, if I have to clutch Rambow's dick for probably a few seconds, I'm prepared to do it.

"Shock you?"

"Not shocked, Alison. After our romps last evening I'm taking notes next time. But I am really concerned for your safety. This lump has probably snuffed two girls just as young and tough as you, and look how those 'tests' turned out.

"I have one firm condition. Well, two.

"First, you let me run this by our lieutenant, make sure he agrees, and is willing to give you all assistance possible."

"That's reasonable. And actually sensible."

Shant nodded. He looked at her.

"Well, boss, what's the second condition?"

He looked at his watch.

"It's still only a quarter to nine. Pap's usually five or ten minutes late.

"And I have my notebook handy in case I learn some new tricks.

"So how be we adjourn to ye olde bedroom for a quickie nap?"

She laughed.

"I don't think you're going to be in any need of a soothing hand job from Madame Alison, new masseuse with Happy Andings. So let's get on with the big boy's fun and games."

Pap was only ten minutes late, and after greetings they moved immediately to the motel restaurant.

Both Shant and Alison ordered full breakfasts. Pap settled for dry toast and coffee.

"Maybe I should try that exercise routine," he said. "Does wonders for the ayem appetite." He grinned.

Alison laughed. "It really does."

After his first cup of perked coffee, Shant went to the lobby phone, the old-fashioned type tucked away nice and private in its own little house.

He got through to Lieutenant Southfield on his first try.

It took a lot longer to fill him in on his and Alison's plan.

At first he was dead against it. Then he was a lot against it.

Finally Shant got him down to "Well, I still think it's crazy. Alison's a competent woman but she has had no experience in this type of stuff. It's police work, not for civilians. This guy may well be a multiple-killer, Michael."

After several more minutes of heavy arguing, Southfield would only agree "unhappily" to it if he heard from Alison directly.

So Shant parked the receiver to look like it was still occupied, which it was, and hustled in to the restaurant and quickly explained to Alison that Southfield wanted to talk to her.

He anticipated another argument but didn't get it.

"Sure" said Alison. And left the table.

By this time Pap had heard an edited version of the plan from Alison.

As Alison left Shant said "Women!"

Pap said "I agree".

CHAPTER 21

"Now, listen, Gibbie. This is very important. Especially to you. And to Happy Andings as well."

GG was in her dominant mood, and she towered over him as he sat relaxed in her office chair.

"If you screw this up in any way, *any way*, you'll never get past the reception area here. Remember, I'm now the majority shareholder and I can legally have you bounced from the premises."

Rambow nodded obediently. How he'd love to kick her right in the pussy. He should never have signed over 70 percent. All she and that midget Tonto had done was help him out a little on an accident situation. Well, two accidents, but nothing really spectacular.

"The only reason I called you, Gibbie, was that a real cutie dropped in earlier, said she was looking for a job. But she had another appointment or something, so she said she'd be back later if anyone wanted to talk with her. I didn't let on I was the boss here. She thought I was just a flunky office drone.

"I know you're feeling down and I thought a new girl might be good for you.

"But no funny business. I'll let you interview her, and if you can talk her into showing you her goodies, or even giving you a quickie hand or blow job, okay.

"Notice carefully that I said 'talk', Gibbie. I don't think this broad has any experience in the whack parlor industry. She may just want to try it out as an adventure or something. There are a lot of young broads like that. Hell, I used to be one myself.

"So go for a simple fun date, Gibbie. And to make sure you don't go crazy again, and really fuck things up for everybody, I'm going to watch you through the secret viewer." (And also get some more footage in case I need it.)

Rambow started to shake his head.

"You know I've watched you before, a long time ago, Gibbie. Back just after I first started here as manager and I wanted to see how a real professional did interviews and stuff. I told you all about it and you said fine." (You thought you were really hot stuff and only too anxious to let me see you and your equipment in action. Hot stuff. I've seen better action from two young boys whacking off together for the first time.)

"Now, if you treat her right, and don't try to force her into anything, we may have a real money earner on our hands. She looked so young and innocent that I know several of our regulars who would gladly pay a premium price for her. If she only stuck even for a month or two, I could underpay her on the basis of she had no experience—exactly why she'd bring a premium—and charge extra, giving us a nice bonus.

"For god's sake, Gibbie, don't go past a hand job. At the most a blow job if she really wants to, but only then, and don't say that's required, just the hand job.

"In fact, Gibbie, say nothing about being even a junior partner. Just maybe act like you're a hired gun to test her and show her what's required on the job. That's how I'll intro you if she comes back, so don't confuse things. Clear?"

"Absolutely, GG. I'll do exactly as you said." And I'd still like to kick you where the sun don't shine.

"I'm not even sure the broad will be back, Gibbie, so why don't you find something to read for awhile?"

GG dug into a stack of soft-core porno mags that she rotated among the rooms. Some of the girls liked to have their customers ready for their magic hands as soon as they had them turn over. It speeded things up and especially the fading girls needed all the help they could get.

GG found an almost new mag—no creases or stains on it—and threw it over to Rambow. He opened it avidly. At WIMPS he didn't really have the opportunity to openly view such literature.

GG got engrossed in HA finances. She kept a separate set of all data in a password protected secret file on her computer, and every day or so she sent a copy after closing to her second computer in her apartment. Like Mark Twain advised, she didn't trust anyone.

Rambow stayed engrossed in his literature.

Alison was trying to get ready for her second Happy Andings visit of the day. She was pretty sure she had snowed that huge manager, Glory, or GG. Despite her apparent low level of intelligence, Alison got the impression that she was far sharper than the image she presented, so she was careful to not overplay the "virgin looking for safe thrills" act.

Now she probably would be faced with Rambow.

Although she had acted casual about what she might have to do, and the danger involved, to Shant, she was nervous.

She'd be alone, probably in that soundproofed room where two other young women had probably died, and possibly expected to fondle the privates of that same murderer.

Should she be sensible and pull the plug now, when it was possible? Admit she had chickened out, to the three currently most important men in her life, Shant, Pap, and the cop?

She knew that all three would never laugh, at least right now and then only with her, about what they would call a sensible choice.

She looked at her bedroom wall mirror.

Sure, she was liable to do just that.

She started to laugh, and had to sit down on the bed before she fell down.

She opened her walk-in closet and looked over her clothes. She had to wear something which would get Rambo into action, and yet appear somewhat innocent and unsophisticated so he might not get vicious.

She picked out a fawn skirt, fairly short, and a sleeveless blouse which was tight enough to hint at the goodies enclosed.

In the kitchen, with a final—no, no, not final, just a regular—cup of coffee, she decided how far she would go. She had her cell with both Michael's motel room and the Lieutenant's personal cell numbers preprogrammed, in a fitted black case attached with a Velcro strap she wore under the name brand label of her scanty panties.

She had no intention of disrobing beyond her blouse, even that was at the extreme limit she had decided on, so the cell should be hidden, safe and accessible. She also wore a powerful police-strength whistle disguised in a large necklace. It might not stop an attack but it would certainly make it obvious, even in a soundproofed room. The lieutenant had assured it had been tested in action and it worked.

She gave herself a thumbs' up gesture in her hall mirror. "Get it done, babe."

About twenty minutes later, with her car parked almost a block away, she entered Happy Andings, a little surprised at the modest and apparently clean decor.

A bell sounded when the door opened, and a few seconds later a short man appeared.

He smiled, not unattractively. "Can I help you?" She didn't look like a customer, he thought, although two of the girls had females as regular clients. He never inquired as to what transpired in those normal length sessions. He was not in the least interested.

"Hi, my name is Marsha. I have sort of an appointment with the manager, a GG?"

"Sure, grab a chair for a minute. I'll see if she's available."

He ducked back of a fairly thick curtain, returned just a minute later.

"She's on the phone right now, said she'd only be a minute. Hang on.

In GG's office she was giving her junior partner his last-minute instructions.

"No violence of any kind, Gibbie. No blow job, unless she volunteers. Remember, I'll be watching, at least until you get things underway in a very friendly way. You're an instructor, nothing more. Clear?"

She stood toe to toe with him; he could see she was not kidding. He nodded.

"Come on in, Marsha. This is Gilbert. As our customers are men, we use him to give a girl her first interview, and explain what the job is like. You said you'd had no experience in massaging so he'll tell you whatever you want to know."

GG walked as Rambow led the way, with Marsha following. She used her key to unlock the door— "This room is used mainly for training, so we keep it locked most of the time"—then pushed it open, and as Rambow entered last she made a point of showing him that she was pocketing the key, not giving it to him as she normally did. She also mouthed "I'm watching".

Alison/Marsha looked around. It looked like a typical sleazy sex room—she'd seen them in the movies, not in real life—and noticed the key byplay.

GG pulled the door closed, hung a sign on it, "In session; do not disturb", and immediately went to the secret video camera and activated it.

If she had to enter this room in a hurry to prevent injury, even death, she planned to kick Rambow in his balls just as hard as she could.

Inside, Rambow sat on the edge of the bed, motioned to one of the chairs for Marsha.

"You'll have noticed, Marsha, we haven't asked you yet to fill out any forms.

"The reason for that, my dear, is that you said you'd had no massage experience. So, you may not really understand what it is to massage a man."

He paused, and was obviously looking for a reply.

"No, Gilbert, I don't really know much about it. Maybe you could fill me in?"

I would certainly love to, Marsha, but later perhaps.

"I'll do my best. If at any point you have a question just let me know.

"Nearly all our customers are men, although one or two girls also service females. That would be strictly your choice. A girl working here always has the right to reject any customer, although then neither she nor we make any money.

"Anyway, a man comes here as a customer because he wants a good massage, and to end up refreshed and relaxed."

Alison nodded.

"First, of course, the man gets undressed, puts his clothes on a chair which is in all rooms, the lies face down on the massage table."

"He takes off all his clothes?" She tried to make it sound just a normal question.

"Of course, how else can a girl give him a full massage?"

Rambow looked genuinely puzzled. "Is that a problem?"

"No, no, I was just making sure I understood. You're doing great in explaining, Gilbert, please continue."

Rambow accepted the praise with grace.

"So first the girl gives him a complete massage on the back side: back, legs, bum, all. Oh, I forgot, you do know how to massage professionally?"

"Well, I've never done it real professionally, but I have given a bunch of massages to my friends and they all say they're great massages."

"Sounds okay. If you work out, after awhile I sometimes give what we call graduate update courses. There's no charge, and quite often with the extra services that she learns she can give her customers, her earnings will jump quite a bit."

"Wow. What are the courses like?" She looked genuinely interested.

"There's no point in going into them now, Marsha. We don't even know if HA can offer you a contract. I better get back to explaining the basics.

"After the girl has completed the full back side, she asks the customer to turn over so she can do the front side."

Alison/Marsha nodded. "Sounds logical."

"Of course, most girls find their performance on the front is a real determiner of both tips—the girl keeps most of these—and repeat visits."

"That's really interesting. Why is that?"

He put two fingers up.

"It's pretty simple, Marsha.

"That's the section of the body the girl does last, so that's closest to when the customer will be paying his bill. And of course calculating what if any tip he will add.

"And second, that's when the girl has the chance to end the massage with a real flourish, making the customer feel really good, and relaxed at the same time."

He paused and looked at her.

"Any questions?"

She wasn't sure how far she should play the role of ingénue. Too much, she figured, and he might be turned off. Too experienced, at least in her apparent attitude, and he might think she was an old pro.

She decided.

"I know that each massage parlor has different requirements for how the massage is ended. Maybe you could tell me exactly what Happy Anding's is?"

"There's no such here as an official policy on that, Marsha. You heard wrong.

"But I will tell you that our customers, certainly the ones who are regulars and who keep both the girls, and HA, in business, are adults. And men."

He looked directly at her.

"What kind of a massage ending do you think you would use if you were hired here, and if you planned on making some good money for both of us?"

Smooth. Rambow had put the onus right back on her.

Again she had to make a choice, and quickly.

She sort of smiled. "From what you have described, Gilbert, I assume the customers would expect something like a hand job. I have even heard some girls talk about where a blow job is standard, but I'm sure HA is above that level."

He nodded.

"Generally, that's correct. I'm also sure some of our higher earning girls have no compunctions about the occasional BJ for good regulars, but that's up to them. I know one or two who feel a BJ is just as easy, maybe even faster, than the basic hand job, and can result in substantially more tips. But again, the rooms are private and the girls only do what they want to."

He moved around the room but didn't approach her.

"With your implied almost total of massage experience, Marsha, do you feel you'd be able to handle" -- he smiled at her— "the work here at HA?"

"Well, I guess like most females, Gilbert, I have a little experience with hand jobs, and as long as the customer behaved himself, you know, didn't try to turn it into something else, if my tips depend largely on that, I think it would be no problem."

She was surprised, she thought that once the talk turned to hand jobs and BJs, Rambow would start to get twitchy. But he really hadn't made a move. If he didn't do something soon, make some kind of move confirming that all their suspicions might have a solid foundation, she'd have to take the initiative herself.

"I know you're the official trainer here at Happy Andings, Gilbert. Would you like to have me give you sort of a sample massage so you could determine if I could do the job?"

He seemed to be considering it. From what she knew, what the fuck was the holdup?

She had thought that once she offered to give him a whack job, he'd have his clothes off and be on the table in a flash.

He continued to pace the room, but came nowhere near her. He looked at her closely.

"We provide the girls uniforms. Short skirts, fairly tight, or tight ass shorts, and short sleeved blouses open enough to display some cleavage. What they wear beneath is their choice. Some do wear lingerie, and some say they can move around a lot easier, and indirectly encourage the customer to develop a hard on faster, simply by some well placed flashes, without. It's up to them.

"You don't of course have yet a uniform, and to get an accurate idea of how you might do here, what would you wear for your trial massage".

He was good, no doubt about it. He was putting her on the spot again.

Another decision. She felt she had him coming along so she'd have to be very careful here.

"Well, I guess I could take off my blouse and skirt, do the massage in my bra and panties. Would that be okay for you?"

Shit, she was saying yes to a lot of things she had been fully prepared to say no to before the interview started. Was this guy actually a crazed sex killer? Or just a real smoothie who sometimes lost total control?

He looked at her again. Then at his watch.

"Oops, just realized there's a call I have to make. It'll only take five.

"If you want you can hang on here. I'll leave the door open, there's a can just down the hall. Stay or come back again?"

What was happening? He was acting more like the virgin in this melodrama. And leaving the door open?

She'd come too far, and all her men had done too much work just to walk away now.

"Sure, I'll hang on for a few minutes."

He opened the door and left it wide. In a minute or two she went quietly to the door and peeked both ways. No bogeymen.

Once he turned the corner Rambow spotted GG's legs poking out from the cramped video camera room. He gave her a pinch on her ass.

"What was that for? And what's happening? Lost your interest in a hand job?"

He pushed her towards her office. She unlocked the door—the bitch kept everything locked—and they both went in and he closed the door.

"Aren't you proud of me, GG?" He grinned like a kid showing his mom his first A report card.

"Yes, yes, I am, Gibbie. Really impressed. Why the change in plans?"

"I don't really know, GG. She's hot, and I can see she's got a great bod. I just got a bad feeling. Like she was up to something. You know how some time you get the feeling a girl is not good, even before she starts.

Like maybe she claims to be the best BJer in town, then on her first trick she almost bites it off with excitement?

"Well, something like that."

He looked down at his crotch. "This guy isn't bothered, though, he's all ready.

"Are there any other girls not busy right now, GG?"

"I just got a late cancellation call from Abe—you know, the big tall guy with a Lincoln beard—and he fell all over apologizing that he'd have to cancel on Stephanie. Some kind of 24-hour flu. He said he'd make it up to her on next week's visit, so you can tell Stefie. I was just about to go and do that, but I wanted another checkup look at you in the special.

"You can take the news to Stef that she'll get a double fee from Abe next week. And you could slide in there on a freebie."

"Stephanie? The brunette with the big boobs?"

"That's her. You've used her before, said she gave great head."

"Okay. I'll go back and tell Marsha, or whatever her fucking name really is, that I want to think about her, that even though she talks a good line I'm a little afraid she'll freeze up on the action line. And I'll tell her something has come up, I don't have time now for her trial. If she wants, I'll have her come back in a few days."

"Yeah, good idea. I was sort of looking forward to see how you'd handle her, she has got a great figure. I was actually surprised when she offered to strip to bra and panties."

"Me too. That's part of the reason I was nervous.

"Okay, GG, why don't you phone Stef on the inside line, tell her I'll be down to see her in a few mins. What room's she in?"

"Five. Have fun. You going to go for a hand or BJ?"

"Both. I'm horny enough now for all two."

"It took a little longer than I thought, Marsha. Look, I want to think about you a little more, I'm just not sure you're HA material. And I don't have time now anyway for your trial massage.

"You can think about it too. I can tell you that all the girls here like the work and the conditions, and the bucks, more than they can make in any other parlor in Vegas, and they rarely quit, usually only because gravity is causing too many sags.

"In a few days, if you'd still like to try out for me, give GG in the office a call and leave a cell number where I can call you. I may be out of town for a day or two.

"Are you still interested?"

"Sure, I think you'll find my trial demo will convince you I can handle whatever comes up here." She grinned to make sure he got the point."

As she walked the block back to where her car was parked, she was furious. That son of a bitch. Turning down a great hand job, and me half undressed to do it. Who did he think he was?

Well, it just meant her attempted semi-seduction of Gilbert Rambow was postponed.

Definitely not cancelled.

And for her test she'd wear the sexiest panties she had.

CHAPTER 22

"Lt. Southfield please."

"He's in his office. I'll connect you."

"Southfield."

"This is Michael Shant, Dan. How are they hanging?"

"Low. How's our sting op on the preacher coming?"

"I'm expecting a call from Alison any minute. She had called earlier and said she was in the special room and that she expected him back, he left to make a call, in a few minutes.

"She said he was acting almost like a normal human, no grab ass or anything. She wanted to make sure we wouldn't move on the plan until she knew that he was starting to get kinky."

"Alison's starting to cool on the sting?"

"I don't think so, Dan. She said it was just almost as if GR had been tipped in advance, he was acting so cool and businesslike. She figured we'd blow the whole plan if we charged in before she had some solid evidence, and she didn't have that."

"Okay, I'll keep the troops held back until she gives a clear 'let's go'. I have two cars very close so if she needs us, we can be there within just a few minutes."

"Good. I better get off this cell, she may be calling me any minute."

"Keep me posted, Mike."

"Dan, sorry to get back so soon. As soon as I hung up before Alison called.

"She said GR had definitely cooled. She was pretty sure he'd received info from somebody.

"When he returned to the special room, he acted like a kid on his first date, very reserved, very cool, even left the door open. Then he brushed her off with some story about he wanted to think about her, that he wasn't sure she was 'HA material', for god's sake, and that if she was still interested to phone GG in a day or two.

"Said he had to be out of town for awhile but they could hook up later, if she still wanted, and if he thought she was a HA girl. What horseshit, he'd take anyone.

"So maybe he did get tipped."

"Not from here, Mike. Only my tightest men were in on this, and I know none of them would say a word."

"Well, unless Pap let something slip, no leak here either, and I know that anything regarding Alison he'd keep his mouth closed tighter than a virgin's pussy."

"These things happen. Maybe Rambow just wasn't horny. When you've had a chance to get more info from Alison, let me know and we can maybe arrange a new sting date.

"Will do, Dan. Talk later."

Shant closed his cell.

Alison had sounded more angry than nervous or frightened. She had said she would meet him at his motel in about a half hour. He'd get the story then.

CHAPTER 23

Pretty Pussy screamed when she saw him.

"Oh, Gilbert, I've missed you so much! Why don't you let me know when you'll be back in the office? I get so worried."

Big Bertha seriously watched the younger woman that she knew was screwing the Boss as often as she could.

Well, Pretty Pussy didn't mind that much. As long as she could give the boss, and sometimes his good friend or two, or three, a good lip-smacking BJ as he sat there looking dignified and preachery, right up to the moment when his whole body tightened and flooded her with his warm sensuous cream, as long as she "got my daily vitamins", she was content.

She knew only too well that she could never compete on looks or body parts with the younger broads. But the Preacher could get a simple piece of ass almost anywhere. So many females actually believed the biblical bullshit, and would do whatever the so-called message deliverer would request, all, of course, in "his holy name".

One time when she had been fondling his dick, just prior to his explosion, and he was in a very cooperative frame of mind, she had jokingly asked Rambow what the holy name was.

As his problem was being resolved, and as she couldn't talk for a minute or two, he had laughed, "It's John Doe. But don't tell anyone."

Once Rambow had disengaged himself from the younger bitch's clutches, BB had moved in, taken his arm, and literally shoved him into her office.

"Boss, a couple of matters which may be important.

"First, there's a registered letter here for WIMPS, from the IRS. As you instructed, I opened that kind of mail."

She reached behind him, managing to rub her large but soft breasts against his shoulder, and grabbed the envelope from the corner of her desk.

"Apparently they are going to do an audit of both WIMPS and you personally. The creep or more likely their machine who wrote it said 'There are no accusations implied in this normal audit. But should any discrepancies be uncovered in either your or your church's records, we do have the legal right to request and examine in detail all such records for the past 7 years."

"Jeesus Keerist! Is everybody in this fucking world persecuting me?"

Rambow rarely swore in the office, almost never using biblical terms which his faithful WIMPS customers would be shocked by, so BB knew that he was really angry.

She lowered her voice, and turned so her back was to the outer office where the PP lurked like a vulture, and gave him a quick sales pitch for her charms as a temporary and quick relief for his problems.

But Rambow, normally easy to persuade he needed the pleasures of a soft, warm, wet receptacle to resolve his difficulties, had been too well serviced by Stephanie, who, given the unexpected treat of a twofer fee the next time her regular Abe visited, had decided to splurge on the freebie for the boss, and had used some new techniques just learned from the current newsstand issue of "Creative ways to keep your man happy with your seductive mouth".

Usually it was loaded with boring old methods she had tried and discarded years ago, but it had a new editor, and she was trying very hard to increase circulation in the face of increasing encroachments by really graphic—and apparently free, except for duplicitous and fraudulent ads which once answered dogged the poor recipient for the rest of his life—hard core porn channels.

"Maybe later, BB", he answered casually. "What's the second matter?"

"A short but really ugly guy by the name of Klassen has been in four, no, five times over the past two days. First time he was alone. The other times he was with King Kong, a guy who looked like he could crush pineapples with a couple of fingers."

"And what did that prick want?"

BB had to slide around Rambow—again comforting him with a solid feel of her quite large boobs—and opened her left-hand bottom drawer.

She pulled out a steno pad and flipped it open to a page she had earmarked.

"Here's in effect what he said.

"Tell that motherfucking cocksucker Rambow that I want my money by Wednesday noon. Cash, every penny. And that asshole had better add in all the accrued interest too.

"Tell him this is his last notice. No cash in full and he can look forward to a good Polish wake, probably attended by at least three people.

"Remember, sweet cheeks"—BB thought that was a nice thing for the slug to say, she'd always been proud of both those little beauties— "no more futzing around. If he hasn't got the full amount, he could sell several of his organs. He won't need them anyway."

BB closed the pad and dropped it on her desk.

Rambow rubbed his forehead for inspiration. Unlike the fable of the magic genie appearing when the lamp was rubbed, nothing happened.

"I'll be in my office, BB. No calls, no deliveries, no visitors, nothing. Got it? My door will be locked."

She nodded. If she couldn't use her many wiles to relieve the boss, she knew that the bitch PP out front didn't have a hope either. Rambow always preferred a quick oral answer to his physical needs. He regarded having to disrobe as an unnecessary chore.

In his office he lay down on the embroidered settee presented to him by the Ladies Auxiliary to the honored and esteemed leader of the WIMPS. He was fairly confident that that worthy and charitable and believing group had no idea that its main use was as a comfortable spot to rest with his trousers down around his knees and BB ministering to him.

But now it was simply a settee.

The IRS. Those parasites were worse than piranhas.

Once they got their greedy claws into the inner finances of the WIMPS, and began to note, and probably trace through their illegal and never authorized wire taps and big bully tactics with several of the small countries he had selected as banking recipients of periodic large cash deposits, there was no telling what they could uncover.

Contrary to one of his "seen the light" parishioner's very firm opinion that hard copy accounting records—and the former but now retired chief launderer for several large and respected mob front companies knew whereof he spoke—should never be kept where the main man resided. (The main man here, of course, was Gibbie Rambow.

"If you have your computer fixed properly by a real pro so that with one key click everything on it is deleted and destroyed forever, then it's okay to keep them close. It's handy, of course, that you don't have to make a quick flight to Belize every time you want to get a fast total of last month's real revenue.

"But if you are foolishly using real books, on paper and all that, you're a goddamned—sorry, preacher, that just slipped out—idiot if you have them nice and convenient where any government prick can get a subpoena on them from a should-be-disbarred judge who sits on some bench as a rubber stamp for what the feds want approved."

Rambow had agreed with that philosophy, but like many good intentions it languished in his To Do file.

Well, now it was too late. He had to get those books somewhere safer than where they were.

And he also had to absent himself from that greedy Klassen. He had obviously invested a few dollars and bought himself some gorilla who when Klassen said "Kill" or "Cripple", would delight in doing just that.

But Rambow had faced and come through problems like this before. Well, maybe not quite as serious as these, but he knew that if the accounting records were gone, the feds could rant and rave but if he stuck to his story— "I just don't know. Numbers and records are just not my forte, strong points that is, and someone on the WIMPS staff has made an error. But we will get it straightened out, officers." (Sure, in a decade or two.)

And if he had to, he'd play his trump card. "This is pure religious persecution." Just as the 'race' card had worked for generations of unqualified illiterates, that persecution angle was pure gold.

The pig Klassen was even easier. If he couldn't locate Rambow for a few days, and if Rambow appeared with an apology and all, or maybe most, of the amount in question, he was sure all would be forgiven. Bookies did not thrive by knocking off or even just crippling good customers.

"Just crippling"? He had better get back down to planet earth. He was in no mood for even thinking of "just" anything.

The more he thought about it the better he felt. Some years ago, when he had spent time south of the border, he had gotten involved with a scam that went sidewise. But in spite of his partners literally losing every dime, he had managed to acquire and hold on to a slummy property on the southern outskirts of Ensenada, Mexico, then a typical sleepy village.

Over the years, as "earnings" from WIMPS increased dramatically, he had hired a local named Luiz Grandiloke, who explained his unusual surname as a combination of Ukrainian and Spanish forefathers.

Rambow had set up a local bank account for him, and Luiz had employed local carpenters and other tradesmen, and now the original slum building was a not bad three bedroom and casita property. It had cost Rambow a lot of money, even during the period when the peso was almost worthless, but now it was his lifeline.

He'd physically grab the one set of accounting records, and decamp with them to his Mexican villa for a few days of leisure and young attractive and willing Latin ladies, where the chances of bumping into any of the WIMPS group, or the IRS leeches, or thug Klassen, were low indeed.

Yes, a few fresh faces, a little or even a lot of troubles-forgetting tequila, and Rambow was confident his normal good luck would get him through.

He smiled. And when he made his grand return, maybe he'd even have that Marsha broad come in and parade around in bra and panties while she demonstrated her hand abilities. She did have a great bod.

He arose from his settee siesta—might as well get started now on practicing his Mexican soiree—unlocked the door, and beckoned to BB.

"C'mon in, BB. I think maybe later is now." She did have beautiful full lips.

She smiled at him, then when he turned back to his office, she stuck out her tongue—soon to be in more active use—at the PP bitch.

CHAPTER 24

After the pleasant session with BB, Rambow felt recharged. But he had to get moving, any of his enemies might show up on the WIMPS doorstep at any moment.

To cover his tracks, he decided to take a short flight to San Diego, then take the trolley to the border. Once across he could cab it into Tijuana, then rent a clunker for the short trip south on the Pacific Highway to Ensenada. The return trip would be just the reverse.

He could have his employee Luiz meet him on the Mexican side of the border, but it wouldn't save much time, and he enjoyed the road along the Pacific almost the way to Ensenada.

He opened the wall safe in his office. He took out his passport and peeled off seven or eight hundreds from an emergency stash he kept there.

There was no need to use Mexican currency. Anywhere in Baja California, the state that occupied the skinny isthmus that ran south several hundred miles, U.S. currency was readily accepted.

He dug out the single volume ledger book that contained all the secrets he didn't want to share with anyone, not WIMPS members, not Klassen, and most certainly not with the IRS vultures.

He pocketed the currency and passport, put the record book into a 9x12 manila envelope he normally used when he purchased porno disks and didn't want any church members to check out his purchases.

He looked for a phone number for Luiz Grandiloke but couldn't find it. Didn't matter, he knew Luiz spent most of his time at the house, according to Luiz "puttering around and keeping things shiny in case the boss dropped in".

Rambow had used the Mexican house a number of times, especially before he acquired Happy Andings and always had a place to either take his women or to use the girls who did housework there. With the HA facilities he hadn't had the need for a private bedroom as much the past few years.

In the back of his mind he saw it as sort of a retirement haven, especially if WIMPS should ever get too much unfriendly publicity, just like that current west coast asshole writer was liable to create.

He knew that with sufficient income he could live very pleasantly in the small Mexican city—expanded since he first acquired the dumpy house--due to the ease of access and the pleasant climate for North American tourists and retired oldies.

Rambow also knew that with just a little extra cash he could easily get local Ensenada officials to overlook any minor complaints from U.S. counterparts. He knew most Mexicans gladly accepted American money, and local jobs, but didn't really harbor much true friendship for their northern "cousins", whom they often found to be arrogant, loud, and generally overbearing towards their "poor" Mexican amigos.

Okay. As always GR had things well in hand. A place to go and cheap fun to be had when he got there.

He'd tell BB that he had to leave town for a few days, she knew enough about his various "business enterprises" to also know that his whereabouts would be "unknown".

While he was gathering his necessities for his "foreign" trip, he heard the outside line ring. A moment later BB came to his door, and knocked lightly before she entered the open doorway.

"Gibbie"—she always felt entitled after a session below Rambow's desk, and purposefully accented the nickname to piss of The Bitch—"that Klassen is on the phone. Said to tell you he was on his way here, and would be here within 45 minutes. Said you'd better have 'every fucking penny' of what you owe him. Or else. He started to explain in disgusting detail what that meant but I put him on hold."

"BB, I have to go sou... away on business for a few days. I'll phone you manana to see how things are. Anybody like that prick Klassen, and certainly any cocksucker from the IRS, you tell them I'm away on business, you don't know where, but expect me to be away for a couple of weeks.

"I don't think it'll really be that long, BB, but I've got to get going. Right now.

"Of course, you're in charge"—he raised his voice so his part time BJ in the front office, Pretty Polly, would hear— "so take care of everything.

"There should be plenty of money in petty cash in case you need it."

He leaned over, gave her a kiss on the cheek and a healthy goose in her can at the same time, swept up his few travel items, and went out the back door, just in case Klassen had lied about how far away he was. It would be just like that prick to do that.

He used the rear delivery lane to cut over to Paradise, and within a minute flagged down a cab.

"The airport, amigo." The driver, a hulking very black man who looked like he'd be almost seven feet if he stood up, looked at him carefully in the rear-view mirror to determine if he had been insulted.

He was apparently convinced that no slur had been intended, so he ground the gears and headed straight west. Unlike most cities Vegas had an airport where you didn't have to pack an overnight bag just to get there.

Rambow didn't need to go home to pack. He could easily carry the record book, and its envelope looked innocuous and grubby enough that no snatch and grabber would even waste time seizing it.

With money in his pocket Rambow would send Luiz, or his not unattractive live-in girl friend, maybe even wife by now, into town to get whatever clothes and supplies he needed. Traveling light had always been one of Rambow's mobile philosophies: all you need is bread and optimism. Anything else you can buy, rent, borrow, even steal. Why act like a fucking loaded-down porter when you travel?

The plane and trip went just as Rambow had planned.

By walking across the "most trafficked border in the world" he avoided the constant traffic snarls, much worse on the U.S. side; once in to the federal republic of Mexico traffic enforcement was far more lenient.

He rented a battered '07 Ford once in TJ.

The main highway south bypassed most of Tijuana. That was just as well, as it was a big, noisy, poorly policed city of millions. No one knew how many, because many of the Central American illegals who temporarily squatted in the TJ outskirts were there to try their skills at climbing or evading the huge U.S. border fences, reminiscent of the infamous Berlin Wall.

Built at a boondoggle cost of billions to U.S. taxpayers, the fences and other "keep out" attempts were just a joke to the hundreds of "coyotes" who made their livings showing the illegals how to get into the land of milk and honey. (More likely nowadays a land of unbuttered bread and day-old beans. Times change, as the Roman and Greek and British empires found out.)

The drive alongside the Pacific was as pleasant as the tourist guides promised it would be. Traffic going south was light, and he pulled alongside the malecon in Ensenada less than an hour later.

He had a quick Mexican rum over ice and bottled water at a small waterfront cantina where the scenic wall was wide open. A rolled-up metal curtain was pulled down at closing, which was probably when the last patron has stumbled out.

He had doubts about the Ford's ability to start again but his fears were groundless. He turned the key and the engine roared, smoked, and coughed encouragingly. Another good omen. Maybe some of that WIMPS crap he peddled might actually make sense.

The house was where he'd left it. Originally in what looked to be a "Condemned, Do Not Enter" zone, it was now book-ended by pleasant two storied houses built of very durable adobe with tiled roofs. Obviously a little Gringo-izing had occurred. He might actually have a profit on his years-long investment. But he had no intention of selling it. He had already been seduced again by the soft tropical air and the relaxed—sleepy? —attitude of many of the area's inhabitants.

No one seemed to be around. If Luiz was puttering about acting like a handyman, he must be doing it inside.

Rambow realized he hadn't brought a house key with him. He wasn't even sure he had one, it seemed that on every previous visit the doors had been unlocked.

He tried the front door and, sure enough, it opened easily.

There were thick rugs covering the entry way so his entrance was as silent as any thief would prefer.

No one in the fairly large living room, and the same in the quite large kitchen. He poked his head into the front half bath room. Empty.

He started with the front bedroom. Zilch.

The master bedroom, centered between the three bedrooms, had its door closed, but he could easily see that it was unlocked; the deadbolt he'd had installed one time to assure him a little lovemaking privacy was pushed back.

He turned the large metal handle. The room was occupied.

In the substantial and canopied bed were two, no three, no four people. Sort of in the center was his "handyman" Luiz. Nuzzling him from both sides were two apparently young and also apparently attractive, and from their bare tops probably nude, girls. Topping off the party was the cook. Rambow could identify her because she still had a large apron pulled up to expose everything except one very large breast which was covered by that apron.

They all smiled at him.

"Boss! How good to see you! You should have told me you were coming, I'd have gotten more girls. But you're welcome to jump in here and share these beauties."

Rambow liked sex in all its permutations, but three women? How did Luiz manage to satisfy them?

"That's a gracious offer, Luiz, but I'm just a little bushed from my quick trip here.

"One of these lovely girls I assume is a maid that I'm paying for?"

Luiz nodded enthusiastically.

"Si, senor, they both are. Maria and Lupita. No ingles, I'm afraid, but they are very friendly."

"Okay, Lupita, get me a cold beer please."

One of the girls stood up quickly, and without any embarrassment looked at her boss.

"Que?"

"Una cervaza fria," Luiz translated, and the girl slipped gracefully over the somewhat chubby cook and stood in all her glory before Rambow. And glory it was. Rambow doubted if she was over 16, could even be just 14 or 15, but she had a beautiful very-adult body.

She nodded her head at Rambow, as if acknowledging his authority, then turned and walked gracefully and slowly towards the kitchen. Two twin cheeks, each moving to a rhythm undetected by Rambow but certainly appreciated.

Lupita returned promptly with a frosty Dos Equis bottle, presented it proudly to Rambow, and made a little bow which almost inserted one of her charming and full breasts into his hand. He thought he'd have a little private talk with Lupita later.

Luiz now stood up, unfortunately displaying his full naked body. The maid, who looked about 50 but was probably only 30, clapped her hands, and Luiz turned partially and bestowed a full mouth smile on her.

"Gracias, Blanca."

He carefully walked over the still recumbent body of Maria, and finally stood on the floor. He scooped up his pants and slipped them on.

"How long you down for, boss? Want me to arrange a real fiesta for tonight? I know a couple more red-hot senoritas who would love to party, and they make these two look like flat chested little girls."

Rambow wondered how Luiz managed to keep such a sexy harem on the hook.

Rambow gave him free rent and board but only paid him a couple of hundred dollars a month, although that of course translated into over 4,000 pesos, but that certainly wasn't enough to attract and keep a handful of lovely ladies hanging around.

"Probably just a couple of days, Luiz. Not really sure right now.

"I do have to go over all the household accounts, so you can get into gear and round up all the receipts to go along with the books which I know you have kept faithfully."

Shant was pretty sure Luiz had. On his last visit he had been shown a large account book with the last entry almost three months before that day's date. He had reamed Luiz out royally, threatened to throw him out the door, and see he never got such a soft touch job again.

Luiz had been actually frightened, Rambow could tell, with the thought he might actually have to get a working job.

He had promised on his mother's grave—Rambow knew she was alive and working part time in the downtown bar area as a cheap hooker—and Rambow had reinforced the threat with a warning that if on his next visit the account book was more than one day out of date Luiz was immediately unemployed.

He was not surprised when Luiz quickly accepted his order.

"Si, boss, I will have everything laid out for you like a pretty embalmer's body within just a few minutes. In the meantime, how about another cold cervaza?"

The little prick was hoping to get me a little buzzed.

"No, maybe later. But have one of these maids," he didn't know which perky breast he should point to, "make a pot of strong coffee.

"I'm going to take a fast shower to wash off the travel grime."

"Perfecto, boss. I'll have Lupita make the cafe. And Maria is a top quality back cleaner, she'll really make things shine." Luiz grinned.

Luiz gave the orders in Spanish and both girls smiled and nodded.

Maria smiled again and took his hand and gently led him to the bathroom. She turned on the hot water, checked it with her dainty hand, then started using the other dainty but surprisingly firm hand to begin undoing his belt and unzipping his pants.

By that point Rambow found himself looking forward to more action from those dainty but firm hands and together they both managed to get rid of his remaining clothes in record time. Maria was already ready for the shower, no clothes to waste time on.

As he relaxed in the warm water, he began to appreciate Maria's ability as a top quality back cleaner. She was also fairly expert at cleaning and shining all other portions of his body. He wondered idly how she'd do as a massage therapist at Happy Andings, then realized the problems in getting her across the border weren't worth the effort.

Besides, it was nice to have such agreeable servants here in Ensenada. And he knew there'd be no need to back up with any heavy-handedness any instructions he gave the girls for whatever personal services he might like. Not like those miserable bitches at HA.

An hour later Rambow was finally finished his shower. About halfway through Lupita, also ready for the shower without having to divest any clothes, joined them and the party continued.

It turned out that neither girl had any experience in using her ample juicy lips on a gringo. At least that was how Rambow interpreted the rapid-fire language which each girl used to show him what she was talking about.

It involved a lot of holding, stroking, and touching an organ already swollen by all the attention. Although Rambow failed to see any real difference between Luiz, for example, and himself, the girls giggled and laughed endlessly as they held his dick and pointed out differences in it—not apparent to Rambow—and vied to see who would be first to kiss, then suck it.

As he finally exploded in Lupita's mouth—he thought it was her—the other maid—Maria? —seemed disappointed that that milestone had been reached by her colleague. But that didn't end the party, and soon

the girls had Rambow reinvigorated, and this time
Maria? got to put the finishing touches on her creation.

Back in what might be the real world, Rambow
pushed the girls out and away, got dressed—both had
offered to do that for him—and headed to the kitchen
table. He got the cook to pour him a mug of coffee—
Lupita had passed on his instructions to the cook
evidently—and the coffee was hot. And strong.

It just about cleared out his tonsils and he talked
in a falsetto for 30 seconds until he inhaled enough
oxygen to counteract the acid, but he had specified
strong. Next time he might find a word with a little less
strength, at least in Spanish, than 'strong'.

Or maybe the cook had witnessed or heard some
of the shower mob scene and calculated correctly that
he would need some strong liquids to replenish all the
body fluids expended in that endeavor.

Luiz had also followed instructions. The big
ledger book was open to yesterday's date and there
were several entries below that.

Okay. Now to start reconciling the ledger
amounts with the receipts, which Luiz had thoughtfully
thrown into an old 20-liter drinking water jug. Not in
any order, of course, and certainly not separated into
any known categories. But at least he had kept the
book current. That was a start, and Rambow knew
enough about employees—American or Mexican—to
know that a start on something was an achievement, at
least for him, the boss. Somebody he was paying good
money to had actually listened to an instruction and
had made a start on following it. One thing at a time.

He went through three more mugs of the coffee,
his body reacting less with each mug, and by the final
one he thought he might even beat what had been
odds-on of an immediate heart seizure.

The two totals were reasonably accurate. The
receipts totalled more or less what the account book
showed.

But there was a problem. The amounts entered,
and verified roughly by scrawled receipts often on
ordinary scraps of paper— "Most stores here won't give

you a formal receipt, boss, you just have to insist that they scrawl the date and amount on the paper, and you even have to give them the piece of paper—were far in excess of the amount Rambow had budgeted. In some cases well over double, and for several recent weeks, almost triple the totals Rambow had estimated.

Even those inflated amounts wouldn't break him, of course.

After all, what were a few thousand pesos here and there, compared to a big bettor like him who currently was dodging a thug who claimed a debt of well over a hundred grand?

Well over, indeed. The last figure Rambow had heard from that fucking criminal Big Bobbie Klassen was either approaching or over a hundred and fifty.

At a certain point Rambow gave up on the big numbers. He knew the WIMPS church was taking in a potful each month from its loyal members, and even with his ownership cut down to 30 percent at Happy Andings, it was throwing off a fat profit each time Gertie deigned to show her "junior partner" the actual books.

But Rambow disliked his employees cheating. What he did was different, he was the boss.

Even though his tirade last visit had scared Luiz, apparently he thought the firing threat applied specifically to the lack of record keeping. Keeping even reasonably honest books was a separate problem.

He had last seen Luiz talking to one of the maids, it looked like Lupita. Talking to her? Not really. He had been standing beside her, one palm firmly ensconced on one of her firm and bouncy cheeks, the other idly stroking the inside of her thigh above where her short skirt—more like a bikini bottom slipped down—ended.

"Luiz!" he shouted. "Get your Latin ass down here pronto."

He heard females giggling on the hall above, then in a moment the sound of male shoes descending the stairs.

Luiz appeared at the corner. Looking as innocent as a jaguar just before it makes its final killer move on you, Luiz said, "You roared, boss?"

Trust him to try and joke his way out of whatever problem he had fallen into now.

Rambow pushed the chair next to him backwards fairly firmly, and it tottered but Luiz gracefully caught it and set it upright.

"Sit down there, Luis. You have some explaining to do."

Rambow turned the ledger book around and pointed to the recent totals which Luiz had underlined at the end of each month. Very nice touch, Rambow thought. I didn't even have to use my calculator.

"Those totals, amigo, are more than double what they used to be, and also about double what I've budgeted for this place. What's going on?"

Luiz's face registered complete surprise.

"You know, boss, that costs here in Mexico are going up just like in the U.S."

"Minor increases in costs are okay. But here"— Rambow pointed his finger— "you entered wages for five people: you, the cook, two maids, and two helpers. What the fuck do helpers do?"

Luiz smiled. "Helpers are girls we have to bring in to help the maids when there's a lot of, say, like cleaning to be done. These girls nowadays are good for a lot of wonderful things"—Luiz grinned and threw Rambow a wink— "but they ain't too much good when heavier work has to be done. So, I get some helpers to help them. Keeps them happy, as you can see"— another wink— "and that's important."

"If you wink at me again, Luiz, I'll consider you're asking me for a date. Who are these helpers you get to help the two very strong young maids I'm already paying plenty for?"

Luiz waved his hands creatively. "Oh, it depends on the work, boss. Some helpers do one kind of work better than others. They sort of specialize, like a doc, I guess you could say."

"Are they females? Young, very pretty, very agreeable, helpers?"

"I try to hire people on your behalf, boss, who need the work, who will get along with the present staff, and who will be nice and presentable if you should happen to visit when they're helping. You know, to maintain your image in the community."

"Sure. My image in the community." He frowned.

"Are these helpers related to you?"

"You know, boss, in a small town like Ensenada most people are related somehow. A lot of inbreeding, you could say."

"Answer my question. Are these helpers related to you?"

Luiz hesitated. "Well, I guess some of them were, boss. But like I said..."

Rambow cut him off. He was getting pissed with his evasions.

"Were any **not** related?"

"I'd have to check the records, boss, but..."

"Anybody not?"

Luiz slowly shook his head. "I can't remember for sure, but I guess most were related."

Rambow paused. He didn't want to let his anger control this argument but he knew he had to win it or next time it would be just a repeat.

"You've been cheating me, Luiz."

"Hey, boss, that's a hurtful thing to say."

"You have been cheating me." He paused between each word, to emphasize his meaning without letting his temper take over.

CHAPTER 25

"I am really pissed off, Luiz. I let you get away with all kinds of things, including fucking all the maids—and the cook! —when they should be working, and eating much better food than they would if you had to pay the bills, and living for free."

He could feel his anger growing. He knew that was dangerous, he remembered what had happened with that second girl at Happy Andings.

He forced himself to throttle back. He did want to strangle the little prick, but he realized that any physical action here would mean trouble, in spades.

Luiz probably had half the police force as relatives. Maybe even all of them.

No, let it hang for the minute. Where could he get Luiz completely in his control?

Of course, that nice little soundproofed room at Happy Andings.

"Okay, Luiz, I'm going to forget all the stealing you've done. Just remember if it happens on this scale again", he knew it was impossible to stop it all, even most of it, the opportunities were too obvious, "you will be in really big trouble with me."

Luiz's macho temperament also got the better of him.

"Listen, boss, I'm not some flunky here. You said I was manager of this house, and I know that any manager has certain rights."

"They don't include stealing." Goddammit, would he shut up.

"Well, first thing, boss, I don't regard it as stealing. And second thing, just don't lean on me too heavy. Remember I have enough on you to cause you big problems, even up north."

"What does that mean?" Rambow felt his anger bubbling again.

"You know. That last trip you made here. Remember how drunk you got with those two sweet teenagers I lined up for you, the ones you wanted to marry at one point?

"Well, that time you had brought your big ledger book with you, and when you were rolling around in the bedroom, sorta drunk outa your mind, I thought you might somehow lose that book, which you had told me a bunch of times was so fucking valuable, that I thought I should help you out in case you lost it or gave it away to your sweethearts or something.

"You know, I was just thinking of you, Boss, so I had my cousin downtown in Ensenada, the guy who works in that quick copy shop, make me a copy of that ledger book."

Rambow was speechless.

He thought back to that trip, he remembered the two young broads, but he couldn't remember ever giving possession of it to Luiz.

He wasn't that stupid. Not the ledger!

He cleared his throat. "That was very thoughtful of you, Luiz. And where is that copy now?"

"Oh, I made sure to put it somewhere safe, boss, so if I, ah, you, ever needed it, it would be safe."

"I'd like that copy, Luiz. Now."

"Well sure, if I could boss. But I gave the copy to my cousin Joey who works in the bank, and he arranged to put that valuable copy in the bank vault."

"So go and get it." He pictured how that little prick Luiz would look lying face down in the HA Special Room."

"The thing is, boss, that where he put is in a sorta special area for employees to use. But they can only get at their stuff once a month, because they're getting it free.

"And he just used that space yesterday, so you'd have to wait until next month before I could get you that valuable copy."

CHAPTER 26

"How does the Rambow sting stand, lieutenant?"

"Pretty well the way it was yesterday, Michael. We're ready here. But the infamous Mr. Rambow is late for rehearsal."

"You mean he's missing?"

"That sums it up pretty well, Mike. I had a loose tail on him, I didn't want any danger of him spotting it.

"But late last evening my man lost him. Rambow was at the Circus, apparently just putting in time, and when a horde of bus tour customers trooped in, he—Rambow—used the opportunity to head towards the can but then detoured before it. By the time my man could safely get closer he was gone.

"I've had a team looking for him since but nada. We had both the Happy Andings and WIMPS offices checked. Just 'out of town on business'. Neither place seems to know where, or when, he'll be back.

"But from the clothes and stuff at his apartment, checked for us by an anonymous helper, it doesn't look like he's scrammed for good.

"If no reappearance, or news, I'll put out a four-states missing and wanted for questioning clip on the police teletype. That may turn up something."

"I sure hope we don't lose him, Dan. We both know he's probably responsible, maybe personally, for the murder of those two girls.

"And I'm pretty close to having a solid embezzlement case on him at that WIMPS funny farm. I've had a CPA guy I know taking a look at the company books, and he says it's a slam dunk to get him in front of a grand jury, maybe even go right to trial.

"But I don't want that prick to get off with a few years when he should be doing hard time for murder."

"Neither do I Mike, and I don't think we've lost him."

"Pap told me just today that one of his snitches has heard that the IRS is also getting interested in the preacher. Appears Rambow heard the same rumour, or maybe even had a direct call from the tax snoops, and decided to hide the financial evidence somewhere away from Vegas."

The two men were in the lieutenant's LVPD office. Southfield was sitting behind his desk, Shant was prowling around.

"That's a good point, Mike. Many people throw a nervous fit when the IRS looms on their horizon. Maybe Rambow did. But if he's hiding stuff it probably means he plans to come back to his loving church. And, of course, the sweeties at Happy Andings."

Shant nodded.

"I talked with my researcher Alison. You remember her?"

"Do I ever. What a dish."

Shant grinned, a little embarrassed.

"She is that. Anyway, she's still primed to do what it takes with Rambow. She was pretty pissed when he let her get away, even after she had offered to do her trial massage in panties and bra."

CHAPTER 27

"You know what a Special Room is, Luiz?"

Luiz shook his head.

"It's a specially soundproofed room at my Happy Andings massage place. It has only one piece of furniture in it. A giant bed. Mirrors overhead and on the walls. Complete privacy even though next door some girl is blowing a customer.

"And the girls—notice the plural, Luiz—I allow in there are the absolute tops. Young, big firm boobs, and pussies and asses that are just crying out for some special attention in the Special Room.

"Anything goes, Luiz, anything."

Rambow could see the sweat starting to bead on Luiz's forehead. He knew that while Luiz had access locally to a bunch of young willing girls, none had any real experience, none knew how to dress—and undress! —properly, and none were experienced in making a man feel on top of the world.

Now if he could only sell the little prick. He had to get him across the border. It would be far too dangerous here in Mexico, where Luiz would be related to half the population.

But he didn't want to oversell the creep. He wasn't a rocket scientist but neither was he stupid.

If he thought that Rambow was up to something, especially to do with the so-called stealing, and certainly with the extra copy of Rambow's ledger, he would refuse to go.

But Rambow could see that his overheated lust was getting the better of him.

"How many girls you got working there at that Happy place, boss?"

"We keep it open 24/7, Luiz. It's always open. On each shift, there are four of them, the girls only work six hours at a time. Beyond that they seem to lose their enthusiasm for playing with our customers' dicks.

"Anyway, on each shift there are four girls on shift, and any of the other girls who want to have appointments with special customers can be there too."

Luiz's eyes were wide.

"So how many broads in total?"

Rambow paused, did some quick mental arithmetic.

"Happy Andings has 26 girls working full time. There's always a few girls who don't hold full time jobs but who want to put in maybe 20 or 24 hours a week, and usually we have several girls who have applied but haven't been interviewed and tried out yet."

"You mean somebody gets to try out each new girl?"

"Of course, Luiz, you think we're going to dump some new broad on our customers, who pay good money, just because she says she can give great hand or blow jobs? Each one is tested with a full massage and whatever her specialty is, hand or mouth. If she does that great, she's in. Otherwise, there's the door."

Luiz swallowed. "And who gets to test them?"

Rambow knew he had Luiz. Now to reel him in.

"When I started, I did all the testing. But now that I'm a little more discriminating, I interview them all, but select only the ripest, the ones with the best bods, the fullest lips, for my personal testing."

He paused. "With normal turnover—these girls come and go frequently—I usually have four good tests a week, more if I feel like it.

"And sometimes with a really stacked girl, I'll have one massage, then tell her I'm not too sure she's ready for the big time at HA, but if she wants to have a rest and then come back later for another trial, I may be more inclined to give her a chance.

"Each girl that I do that to comes back and really throws in extra effort, so the end result of the second trial is a really great hand or blow job.

"And often a girl who on the first trial said her specialty was hand jobs will change on the second to blow jobs, and do a really great job on my dick."

Luiz was sweating freely now. Rambow knew that his secret passion was blow jobs, but few of the local girls were good at that; they thought that screwing was the ultimate physical pleasure they could offer.

"And quite often, if I have a friend in town, or some business guy I'm trying to impress, I'll have him come over. I'll introduce him briefly to the new girl as a possible investor and I want to show him exactly how HA works.

"If he wants, he gets the complete privacy of the Special Room. Some guys would rather watch me get massaged, they just want to watch. Or they may ask me to watch them. They say they want to be 'safe' with the girl, but that's bullshit, they're just voyeurs,

"The girls don't care. They're auditioning for a job at the cleanest, safest, and highest paying massage parlor in Vegas, and they do what I tell them."

"You don't screw them, boss?"

"No, we don't allow that. It has too many problems. With hand and blow jobs, the guy is just lying back like it's part of a regular massage. Some cop busts in, that's what he sees, a guy getting a legal massage in a licensed parlor. No sweat. But full screwing takes too long, and has far too many possible complications.

"And I find that a great blow job does the trick. I don't need to be inside the broad to have a full orgasm. And that's what our customers feel too, we've never had a customer try to increase a blow or hand job to a full fuck. They know and agree with the rules."

Luiz cleared his throat.

"So if I went up there with you for a little visit, you'd be able to get me some nice freebie massages?"

"Who's the boss of Happy Andings, Luiz? You're looking at him." Rambow didn't feel it necessary to go into the recent new shareholder percentages. "I pay, and get to tell, those 26 or whatever number of girls what to do, and when. I just say, 'This guy is my business colleague. Give him one of your best massages.' And the girl you pick out does just that."

"How many massages could I have, boss?"

"Well, within reasonable limits, Luiz, about as many as you can handle. Unlike the local girls here, the HA girls are pros. They all have great bods, and they all do great hand or blow jobs, because that's how they make the big bucks. A couple a day, Luiz, and you'll be nicely tired out."

"How come some do only hand jobs, others do blow jobs?"

"The girls pick a specialty when they start. The hand jobbers get a little lower fee per massage. A customer chooses when he pays his fee what he wants, and he pays more for a blow job. Some girls just can't give a good blow job, but they're great with their hands."

"Any do both?"

"Sure, most of the blowers will start with a hand job, and get the customer close, then switch to mouth work. Of course, if the customer said 'Only a hand job today', a blower would do that, and still make the higher blowjob fee."

"How long a visit up there would I have?"

Rambow knew Luiz was busy adding up the total numbers of massages he could cram in.

"I think you could be away from the house here for five or six days, right?

Luiz just nodded. Rambow he was multiplying five or six by two, no, make it three, massages a day.

"Goddammit, GG, this is important. This prick Luiz, the guy who takes care of my house down south, has made a copy of our original HA ledger. You know the damage that would do, to HA, to you, now that you're the major shareholder, and to me, at WIMPS."

GG stared at Rambow. She was certain another big problem loomed.

"So why did you bring him here, and from what I hear, ply him with free massages?"

"I brought him here to eliminate him. There's no way I could do that in Mexico, he's related to every cop in town. I'll have Tonto give me a hand. He can dump and bury the body like he did with the gir, ah, others.

"Then little Luiz will be just another illegal who decided to stay and enjoy this wonderful country. There shouldn't even be any connection to me. If there is, I knew him a little from my Mexican visits, and so I invited him here for a visit. After a day or two he disappeared and I haven't seen him since. No idea where he might be, probably joined a group of other illegals, likely headed to LA where no one even speaks English any more.

"And that will be the end of the ledger problem. You'll have to start keeping whatever records you want fairly accurately, we'll just cross off the last few years: 'Sorry, the records have disappeared, probably an irate girl who was fired for not doing her job properly. But all recent records are here, nice and neat in this book.' How does that sound, GG?"

"Like shit, Rambow. But I guess we can get away with it if we stick to it. HA might get a fine from the IRS if they do an audit, but otherwise books here in Vegas re disappearing all the time. Not really much the authorities can do."

She stretched, she'd been listening to Rambow for a couple of hours. Seemed more like days. What did she ever see in him?

"And just how are you going to eliminate your problem?"

"I'm not sure but I'll keep it simple. He's too wiry to tackle, but I have a revolver that I took from a guy years ago for a debt. Never been registered so I can throw it away after."

"You're going to fire a gun here?"

"In the Special Room, where I'll have him waiting for his next freebie, no one will hear anything. The gun is a 38 and the guy who gave it to me said it wasn't powerful, just strong enough to do the job at fairly close range."

"I don't like it. At least make it in the early evening when we're not busy. I'll keep the room adjoining the Special empty for awhile. I'll tell the regular girl in that room I want it cleaned because a customer complained he saw dirt. As though our customers are looking to check on dirt.

"And I don't want to know any more about it, Gibbie. Keep the details to yourself. If you use Tonto tell him to not say anything to me.

"Is that clear? I'm speaking now as the majority shareholder, one that can fire your ass out of here if I want to. Remember that. You'd be losing all your 'sample massage' tryouts, you'd have to get that broad in your WIMPS office to blow you."

Rambow hated to have to take orders from this bossy broad that he had actually started in the business. But he nodded to GG.

"Where is Tonto today, seen him around?"

"He's here somewhere, he always is. I think noises may be his weak spot, I think maybe he listens outside the regular rooms to hear the tales of passion unfold."

"Tales of passion! That little creep is probably whacking himself off as the customer comes inside."

Rambow left, aiming to get Tonto on board. He hadn't yet decided on the actual method of elimination. He sorta liked the concept of creeping up on Luiz when he'd be lying naked on the table in the Special Room, waiting for his next freebie massage.

CHAPTER 28

"She missed our appointment last evening, lieutenant, and that's not like Alison. I'm worried."

"I understand, Mike, but there's nothing we can do, not even file a missing person report. She's been gone, what, 10 or 11 hours? An MPP requires somebody missing at least 48 hours.

"And you know that Alison, like your other researcher Pap, is independent. She may have contacted Rambow at Happy Andings and already arranged an appointment for her trial massage. And she may be staying away from you, and even me, because she doesn't want to screw the sting to Rambow."

Shant slowly nodded.

"Yeah, Dan, she is independent, and I agree that she may be proceeding in the manner you just outlined."

He forced a smile. "Okay, Dan, I'll try to be cool for a while longer.

"I just hope Alison hasn't done something silly and got herself into a jackpot with that nut Rambow. We both know he was probably at least implicated in the murders of those two young women.

"While I think Alison could handle herself in most situations, who knows what that creep could come up with."

"I agree wholeheartedly with what you said, Mike, and rest assured that I have units here at LVPD ready to roll if she gives us the word."

CHAPTER 29

"I already have that prick Luiz lined up for his elimination. I can't see any problems with using my gun. It's not traceable and won't make too much noise."

Rambow was walking around the massive bed in the Special room, talking to himself. The outside door had been carefully closed.

"Tonto has said he'll help just like with those two broads. For a fee, of course. Some day I may have to arrange his elimination too, but not now, he's too valuable in getting rid of bod, ah, stuff I want disposed of carefully."

He touched the clean sheet on the bed; the cleaning woman automatically changed all bed and table sheets every shift, oftener if needed.

If he had Galindo lying here, he patted the bed, and naked of course, I could simply walk in with the gun hidden in a pocket, start telling him his 'date' was getting ready, stick the gun behind his ear and pull the trigger. And any blood would be contained in that top sheet specially made of waterproof material; it was often needed here at HA.

Adios ledger book problem, that copy in the bank vault in Ensenada even if found wouldn't make any sense to anyone down there.

But that still left that slinky looking broad, the one who offered to do him in her panties and bra. He didn't want to forget her.

She was supposed to leave her cell number here; he'd check with GG.

If she had it, he'd get GG to set up an appointment with her. Might as well see some free cheesecake to take his mind off his troubles.

And with the fucking IRS, the Mexican, and that prick bookie Klassen, he did have troubles.

"Nice to see you again. You're still interested in an exciting career here at Happy Andings?"

Alison forced a smile. "I'm not sure I'm looking for a career but I could use some bucks."

"That's a good attitude. We actually have few—well, none—of our masseuses who retire on pensions at age 60. Somewhat shorter career spans here than in the parasitic civil service."

Rambow stood up. "If I remember, you said you'd do your trial massage in panties and bra. Right?"

Why on earth had she ever agreed to that?

"Yeah, if you think that costume is necessary?"

"Not only necessary but essential. About the only rule we have here at HA is that when someone gives their word, they live up to it.

"So, you can hang your clothes and purse here in this Special Room closet. You can see that it has a lock, with the key in it. When you've put your stuff in it just lock and take the key, and put it somewhere safe."

Alison wondered where she'd find something safe in a bra and panties. At least Rambow was giving her a secure place for her clothes and wallet. She had lots of I.D. in that wallet and she didn't want him finding out her real name and other key data.

Rambow moved to the hall door.

"I'll give you some privacy now to get ready. When you are, just crack this door a little and I'll soon see it and be back for your trial demo."

He left and firmly closed the thick door behind him. There was a latch on it and she pushed it closed so she'd be able to partially strip in privacy. What on earth was she doing here, getting partly undressed for a jerk who may even have been involved in two women's murders? She hoped Shant appreciated her sacrifices. And she hoped he would be properly thankful later, when the lights in his motel room were low and the bed was handy.

She stripped off her skirt and blouse and hung them in the closet. She added her purse, then closed and locked the door and withdrew the key.

In the hall outside Rambow heard the closet door being locked. He took out his key ring, selected a large triangular key, and quietly slipped it into an almost hidden lock.

He turned it, slowly pulled the door open, and was looking at the back of the closet, from a door which was fitted so tightly into the normal woodwork that only a very close and detailed inspection would uncover it.

He quickly located Alison's purse, opened it, and withdrew her Nevada driver's license. There was also a small black pocket which held her business cards. She billed herself as a 'Freelance Researcher'.

Indeed.

Shant replaced the items as he had found them, then quietly closed and locked the hall access to the closet.

She was obviously working for that sleazy west coast writer Shant. She hadn't learned very much yet, although Rambow was sure she'd try grilling him when she thought he'd be paralyzed with lust over her partially nude body. If she only knew how many women he saw, and completely nude at that, in just a week of 'interviewing' at Happy Andings.

Even if she was the most luscious broad in all of Vegas—and there was a great deal of competition there! —he wouldn't foolishly tell her anything she wanted to know.

He'd just get a probably lousy hand or blow job from her, then after apparently considering it seriously, tell her she wasn't up to the standards he was trying to maintain at H.A.

Might as well give her an inferiority complex, she deserved it for trying to spy on him.

He paced the big hallway onto which all the massage rooms opened. He was just about back to the Special Room—he noticed the door was lightly open, she was ready to show him her assets and her talents— when he pulled up.

He was soon going to have to dispose of Luiz. There was no way he could let him return to Mexico with his carefully secured ledger book there.

So then, why not just keep the researcher broad, maybe even have some sport with her, and get rid of her at the same time as Luiz?

Maybe even plant them together so they wouldn't get lonely in that cold and dismal park where Tonto was getting rid of bodies.

Sure, he thought, as he walked toward the Special Room. Two doors from it he pulled up again.

On the so-called article he was supposed to write on Rambow, that Shant represented some big magazine. It probably had lots of money floating around to cover expenses of writers and other suppliers of crap for their brain-dead readers.

He could hold the research broad for ransom. He really needed some quick cash, certainly for that bookie thug Klassen who was now threatening to break both his legs.

If the ransom scheme failed, he could just snuff her along with Luiz.

If it worked, he could at least ease the pressure from Klassen, and then let her go.

She wouldn't have learned anything, and if she bitched about her enforced stay, he'd just say she got turned on by him and begged to stay with him for a few days so she could enjoy some of his fantastic screwing abilities.

Sure, anyone would believe that, he already had a solid Vegas reputation—outside of WIMPS circles, anyway—as a stud.

He nodded. The broad was already in the Special Room, and when he locked the hall door on her she could scream and shout as she wanted, no one would hear her.

And GG was already keeping the adjacent massage room vacant for 'cleaning', so no one would even hear very muffled knocks on the adjoining wall.

Sure, that all fitted together. He could even have that moron Tonto make the ransom call so Rambow's voice couldn't be traced back to him.

At the door to the Special he paused yet again.

If he was going to at least kidnap her, maybe even snuff her, he might as well get a free massage from her, especially in her underwear.

He grinned and pulled open the door. He had the only key to that room's very sophisticated lock in his back pocket, he had never returned it to GG.

Everything was a go.

"Okay, Ali…, ah, sweetie"—he wasn't supposed to know her real name— "all set for your Academy performance?"

She noticed the slip. Had he found her real name? How? Or did he have a favorite masseuse also named Alison?

She doubted that, but she didn't want to trigger any problems.

She had been leaning against the giant bed, there was no other furniture in the room.

She pirouetted in front of him. Might as well give him the full treatment, although she sure didn't look forward to having to put her hands all over his body.

But she claimed to be a researcher, and that's all this was, research. Unfortunately of a particularly distasteful kind.

"Okay, Mr. Rambow, I guess you have to get undressed now. I imagine you'll want to keep your undershorts on to maintain your managerial dignity?" She wasn't holding her breath for his answer.

"Certainly not. A full massage is just that, and with any clothes at all on it's just not a full massage, is it?"

Like she expected. He was going to be completely nude.

She turned her back as she heard him start undressing. God, what a fucking mess she'd got into, all over that Shant.

On the other hand, if she viewed it strictly as "experience", something she could laugh over with her friends years from now, when the humiliation had worn off, then maybe it was not all that bad.

After all, how many researchers got to give a probable murderer a hand job? Or, she groaned, even a blow job if he insisted on seeing her full range of talents.

She heard what she thought were shorts being pulled down. Soon, she thought, she'd have to face the music. Literally.

As if he had heard her thoughts, Rambow said "Ready".

She turned slowly, hoping that a sudden earth tremor or quake might solve her problem. It didn't.

He was naked, and facing her. She tried to look into his eyes, then realized that only too soon she'd be staring at what was currently a pretty limp dick, probably by then in an "at attention" stance.

"Okay, lie down there on the bed. On your stomach."

He did a quick jump onto the massive bed and rolled over with his ass up.

She didn't really know much about professional massaging. A friend of hers who had been in the business told her once "It's not all that difficult. Most people just want to feel someone's hands on them. Start softly then increase the pressure.

"If it's a guy, use light fingers, including nails, on his legs.

"By the time you tell him to roll over he'll have a solid hard on. If you're going to do something constructive about that fairly obvious problem, continue to massage his chest, then his front legs, in the same manner: light to firm strokes on his chest, then light fingers and nails on his legs. By the time you get to the main event, whether you use your mouth or hands to resolve the issue, he'll be hot enough that either one will get things solved very quickly."

She figured that advice was as good as anything, so she started on his back. He didn't say anything or even move as she started with light strokes, then increased the pressure.

After what she thought was an hour, but was likely only a few minutes, she moved down to his legs. She had fairly long nails, and after a few basic strokes she started using them lightly on his thighs.

He moved his legs a little but was silent.

So far so good.

She gave his ass a few quick squeezes. Then, taking a deep breath, she said "Turn over".

He did.

His cock was already half erect. He just looked down at it, then at her, and smiled.

"Not too bad so far. Now is the most important part in being a good masseuse."

She tried to ignore his dick, and fortunately the bed was completely open on all sides, so she could easily move around it.

She tried to prolong her efforts on his chest but eventually came to the conclusion that it was time to move on. Rambow hadn't spoken since he first turned over.

In one way she was glad of his silence, in another she thought that his talking would make things easier.

She moved her body along the bed and began on his legs. He slightly spread his legs as though to make her task easier. All it did was expose more of his sexual equipment to view.

But she knew she couldn't complain, he hadn't made any attempt to touch her. If he had, she would have seized the opportunity to end the massage on the grounds of unprofessional conduct.

She deliberately dug her nails in a little as she stroked his thighs but all that happened was she saw his cock stiffen more.

Well, if her friend had given her accurate information, the harder and faster the dick got the easier for her to get him to the massage-ending climax. She hoped.

She knew he was looking right at her but she resisted the urge to look up at his face, anywhere actually but what she'd have to look at next.

She finished his legs. When she was stripping earlier, she had seen a small bottle on the floor beside the bed. She assumed it was some kind of oil. Now was the time to use it, anything to make the finale faster.

She picked up the bottle. Yes, it was marked "massage oil". She shook some onto her left hand, then rubbed it into her right as well.

She grimaced internally, then leaned over and grabbed his now very firm cock. She lathered the oil on it from head to base, making it slippery and shiny. Actually improved the appearance a little, she grinned to herself.

She began to stroke it in the classic hand job style when he spoke.

"Normally"—she paused in her stroking—"applicants for jobs here at Happy Andings are required to do a full blow job, as that is often the difference between a barely acceptable and a great masseuse. And it seems to me that you agreed to do a full massage, and as you know that means a blow job."

He stopped talking. She didn't know what to say, she thought back to how she had accepted the "demo trial" condition. Had she agreed to a blow job?

She sure didn't want to walk off the job now, now that most of the heavy work had been done. Should she agree to a blow job?

Rambow smiled.

"But I've already had two other blow jobs today from other applicants and I'm a little tired.

"So I'll let you continue with a straight hand job, with the understanding that if I do offer you a job you'll have to at some point show me you can give a fine blow job.

"While some girls here have regular customers who actually prefer hand jobs, all the masseuses have to be fully qualified on both hand and blow jobs.

"We certainly can't have a good customer who has paid our healthy fee getting a little shrinking violet who tells him at the crucial moment, "Oh, sir, sorry, I don't do blow jobs, just hand jobs. Should I continue?"

"He'd never return, and our HA business is based on customers who do return."

Her hand was still holding his cock.

She was reasonably sure her researching activities wouldn't extend to a full-time job at Happy Andings, so she probably wouldn't have to go the blow job route. Wonderful. It was bad enough just holding his cock without having to suck it.

She replenished the oil on both her hands and on Rambow, covering everything she could see.

His dick was now at what looked like full readiness.

She started to squeeze and stroke vigorously. She could see that his whole body was tensing, so he must be approaching his climax.

"Go a little faster, Alison, if you please."

He was a gentleman right to the end, and the end was upon them.

His semen shot up in a miniature fountain. She had been careless about aiming, and the spray went largely onto to her chest and bra. Shit.

But at least he had climaxed. Once the stream ended, she released his now shrinking organ and grabbed a handful of tissues, then mummy-wrapped his dick and balls. Let him do the final mopping up. She tried to clean her underwear.

She went over to the small sink and thoroughly soaped, washed, then repeated. When she turned to grab the towel he was looking at her face.

"That wasn't so bad, was it, Alison? I imagine you even enjoyed the fountain display a little. But I know you'll be too shy to admit that."

He wadded up the tissues and left them in a ball on the bottom of the bed. He got up, found his clothes, and without turning his back got dressed.

She went to the closet, opened the door and retrieved her skirt and blouse, then leaned against the closet door until Rambow was fully dressed.

He walked over to the hall door but didn't unlock or open it.

"Well, as you probably already know, Alison, I'm afraid that you didn't pass that test. I wouldn't want you servicing HA customers with that poor level of ability."

She felt like saying fuck you to him but figured it was wiser to stay silent.

"I know you are disappointed, and perhaps it was just stage nerves on your first professional appearance." He smiled and she was immediately conscious of something unpleasant coming.

"So that I am fair as possible to first-time and just starting out masseuses, I do go overboard in trying to help them get over their nervous feelings.

"And of course, Alison, I will do the same for you."

He paused and she was now a little frightened.

"So, here's what I will do on behalf of Happy Andings.

"I'll give you a little time to rest up and think about how you can do better than your performance. I know you can, my dear, so how be I return in a short while and let you have another trial?"

She felt her self control rapidly disappearing.

"No way, Mr. Rambow. I did my best, and you say I failed. Okay. I'll have to get more amateur practice jerking off my friends before I can make it to the HA big leagues. So be it."

She took a deep breath.

"That means I'm withdrawing my application to join the happy team here at Happy Andings. I appreciate your patience with me, and perhaps some time in the future, after I've honed my massage abilities, we might try this again.

"For now, however, I want to leave. I have an appointment to keep and if I'm too late my friend will get concerned."

Rambow smiled, much as she imagined a shark smiled just before he bit off a juicy leg.

"Oh, I imagine a friend will wait to meet with you, Alison. I know I would.

"But in view of the time and effort I have put into your application, and the trial massage that has taken longer than I expected, I have to insist that you take your employment app more seriously.

"I'll be back later for your re-trial. It of course will be for a full massage. That's a complete blow job, as we discussed originally. You can think about some interesting moves to make. Remember imagination is just as important as hand skills to a great masseuse."

She was now really pissed off.

"Let me out of here right now. Otherwise I will consider it kidnapping, and that's a pretty serious offense, even for a TV preacher."

"I don't think anyone else would even think of it as kidnapping, Alison. You came here voluntarily, filled out an application form, even though you lied on most of the questions, and you had friendly and relaxed talks with both the receptionist and the manager about your interview with me.

"The HA official records will show you were interviewed, did a trial massage because of your lack of experience—something every newbie goes through—and failed it.

"When I told you of your failure, you begged and pleaded for another chance, said you really wanted to join our HA team.

"Because of your apparent sincerity, and because in my experience many newbies do freeze up on their first management-witnessed massage, I agreed to give you another chance.

"Because of my busy schedule I suggested another day, but again you tearfully said you wouldn't be able to sleep knowing you had failed.

"When I explained I had other appointments, and it might be several hours before I could give you a new test, you asked to be allowed to stay right here. You said you'd think about what you had done, and try to think of better ways, so you could pass the re-test."

Alison colored. She realized that what Rambow had just said might be construed just that way. What a fool she had been, thinking she could trick this slippery con man on her own. She should have brought a girlfriend or someone with her.

Rambow looked at her.

"I see that you understand the situation. So just relax, and think about passing the next trial. Although I am really trying to help you, the number of trials I can allow is limited."

To how many, she thought. Does he plan to keep me here, just using me as a diversion when he gets bored. Or horny?

She knew she had to get out of this fucking prison box.

"And because you were careless in soiling your underwear, your next trial will have to be in the nude. That should actually make you more relaxed, as of course I will be too."

Rainbow took his key ring out of his jacket. He opened the closet door, then closed it tightly and locked it.

"Why did you do that?"

"We're having it repaired soon and the carpenter wants it sealed for awhile to make sure it's dry."

She didn't believe that but what was the difference. She was still locked in the Special Room.

At the hall door he unlocked, but held it only partly open, then turned to her.

"Spend your time on planning your best massage moves, Alison. I'll be back in a while." He slipped out the partially-open door, then locked the door from outside.

Rambow smiled as he walked down the hall. Alison was safely under wraps until he decided what to do with her: hold for Shant's magazine to spring for a ransom, or just get one more massage out of her then kick her loose.

The ransom would help a lot with his current cash shortage but it also presented substantial problems and possibly risks.

Next up was the crooked Luis. He had to make him disappear permanently—that record book he had was far too dangerous—just like the stupid TV movie portrayed it.

He wanted to find Tonto for his part in that adventure.

The little guy was proving very useful. Just as long as he didn't get big ideas about his importance in these `disappearing` activities.

"Tonto, just the guy I was looking for." Rambow threw his arm around the short man's neck and literally hauled him into an empty massage room.

"We have a little problem, amigo."

Tonto knew immediately that Rambow had a big problem and expected him to help, or even totally, resolve it. The short man also realized he was building a lot of knowledge about Rambow's very definitely illegal activities, knowledge that someday, not really too far off, would be worth real bucks.

"Here's the situation, buddy. You've probably seen that Mexican guy I brought back with me from my Mexican house, he was sort of keeping an eye on things for me down there.

"Well, he's gotten just out of control. He's taking advantage of my offer of some free massages, turned it into almost a dozen free full massages, and when queried by the various girls, simply said that "The boss will take care of things."

"I was prepared to cover him on one or two freebies, but shit, 11! And he doesn't show any signs of slackening off.

"I've decided that he needs a rest in our special park."

Tonto's eyes widened.

"You mean you're going to knock him off, boss, simply because he's run up a tab on massages? Seems a little drastic, doesn't it?"

Rambow hesitated, then realized he'd have to open up a little for his henchman.

"To tell the truth, old buddy, he's also playing games with some, uh, sort of confidential stuff I let him hold for me. Let's just say that Luis, that's his name, is past his "Use by" date."

Tonto nodded. After all, with the two recent female additions to the park, what was one more?

"Here's how I want to handle it.

"Get him into the closet in the special room. Enter only from the hall side. Once he's in, quickly lock the hall door, the inside door has already been locked."

"But how do I get him in there?"

"Just tell him I've got a special girl coming just for his pleasure. But she likes surprises. After he's in there we'll bring the girl into the room, then open the closet door and he'll jump out. Surprise!"

Tonto looked uncertain.

"He'd have to be sort of stupid to believe that."

"He is. Now one more thing. Before you close and lock the hall door, tell him that I said it might be awhile before the special girl got here. Then you give him this Coke bottle, it's still sealed, to slake his thirst. He loves Cokes.

"This is for your info only, Tonto. That Coke has been fixed, it has a powerful barbiturate mixed into it. It'll put Luis out for several hours at least. Once it gets dark you can drag him out and take him to the basement room.

"Once he's tied up there, make sure both hands are feet are tied, I'll come down and whack him a few times with the club that's there, then you and your truck buddy can take him to the park and plant him."

As long as Rambow did the actual killing Tonto was willing.

"Okay, boss, I'll have my truck buddy standing by for my cell call this evening. Can I have some money, say a C and a half, to cover him."

"I'll tell GG to give it to you out of petty cash. Do a good job, like before, Tonto, and there'll be a nice bonus for you when the job is completed."

Rambow was finding it easier each time. This eliminating Rambow's problems was not difficult at all.

CHAPTER 30

"Lt. Southfield, please."

The operator asked him to wait just a few seconds, then connected him.

"Southfield".

"Dan, this is Mike Shant, how's it going?"

"About the same as always, Mike. A lot of bad guys out there, and no matter how hard we try we can't seem to reduce the totals much. How're you doing?"

"I'm okay but Alison's still missing. Any news there?"

"I was checking with the desk sergeant just before you called. Nothing, and he checked all the usual places, hospitals, drunk tanks, accident reports, even the morgue. Nothing."

"I'm concerned, Dan. She didn't leave any message and I've tried her cell a couple of times but it's turned off."

"Not necessarily a problem. Could be she didn't want any give-away noises. She may be chasing down something she found, and she felt she had to pursue it right away. I know that's how a lot of the reporters are, they get what seems like a hot lead on a story and they forget they were supposed to get married—or divorced—today or yesterday. Doesn't mean a whole lot, I've found.

"Over the years we've had a number of 'missing reporter' reports filed by anxious relatives or even newbie editors. Without exception every one turned out like I said earlier, the guy, or even the girl, was just off on some supposed hot story."

"You think it's still too soon to send a few boys in blue into Happy Andings?"

"Yeah, I'm afraid all that would do is alert our friend to our interest, and his lawyer would be on us in minutes. No, the best thing is to wait a bit, Mike. I know that's a lot harder than rushing into action, but usually it's the wisest choice."

"Okay, Dan, but shout if you hear anything. I'm going to get Pap to check out some of his 'underground' sources, maybe they can come up with something."

CHAPTER 31

Cindy was off with a touch of flu, Vic, one of the waiters, had told Shant as he entered, but when he held up two fingers the relief bartender nodded and soon had sent a waitress over with the drinks.

"How does he know what I wanted?" He looked quizzically at the attractive brunette in Cindy's regular brown mini-skirt and low-cut blouse uniform.

"She makes sure all regular relief employees have a full list of what our best customers will likely order. And you, Mr. Shant, are certainly one of our best customers. And mine, too."

She smiled and sort of curtsied, giving him a nice look at her fine upper anatomy.

"Are you two planning something I should know about?" Pap leered better than Groucho Marx and slid into the booth.

Shant smiled.

"Nope. It's confidential. We're arranging a secret tryst later, and three would be a crowd."

The waitress smiled again, thinking she'd gladly see what a tryst really was, if only he would ask her. But it looked like they had some serious talking to do, so she walked back to the bar where there was another order waiting for her. Maybe another time, she thought.

"Any luck, Pap?"

He shook his head. "Mike, I've hunted up almost all of my snitches. Most of them looked at Alison's photo, and some of them had seen her either with us or just around. But not one said he'd seen her in the last few days."

"I didn't have much better luck with our cop friend. He said he had checked all the usual spots but no sign of her."

"What did he think of just busting in to the HA and taking our chances that Alison would be there somewhere?"

"Not a hope, at least right now. Without a solid complaint from someone, actually naming the HA as a probable culprit in whatever the crime is or might be, Dan said all that would accomplish would be to warn Rambow of our interests in him. And, he said the resulting lawsuit would not be pretty."

Both men thought about the problem of the missing researcher. Each had a solid drink to loosen up the brain cells.

"Are you reasonably sure you've checked all your snitches, Pap? I know you have a literal army of them."

"No, I missed a couple, and I'll stay looking for them, but they're more into hard criminal activities, and I doubt they'll be much help.

"I did pick up some rumors about Rambow, though. Several pretty reliable tipsters independently said that the news was that Rambow was in serious trouble, both financially with heavy creditors, including of course the friendly old IRS, and shylock enforcers who would gladly break anybody's legs for a C note or more.

"And even more vague reports from one snitch who has a pretty good ear to the massage parlor and body shop industries. He said the word is that there may be missing masseuses at HA."

"Missing? Like how missing?"

"Well, he was careful with his words, but the feeling I got was that missing as in disappeared, sort of like the bad guys say when someone has departed this vale of tears."

"That doesn't sound good, Pap. We're going to have to take some hard action, and soon.

"You keep on with your missing snitches. Let's get together later at my motel and see if we can't get a Plan A, or even B, underway."

CHAPTER 32

Time was wasting, Rambow thought. Tonto had reported that his first part of the Luis-disappearing-act had been satisfactorily completed, and Luis was now bound and gagged in the basement room.

It was time now for his performance. Not too long ago he would have flinched from beating a man to death, now it didn't seem all that bad. After successfully disposing of two girls who had outlived their usefulness to him, he felt that offing one stealing employee would be a snap.

He knew that in that basement room there were several old 2 x 4s from previous renovations. One of them would do fine.

Luis was awake and through all his bindings looked at him as though he would personally wring his neck. That made it even easier. Rambow selected a piece of lumber from a pile in the corner, hefted it like a baseball bat, and walked in front of his captive.

"I'm doing you the honor of letting you see your punishment for your rotten lying and stealing, Luis."

Rambow swung the solid wood club straight at Luis's head. There was a squishing sound which left no doubt as to the accuracy of his swing. To make sure he swung again, and again. Actually felt good. That would teach Luis to try and cheat him.

Rambow had carefully stood back so there was no blood on him. He dropped the 2 x 4 piece of lumber near the body. Tonto could take everything when he trucked the body to the park.

"Tonto, it's all yours. Clean up and take away everything there. Use the same place as before. And keep up the good work, shortie, and you'll get a real nice bonus."

Shortie, that's what that asshole Rambow called me. Tonto had just phoned his truck friend, who told him another big moving job had come up, and he couldn't make it that evening. Would tomorrow be okay?

Sure, why not? This body wasn't going anywhere, and no one ever came down here.

That will give me time to have a few drinks. He laughed, and looked at the disfigured body. And I won't even have to share with you.

But before I get started, I'd better get my little camera out and record this for my personal file on the great Mr. Rambow. Who knows, someday he may think that I'm no longer needed, so having these photos showing all his handiwork, including those two pretty girls, will change that idea pretty damn fast. And should mean a really big bonus as well.

With thoughts of money and the pleasures he could buy with it, Tonto found his vodka bottle. No glasses down here, but none were needed.

He upended the quart and took a healthy slug.

"That's to you, boss. And the next few as well. All from Shortie, you prick."

CHAPTER 33

"How's it going, Pap?"

The older man smiled, did a fast two step.

"Not too bad. And now that you've brought it up, yes, I will have one."

Shant smiled too and headed for the bureau stand which served as bartender central.

"Any news?"

Pap took a healthy drink, wiped his lips daintily, then smiled.

"Well, not directly about Alison. But maybe close to that subject."

Shant took his drink and sat on the edge of the bed, leaving the one comfortable chair for his guest.

"Okay, Pap, tell me all."

Pap took the chair, sat down, arranged the crease in his pants to suit himself, then looked at Shant.

"Did you know that a big Florida paper has asked me to take a few pix of the local massage parlor business? It's on spec, but if they like them, they may go for a healthy assignment.

"It seems the Old Duffers state is considering passing some enabling legislation for supervised massage parlors. Appears the oldies want to get their needs serviced but don't feel it takes an actual hooker to do that any longer.

"So the paper is planning a special edition on this subject, with pro and con comments and a lot of other nonsense. Guess who they picked for the on-spec pix?"

Shant shook his head in admiration.

"It's all a scam, isn't it? You set it up."

"I've had a good teacher, my friend. I've picked up more on scams and other effrontery from you and your subjects than I did in all the years photographing the dark and dirty streets for various Vegas publications."

"Is any of it true?"

"Sure. At least the part about Florida being the state for old farts. Like me, I guess. Maybe I should move there.

"But there is some validity to the general idea. I know an old buddy who's city ed on one of the Florida biggies, so I phoned him and asked him pretty please if he'd back me up if anyone checked. Since I once rescued him from a notorious brothel just minutes before the fuzz raided, he owes me a big one. Since that escapade he went on to marry a local heiress, and he knows that would never have happened if his mug photo had appeared in the local paper as a found-in at the local pussy parlor.

"And when I talked with him, I asked for a local subject that sort of tied in with massage parlors. He said the idea I mentioned has been actually kicked around in the state legislature off and on for years, so it's credible.

"In fact, if I can get some interesting pix, he might even consider a story or two along the lines I proposed. So my creative journalism career may be off to a new start.

"I hope so, you old fart, it would be a total waste of your creative talents otherwise."

Both men took healthy slugs in honor of Pap's new career.

"That's a great start, Pap, but you still have to get into Happy Andings. Know anyone there?"

Smiling like a tiger that has just spotted his fat missionary buffet, Pap nodded.

"Like I said, I've been around this burg for quite a while, Mike. I've met lots of people in lots of different places. In the olden days, when people actually read newspapers, and didn't just stay Siamese-twinned to some TV or portable phone gizmo, a lot of those people were happy to meet a real live newspaper fotog.

"One of those people was a pretty girl named Gloria. She was trying out for a Miss Vegas contest, with the grand prize a trip to Hollywood and maybe even a legit screen test. She came in second, should have won, because one of the judges was screwing the 'winner'."

"And?" Shant was waiting for the punch line that he knew his old buddy would have.

Pap paused to refresh his drink, looked at Mike who shook his head. Pap could have been a pro entertainer, he knew how to keep his audience panting.

"Gloria has morphed over the years into GG. And she's now the manager at Happy Andings."

"Jesus Christ, Pap, you do take the cake. Have you talked to GG?"

"I sold her the full gallon of snake oil, Mike. I said everything I told you earlier, then added that I wouldn't take any pix showing any customers' faces, and only girls who okayed it.

"She said every girl would do that, then smiled as we reminisced a little about how things might have turned out different for her except for that judge dipping his wick into one of the contestants."

"She didn't associate you with me, or the story I'm doing?"

"No, as soon as I got her into the good old days routine, she believed my story totally. Didn't mention either one."

Shant looked at Pap. He knew there was a great story there, maybe even half a dozen. Someday he'd get to at least one of them.

"That's wonderful, Pap. And your efforts on this make up for the horribly overpriced bills you're submitting for your snapshots."

"Snapshots! Overpriced! You young whippersnapper! I'm giving those photographic works of art almost away to you."

"Okay, then let's drink to fair pricing, old partner."

And both men laughed and did.

Later Pap outlined his plan. He would drift around the HA shop, taking some sample shots, and by photographing and chatting with masseuses who were between customers try to get a feel for what was going on there. And, if possible, find out where Alison might be being kept, if she was even there.

Before he started his new gig, Pap promised to phone Lieutenant Southfield and pass on the info his snitches had told him about Rambow's increasing problems.

Both knew it wasn't yet enough to tease the LVPD into a raid but it all helped to reinforce the case against the TV preacher cum whack parlor operator.

CHAPTER 34

Pap showed up for his first shift at Happy Andings outfitted as Hollywood movies used to portray press photogs. He had more equipment than a 10-man expedition to the Himalayas.

It was early afternoon and the after-work rush hadn't started, so most of the girls were free—and happy—to talk with the professional photographer. Many of them still had dreams of being swept off to the fantasy land of Hollywood by some casting director. They were even prepared for the stereotyped casting-couch approach, it wouldn't be much different than their jobs at HA.

And Pap had learned over many years the art of talking to women, especially females who thought he might be able to help them in their careers, even if those existed mainly in their dreams.

As he had explained to Shant one boozy night, "Let them talk. No one ever really listens to them. Nod frequently and look right into their eyes, not at their boobs or ass. Smile when you think it's required, frown with them if needed.

"You'll make out like a magician with whatever line you're pitching."

Shant had never found any reason to doubt the alcoholic-flavored but time-tested accurate advice.

At first the girls were reluctant to open up, but when Pap said that GG had personally okayed his pictures and presence, they got a lot friendlier. They tried to quiz him on his pro background "Have you worked in Hollywood? Who did you shoot?"

He answered these queries quickly and satisfactorily and with considerable literary license, then switched the subject to any current unusual or out-of-the-ordinary happenings at HA.

"It's funny you mention that, Pap," a busty brunette with powerful arms—probably from all the exercise she got—said. "Just in the last few days I've noticed that the Special Room, it's used for big shots and group things, probably orgies, has been locked up. Not only that but Wendy, who usually services all her customers in the massage room right next door, has had to use a room way closer to the front door, and she says the noise is a lot worse."

Pap nodded and avoided looking at her 42s. Follow your own advice, old man, he thought. He looked directly at her big brown eyes.

He fiddled with one of his cameras, not wanting to give special attention to this current very interesting subject.

"Oh, is that something different? And would you mind turning a little to the right, dear, and smile, so I can get a good shot of your profile?"

She simpered and quickly turned as he had directed and smiled. But she was able to continue talking with a big smile on her face.

"How's that?" Pap nodded approval. "Well, yeah, it is different, Pap. I've never seen the Special closed that long. Even when the boss, Rambow, not GG, is having some friends over for an orgy, it never lasts more than a couple hours. Most men think they're going to last a lot longer than they really do."

She looked at Pap and really smiled.

"Not that I mean all men, Pappy. Just the ones that Rambow seems to know."

She smiled at him again. He was older, sure, but a nice guy. And from what he'd said earlier, he still had some hot contacts in the LA area. Maybe she should invite him to her place when she finished her shift. Easier to talk there, she'd say.

And she was sure that Pap would enjoy a real friendly, leisurely massage while they talked. She knew she could make it last as long as he wanted.

She made the offer and Pap accepted, subject to being able to complete this assignment promptly and without any holdups.

She looked at her schedule. A regular, a good tipper, was due momentarily, and she didn't want to brush him off.

"I have an appointment, Pap. Why not find Wendy, she's a cute blonde. She loves to talk and I'm pretty sure she's free until the next hour. She's the one who used to be in the massage room next to the Special, but since it's been closed, she also had to move. She's up near the front, on the left. If her door is open it means she's not booked. Tell her I recommended her, we're good friends."

Pap gathered up his gear, thanked Marie for her time and her offer to have him visit her at her apartment later—subject to his professional job demands, of course—and headed up to find Wendy.

Most of the massage room doors were closed, meaning the girls were servicing customers.

But he lucked out. In a room just one back of the reception area he found Wendy, who was indeed quite a cute blonde.

He poked his head into the open doorway.

"Wendy? Hi, I'm Pap, here to do a photo series for a possible major NYC mag. I was just talking with Marie but she had a customer coming in. She suggested I visit and take some shots of you next.

"How does that sound?"

"Sounds great, Pap. Marie and I are pals. Come on in, I'm not booked for almost an hour. How can I help you?"

Pap took a fast look at the cute blonde and thought of several ways she could do that. But for now he was all business.

"I've cleared this all with GG, Wendy. I'm on assignment for that magazine, they're interested in doing a major article with full photo coverage of a licenced massage parlor. My job is to get some introductory pix. None of customers", he smiled. "Just girls and where they work.

"If the mag likes my pix, they'll have me do a repeat visit with a couple of assistants to help with posing and lighting.

"It will be a big job, Wendy, and the nationwide publicity could help any girls who want to move into modelling or film work."

"Hey, that sounds interesting, Pap. I've been massaging now for three, almost four years. The pay and the hours are great, and Happy Andings is probably the best parlor in Vegas.

"But the job is getting a little boring. I'm only 24 and I would like to at least get a shot at big time modelling, maybe even films. I have been told I have the facial structure, and the great boobs and legs, to make it in either career. But until a girl actually tries out, she never knows if she could make it, you know."

She moved around the table and sat on it closer to Pap. She patted the place beside her. "This is more comfortable than standing, you can see we don't have chairs here. We don't normally encourage men to sit down. Our job is to get them lying down. And naked," she grinned. "I'm sure you've had your share of full body massages?"

He nodded. "Some, but it's like those famous candies, you can never have enough." He laughed and Wendy joined in. She really was an attractive woman.

"Well, maybe some time we could correct that, Pap. I'd be glad to have you over to my apartment almost any evening that I'm not working that shift."

"No jealous boyfriend?"

"It's just about impossible to have one of those in this job. He'd spend all our time together asking me who and what I did that day.

"So I've found it's best to keep male relationships casual.

"I figure I actually see enough men here on the job to satisfy any curiosity I might have, and when I've moved on to some other career—like the ones you mentioned—then I can worry about the boyfriend bit."

"Sounds pretty sensible, Wendy, and I hope I can drop over some time soon. I always like to get background info on the women I photograph. It makes me understand them better and it actually helps me to portray them more accurately.

"For now, how about a few pix of you, just walking around here, may be changing the bed sheet for a new customer, straightening that attractive HA uniform you wear? Is the buttoned blouse and short skirt the standard?"

"Yeah, the idea is that for regular customers a girl can leave several buttons on the blouse open, so he gets a look at her goodies. The skirt is short, as you can see, so that every time I move around or bend over the good regular customers gets a shot of my pretty bikini.

"As I'm sure you know, there's no screwing allowed. It causes too many problems for both customers and us girls. But it helps to build the tips if the good guys get some nice stuff to look at when they're getting close to the final moment."

She looked at Pap and grinned. "I don't know why I'm talking like a virgin schoolgirl, if that species isn't extinct.

"In plain English it helps some customers to get it up and hard, and during the final strokes before they come, it also is nice for them to see that the girl massaging them has a good body. I hope you're not embarrassed, Pap."

He laughed heartily.

"Not a bit, Wendy. I've done a couple of assignments on the legal brothels here in Nevada, and when you've talked with those girls, and even been able to take some action pix, it would be difficult to ever blush again."

He unlimbered one of his miniature units.

"How about unbuttoning the same way you would for a good tipper, and bend over the table." He moved around to the other side.

"I'll get the shot that a customer would see. So look right at the camera, Wendy, a small but not big smile, and move your hands as you would on a customer. They won't show, of course, but I've found action shots are much more effective when the woman actually makes some moves."

He crouched down and aimed up at Wendy. She had unbuttoned three of the five blouse buttons and he got a pretty good view of her firm breasts unburdened by any bra.

He clicked off two, then moved down the table, motioning Wendy to turn only her head, and took several more.

"Great. Your moves look good, and while I'm not a trained talent scout, Wendy, I do say that your movements when I'm taking pix are natural, and that's a big plus."

"I liked the way you gave such clear, professional directions, Pap. I have to admit that aside from the usual sleaze balls a girl meets in any bar in Vegas, 'the ones who are really Hollywood producers', you know what I mean, I haven't had much experience with photographers. Did you really think my moves looked natural?"

He nodded, he wasn't trying to lead her on, but she did have a natural way of moving into a natural but eye-catching pose.

"Do you have any uniform changes?"

"Yes, we also have short shorts we can wear. Would you like to see them?"

"Sure, I like as much variety as possible in test assignments like this one."

She went over to a small dresser underneath the wash stand and pulled out something.

She held them up, they looked big enough to cover part of a very small pet mouse.

"Shall I put them on?"

He nodded and began reloading a second camera.

"Do you want me to leave?"

"Certainly not, Pap. If my photographer can't see me in panties what's this world coming to?"

She bent over, slipped off the skirt and pulled on the shorts, which barely covered the bottom of those pretty panties. She patted the rear to make sure there were no wrinkles and then smiled.

"What do you think?"

He took a very appraising look at her whole body. Her legs were almost excellent, and combined with those firm but not huge breasts clearly showed that Wendy was indeed a very good-looking woman. And he told her so.

But he had to get back to the more serious business.

"Really great, Wendy. Now I want you to walk around, look in the mirror, bend over the table, and do whatever feels natural. I'll be taking pix so just ignore me. I'll talk to you, just about general stuff, to keep you relaxed."

He started to take shots and she moved around easily in the limited available space. Maybe she was a natural.

"Marie mentioned you normally are in room next to the Special. How come you're up here?"

"That's a good question. "

And she answered it at length over the next 40 minutes.

When her next customer showed up she was still talking, but Pap silenced her.

"I think those pix are good ones, Wendy. And if I get the chance, I'll take you up on your invitation to talk more at your place soon.

"But for now, you've got work to do, and so do I. I'll be in touch. If you give me your home or cell number I'll call if I have free time to do a more pro series of shots.

She quickly grabbed a H.E. brochure and carefully printed both her numbers.

He waved at her and gathered up his safari-expedition outfit. He had a lot to tell Mike.

In Mike's motel room Pap unloaded the info he'd picked up, mostly from Wendy.

"She's convinced that there's someone in the Special Room, Mike. She's been up to her old room next door to it several times. She listened at the connecting wall, made a bunch of loud taps on the connecting wall, and she thinks she got some answering knocks. But they were too faint to really tell.

"And on one of her visits to her former spot, she ran into Rambow in the hall. He almost blew a fuse, she said, and asked her what the hell she was doing there.

"She just smiled—she said she usually is one of his favorite masseuses, and he uses her often—and said she was picking up some makeup she had left in her old room.

"When she asked him when she could move back to it, he settled down a little and told her it wouldn't be long. She said he almost smiled when he said that, and Wendy felt he was up to something not kosher."

Shant finished his drink, and look questioningly at Pap. He nodded.

As Mike rose to mix two more, he partially turned to Pap.

"Well, I have to agree with you, Pap, that Wendy's info is important. So what's your conclusion about all this stuff going on at Happy Endings, Sherlock?"

"I'm damned sure he's got Alison locked up in there, Mike. And from the way he answered Wendy's question about when, I think we have to make a move. And fucking fast!"

Mike frowned. "I agree. But we can't bust in on our own, we need the cops along. I'm going to phone Dan Southfield right now. I'll emphasize those knocks Wendy heard, maybe make them just a tad louder than she remembered."

He wasn't at the station but Shant had and used his home number.

"Dan? It's Mike Shant. I have some new info on our missing researcher. You haven't heard anything? Okay, Dan, Pap and I will meet you at your office. Half an hour? Good, Dan, and thanks."

"He said he has nothing and now he's really concerned that Alison may be in major trouble. He was the one who suggested a meeting right away at the LVPD.

"While he didn't make any commitment, Pap, I got the feeling he's ready to take action.

"Drink up, old buddy, we're off to see the cops."

CHAPTER 35

"Pap, you're sure this Wendy said she heard replying 'knocks' from that special room?"

Pap didn't hesitate.

"Absolutely, Lieutenant. She was sure of that." A very minor exaggeration, he rationalized, nothing in comparison with saving Alison's life.

Southfield sat back in his desk chair and looked into space for a few moments. Then he straightened up and looked at both the men sitting in front of him.

"Okay. I'm sold. I believe there is now sufficient evidence—Alison missing for two, almost three days— along with reports of funny stuff going on at HA. A full three days would mean we could move on a Missing Person basis. But just shading that legal glitch, I feel the statement of an impartial witness—Wendy—is enough to make the few hours legally insignificant."

Both men smiled and held up their hands as boxing winners.

"And because there is the definite possibility of foul play here, I'm going to authorize a full raid augmented by SWAT personnel.

"It'll take me several hours to set this up. It's now"—he glanced at his watch— "almost nine.

"Let's set kick off for high noon, just like Gary Cooper would in those old cowboy thrillers.

"I'm going to let you guys tag along, mainly because you both know the physical layout of Happy Andings. But as observers only, you understand?"

Both men nodded obediently, if somewhat dishonestly. With Alison's very life possibly at stake, neither man was willing to stand back and just watch.

"Okay, try to stay out of trouble for the next couple of hours"—he looked directly at Pap, who did blush modestly, in spite of what he had said earlier to Wendy— "and hook up with me here at the station right at noon sharp.

"I'll be in the rear parking area where our troops will be assembled. Look for the cop car with a 'Commander' flasher on top."

"Pap, do you have one of your sub-miniature cameras in working order?"

Pap nodded. "Of course, I always keep all my equipment in good working order." He should have slipped that line into his conversation with Wendy. Maybe he would next time.

"I want you to take all the pix you can. Remember, I'm still on assignment here, and if we're lucky, and find the preacher man up to bad stuff, your pictures will be very important.

"Can you take some shots without making any of the cops nervous?"

"I could take secret shots if I was in the front row of a marriage ceremony, and nobody would even see me move."

"Good enough. Get some great stuff and there's probably a bonus in it. Enough to keep you in booze for at least 48 hours."

"I'm insulted, unless you mean your fabulous bonus has only two numbers in it."

The men stopped off at an off-strip restaurant for a late breakfast. At all the strip joints it would take half an hour just to get a waitress.

After a filling meal the men went back to Mike's motel. Pap snoozed and Mike did some writing on his assignment. He checked to see where Rambow's advance printed schedule showed he was due to be this afternoon.

The right reverend Rambow was due to preside over a 'thanksgiving and outpouring' ceremony at the WIMPS head office. Shant figured the outpouring part involved Rambow's followers again unloading their wallets. All in benefit of the great man himself, of course. That occasion might be a very appropriate place to collar him, should the evidence warrant cuffs to go along with his phony clerical collar.

CHAPTER 36

The back lot at the LVPD was crowded with cars. Some looked parked, six others were lined up near the main exit gate.

At the head of the parade was a regular four door cruiser. On top of the roof was a portable lighted sign which showed 'Commander' in barely readable letters.

Mike and Pap headed to it.

Lieutenant Dan Southfield was in the shotgun seat, and a sergeant in uniform was the driver. Dan motioned to the two men to get in the back seat.

"When we get to HA, we're going into surround formation," he said when they were inside. "This car will stay in front along with three others, one of which has the SWAT team. The other two cars will cover the side and back of the building.

"You two stay strictly with me. I have a warrant to enter and search the premises, based on Mike's complaint.

"We won't use the Swatters unless we're refused entry. Once inside both of you stick beside—behind—me while we start processing each room. We'll start with the special room. From there my men will disperse to search all areas as quickly as possible.

"If Rambow is on the premises one of my female cops will try to engage him in conversation until the search is completed."

He turned to his driver. "Let's go, Steve."

The six-car convoy headed out, no sirens. The noon time traffic was light and within a few minutes Happy Andings was in sight.

Two of the police cars peeled off and headed to the side and rear of the building. The command car drove right up to the entrance walkway, the other three cruisers covered the remaining side and front.

Southfield and his sergeant got out first. They stopped just outside the door and a Swat unit formed up behind them.

Shant and Pap slipped through the heavily armed and outfitted Swat team and stood to one side so they wouldn't interfere with its entrance.

Southfield looked over his troops, then nodded and opened the door. The first six officers crowded into the reception area. The cutie on the reception desk looked up in alarm at the invasion.

"Don't worry, miss. We're the police. Is the owner on the premises?"

"Mr. Rambow? No sir, he's not."

"The manager?"

"Yes sir, she's in her office, I believe. Shall I ring her?"

"Yes, and ask her to come out here, right away."

Within a very few moments GG rushed into the area.

She appeared calm but concerned.

"I'm the manager. My name is Gertie Glein. What's the problem?"

"I have a search warrant"—he produced the document and gave it to GG— "signed by a municipal court judge. It's based on a complaint signed by a Michael Shant, who says his employee, an Alison Adams, has been missing three days and was last seen on these premises.

"Do you understand the warrant?"

GG nodded. This was not good. She knew that Rambow still had that broad stashed in the Special room. But she couldn't very well stop this army of cops.

"Yeah. I guess the place is yours, Lieutenant." She'd had enough contact with the LVLD over the years that she recognized Southfield's bars.

"Okay, sergeant, first stop is the room at the end of that hallway." Southfield pointed to the sketch map that Shant and Pap had made for him.

"We think the door may be barred." He looked at GG.

"Want to give us the key?"

"I don't have it, there's only one, and the owner, Mr. Rambow, has it."

"Okay, sarge, take a couple of Swatters with you and their ram and get that room open. The rest of you men can start searching in your assigned map areas. Check everything carefully, and try not to disturb more than necessary any massage activities going on. We're not here looking for possible vice violations, we're here just to search."

The men, now more than 16 in the crowded reception area, moved off to their pre-assigned areas.

"Where is Rambow hanging out these days?" asked Southfield.

GG realized she'd better start buttering her toast with this cop. She knew that broad in the Special, if she was even still alive, would be found soon as those cops with the battering ram got to work.

She also realized that she was not in a great bargaining position. She'd already ID'd herself as the joint's manager, and she'd be the one on the first firing line. She felt pretty sure no one except Rambow knew that she was also the majority stockholder in HA.

"I don't really know, Lieutenant. I imagine he's at his WIMPS place, trying to get his followers to ante up even more bucks. He's here often, but just not today, so I...."

There was a loud shattering sound as the reinforced Special room door was breached. Then some cop shouted.

"Lieutenant! You'd better come here. Right now!"

"Watch her", Southfield shouted to a cop standing guard at the door, and raced into and down the corridor. He could see part of the shattered door lying in the doorway.

Right behind him, and ignoring another cop's upheld hand like a traffic signal, were Shant and Pap. Together the three men crowded into the room, avoiding the wood and splinters in the doorway and inside on the plush carpet.

"Mike! What took you so long?"

All three gawked at the caller, as did every other cop near enough to see into the room.

On the far side of the massive bed Alison Adams stood, partly crouched as if for protection. She wore a bra and panties.

"Jesus, Alison! Are you alright? Are you hurt? Where are your clothes? Who's responsible?"

The questions were fired indiscriminately by both Shant and Pap, and even Southfield joined in.

"Who's the prick responsible for keeping me locked up in here for two, maybe three, days? Rambow, that's who."

Southfield turned to one of the officers in the Swat team.

"Get an ambulance down here immediately, full siren and lights. And you," he pointed to another officer, "get out to the reception area and tell the manager, Gertie Glein, that she's under arrest on suspicion of at least accomplice to felony kidnapping. I'll be along shortly to process her."

Alison had run around the bed and threw her arms first around Pap, then in a more intimate manner around Shant. She started to smother him with kisses, but hesitated and silently sounded a 'thank you' to Southfield. Then she got a little more serious with Shant.

The officers all tried to look elsewhere but Alison's very attractive bod proved too much of a temptation, so Southfield ordered them all out into the hallway.

"Sergeant, establish this room as a crime scene. Nothing touched, no one in. The rest of you men carry on with the searching, there's still a lot of rooms to check."

"And there's a basement, all locked up too, so we'll need Swat down there," the sergeant added.

Southfield left the Special room to his crime scene crew and returned to the reception area.

"Gertie Glein, I am placing you under arrest. The charge is accomplice to felony kidnapping, that's a capital crime. Officer, put the cuffs on. Then sit her down there in that chair and watch her—carefully— until we can take her back to the station for formal booking."

He looked at GG. "You are entitled to call your attorney, and a phone will be made available at the station. Officer, read her her rights."

There was another crash, this time more muffled. It appeared to come from the basement.

For a moment everything seemed to pause. Even the cop who was handcuffing GG paused as if to see what would be next.

What was next was another shout, somewhat muffled by the distance.

"Lieutenant. You're going to want to see this. We've found a body."

Another voice chimed in.

"And it's pretty clearly a dead one, boss."

Southfield ran to the hall, looking for the basement door.

After the coroner, immediately summoned by the Swat team leader when the body was found, had quickly inspected the body, it had been moved to his facility for a post mortem exam. It was obvious that the man's head had been beaten in. The sergeant had started on the extensive paperwork needed in both kidnapping and murder charges.

Southfield had looked over GG carefully, and concluded she was certainly big and strong enough to do the beating, so felony murder had been added to her kidnapping charges.

The prisoner had been transported to the LVPD station. A crew of police officers remained at Happy Andings to wrap up the search and to lock down the entire building. Customers who had been found in the earlier search, some in the final moments of their massages, were allowed to dress and leave, after full ID had been shown and recorded.

Shant and Pap hitched a ride back with the lieutenant, who had too much on his mind to worry about them. After GG was formally booked, and called a lawyer who said he'd be over as soon as possible, she was searched again and moved to a solitary cell. Nothing was too good for an accused murderer and kidnapper.

CHAPTER 37

Shant poked his head into Southfield's office. The lieutenant was almost buried in paperwork and barely looked up.

"Dan, could I talk with GG for a minute? I know she's not totally responsible for both those charges, and Alison agreed that it was Rambow alone who kidnapped her.

"Maybe I could get her to shift more of the blame to Rambow."

Southfield sighed. "Okay, Mike, but from outside the cell. And remember her mouthpiece is coming, so speed it up."

"Thanks, Dan. I'll get back to you later."

Shant corralled Pap and the two of them told the same sergeant who had been on the raid that the lieutenant had okayed them talking to GG. He nodded and took them to outside her cell and left them.

Gertie sat slumped on her bed. There were no chairs in the cell.

"GG.

She was bowed but not broken; she was a tough broad.

She peered through the bars.

"You're the two dandies who started all of this, aren't you? What the fuck do you jerkoffs want now?"

Mike answered.

"We didn't start anything, GG. I came here to do a legitimate article on Rambow, but the more we dug the dirtier the story got."

He looked at Pap, who nodded to indicate Mike should keep on.

"But this hole is big, GG. This is no two-bit misdemeanor, this is the big one. The charges are kidnapping and murder, at least one count of that, but there's still a couple of missing girls. And they have been placed with Rambow when last seen alive.

"Loyalty is all well and good, but unless you want to prance down death row holding hands with a real sleaze ball, you should start helping yourself, not a so-called preacher who appears to be trying to slip through on these crimes."

She was at least listening to him but she hadn't said a word.

"Right now, GG, the lieutenant in charge of this case is open to listening. He knows down deep that Rambow is the real criminal here. You may have looked the other way on some of his dirty deeds but you didn't commit them, he did.

"I think, and it's just thinking, GG, not a hard offer or anything, but we—Pap and me—do think that if you told the truth about Rambow, how he had lured and kidnapped that girl Alison into his secret room prison, and whatever else you know about the man murdered and found in the HA basement, he might be willing to discuss your co-operation with the DA."

She finally stood up and exercised her arms a little. She was a big strong woman and there was no doubt that she could have killed that guy in the basement. But Shant, and Pap, doubted it, she really didn't seem that kind of woman.

"I've got a shyster on the way. I know he'll tell me to say nothing. Why should I talk?"

"Because any lawyer, unless he's your oldest and best friend, is going to be drooling over this headline-grabbing case: 'Preacher and girlfriend charged with kidnapping young pretty girl and murdering man'.

"Those kinds of cases come by once a decade, maybe once a lifetime. Your guy will try to help you, but he'll also be busy helping himself to as much of that publicity cream as he can. You know that, GG.

"Right now, the cop in charge just wants to make the guilty party—Rambow—gets what he deserves. You're just a supplementary person.

"But once you get lawyered up it will be out of the cop's hands. In fact, outa everybody's hands.

"Now is the best time to start helping yourself, GG."

She turned around a few times, there wasn't much to see in the 8x10 cell.

She made a decision.

"Okay, Mr. Shant, you've convinced me. Get that cop friend of yours down here pronto and I'll fill him in on what I know about Rambow. And also about his helper, Tonto, the midget who's a sort of handyman at HA."

Shant made eye contact with Pap and turned his eyes upward. Pap understood and headed quickly to the hall and the locking door.

"Lieutenant?"

Southfield looked up, already bleary eyed from the paperwork avalanche on his desk. "Make it quick, Pap, I've got hours ahead of me on this crap."

"Well, you might want to take a break, Dan, and walk downstairs for some exercise."

Southfield looked on the verge of anger.

"Why the fuck should I do that, Pap?"

"Because Mike has just got GG to agree to spill the beans about Rambow, and his helper. Provided you talk with her before her ambulance chaser gets here and...."

Before Pap could finish his sentence, Southfield had leapt up from his desk, buzzed to have a steno clerk downstairs immediately, and had rushed past Pap.

CHAPTER 38

"That was some dramatic conclusion, Pap. Sort of the stuff you'd expect in a mystery novel.

"When GG decided to spill the beans, she sure knocked over the whole damned pot," Pap agreed.

"I just spoke briefly with Dan. He said they had enough from her, signed and witnessed, to shift the kidnap and probably the basement murder onto Rambow's deceitful shoulders.

"The cops are just waiting for a signed arrest warrant for Rambow. Everyone involved wants to make very sure all the Ts are crossed and the Is are dotted. This is no time for a clerical screw up," Shant said with a big frown.

"And that ending will hurt your magazine story, right?" Pap could barely hide his grin.

Mike smiled.

Pap continued, "Sure, it will ruin and turn a straightforward success profile into a solved murder and kidnap case, largely with all our help. Possibly get some undeserving writer an award or something," Pap grinned.

"At least something more tangible than a scrap of paper, we all hope. Something like a nice fat bunch of crispy negotiable bills."

"How can you be so mercenary, Pap, when journalistic literature is involved?"

Mike paused.

"Well, maybe big fat bonuses all round might be some consolation at that. You could put yours toward that AA course you've always promised yourself, and Alison could buy some new bras and panties. Maybe she'd like us to help her shop."

The two men relaxed. They were having coffee in the officers' break room at LVPD.

Shant straightened up from his slumped position.

"But there's something missing yet, Pap. The cops have no hard evidence linking Rambow to those two missing girls."

"What about that shortie, what's his name, Tonto? Isn't he talking?"

"Claims he knows nothing, that he only helped Rambow move a couple of rugs from the basement."

"I know the cops are busy processing Alison's kidnapping and the basement guy murder. But couldn't your silver tongue work any wonders?"

Shant looked at his old friend.

"You know, you may have something there, Pap. It did seem to have some influence on GG, maybe Tonto will also succumb."

He nodded to Pap. "You see if you can get an okay from Dan. Don't make a big deal of it, just say we want to talk with him. We'll stay outside his cell so it shouldn't really be a problem. I understand the little guy has refused any legal assistance, says he's innocent of everything and doesn't need any shyster to screw matters up worse.

"I'll meet you at the cell block."

A few minutes later Pap showed up, smiling broadly. In his hand he had a sheet torn from a memo pad. On it Southfield had scrawled "Okay to let these 2 talk to Tonto from outside his cell", and scrawled what might pass as his signature. He was obviously preoccupied with GG's confessions.

"Tonto, we were talking earlier with GG. She has opened up a lot, and the DA is evidently working some kind of plea deal for her.

"She mentioned that she thought you'd be smart to do the same thing."

Tonto grinned. "Sure, I bet she did. What does that broad know about me and what I might or might not know?"

"Well, she knows one thing, amigo, and that's what your nickname really means. I understand that Rambow was the one who first used it on you?"

"So what? I know what it means, it's the name of that guy who used to be the Lone Ranger's sidekick, helping him out of jams."

"You think that's why Rambow named you Tonto? You might want to look in a Spanish dictionary some time, amigo, it really means a fool, or stupid."

Tonto's face darkened.

"That's not right, it can't be. Rambow wouldn't call me that, unless he...."

"Yeah, unless he meant you to be just that, a fool. Pap, show our friend here your Spanish dictionary."

Pap pulled a pocket version out of his side pocket, flipped the pages to T, and found the word. He held it close to the bars so Tonto could see what his name really meant.

"Fucking Rambow! What a prick! Here I thought he was my buddy, and all along he played me for a, a, a, fool." The last word almost didn't make it out of his mouth.

"That's the least of your troubles, Tonto. GG also said that the Special Room has a hidden secret camera installed that automatically snaps every time that door is opened, and continues snapping until the door is closed.

"When the cops get around to examining those tapes, are you going to be in any, Tonto? Any that might indicate you actually did the dirty work on those two girls, both of whose bodies have been found, incidentally. A walker out with his terrier found them, and they've just been identified as the missing girls, who incidentally also will show up, according to GG, on those secret films."

Tonto's face blanched as though he'd bleached it.

Neither of the two men spoke. This was the time to shut up.

Tonto turned around in the narrow cell. He stayed backside to the bars for several minutes. Finally, he turned to face them.

"You said the DA was cutting some kind of deal with GG?"

Shant and Pap both nodded.

"Do you think, if I told him the truth about what Rambow did—all he paid me for was just to help him get rid of those rugs, I didn't really know what was in them—and he did whatever happened to the girls. I didn't touch them, I swear."

Pap said, "Tonto, we're not lawyers. You might be advised to get one, they'll get you one free. But listen, son, I do know that the lieutenant in charge of this case is not a bad guy. If you fill him in on any missing details before they come out some other way, I'm pretty sure he'd put in a good word with the DA."

"GG did that, Tonto, and she's probably a lot better off for it."

Shant turned as though to exit the cell area.

"By the way, Tonto, would you like to have us tell the lieutenant that you've had second thoughts about your statement? I know there's a clerk steno around here somewhere, and if you cleared up what actually happened, before it all comes out in the wash, you'd be like GG, a lot better off."

He hesitated on the first step, and waited just a moment. Tonto was silent.

Mike nodded to Pap, and tilted his head upwards to indicate they should split.

They got as far as the third step.

"Wait! Wait a second. Okay, pass the word to the cop. I'll give him everything I know.

"That fucking Rambow—call me stupid, will he? —is not getting me to take a fall for him."

"Dan, if you can corral that guy with the tape recorder, and pull yourself away from all that fascinating paperwork, you'd probably find that Tonto is in a talkative mood. His exact words, 'I'll give him'— "meaning you, Dan"—everything I know'."

Dan's mouth was wide open again.

"Jesus Christ, I might as well put in my papers. With you two guys on the loose the LVPD doesn't really need to pay us dicks these exorbitant salaries."

He was on his feet quickly, pressing intercom switches and moving rapidly towards the door and, Shant assumed, the cell block below.

CHAPTER 39

Southfield's office at LVPD overflowed. There were cops in uniforms, plainclothes detectives, and even a couple of suits who looked like they might be from the DA's office. All concerned wanted to ensure everything on this important bust went smoothly.

Southfield held up his hands.

"Okay, we've just got a report from traffic. Rambow's at the World International Moral Protection Society, or WIMPS, offices and church hall just off LV Boulevard.

"We don't anticipate any resistance but he's evidently got several hundred of his followers there, someone said it was a pledging or giving money kind of deal.

"The uniforms will cover the perimeter of the building. You three sergeants will come with me—and cuff the suspect—along with the DA's men, when we make the pinch.

"These two men," the lieutenant indicated Mike and Pap, "who have been very instrumental in bringing this case to a successful conclusion, will be allowed into the building, after we're all in place. They'll stay at the rear. And Pap, please be very quiet if you feel it necessary to record the scene for posterity."

The parade up Paradise started. They turned west to hit the WIMPS building without having to disrupt traffic on LV Blvd.

But the word was already out, and local newsmen and a couple of television vans tailed the official procession.

Two of the cruisers pulled into the access lane behind the WIMPS building and a handful of uniformed officers got out and assumed coverage positions.

Even before they had properly positioned themselves paparazzi morons were besieging them with questions: Is the preacher here involved in something? Something like the catholic priests and their need for young boys? Or was some girl kidnapped and raped repeatedly? Tell us all about it!

It was obvious that their entire recent news had come from glaringly loud daytime TV 'news' as delivered by some talking head with her IQ even lower than her age.

The main police crew got out of their double-parked vehicles which their drivers then used to effectively block all through-traffic on the street.

Even over the normal Vegas street noises a loud deep-pitched voice could be heard from inside the building. It beseeched listeners to 'dig deep into their pockets so that our wonderful and essential work can continue'.

Southfield marshalled his troops into a compact group, then pulled open the ornate large door.

Once all the men, including Shant and Pap, were inside, he started up the aisle. At the end of it, standing on a platform to give himself the spotlight, Rambow stopped in the midst of a new plea for funds.

"What is the meaning of this? Do you people know this is an accredited church here, and that a major charitable campaign is underway right now?"

He stepped off the raised platform and blocked the aisle.

"Who's in charge here? What the f..., what's this all about?"

Southfield walked right up to Rambow, who was wearing some kind of clerical dog collar along with a solid black vest.

"Are you Gilbert Rambow?"

"Of course I am, I'm the official minister of this accredited World International Moral Protection Society church. What do you want?"

The lieutenant reached into his suit jacket pocket and pulled out some papers.

"Gilbert Rambow, or Rheambault, your real last name, I have here a warrant signed by a Nevada state judge.

"You are charged with the kidnap and forcible detainment of a woman named Alison Adams, of this city, and the premeditated murder of two other women and one man apparently a Mexican citizen. The two women have not yet been identified."

Rambow had suddenly lost his enthusiasm for public speaking.

"I am placing you under arrest on those multiple felony charges."

He turned to the nearest sergeant.

"Sergeant, please cuff the suspect and read him his rights."

When those chores were completed, efficiently and satisfactorily, another sergeant held Rambow's left arm just below the shoulder, while the cuffing sergeant did the same with his right arm.

Southfield turned, and the crowd of officials fell into place behind him. They headed for the door.

During the short procedure the entire congregation had been silent. Now they arose as one, and began talking, often shouting, to their nearest neighbors, and to the world at large.

But none of the police officials, or the DAs men, said word one. They marched in silence to the door and exited in silence.

As Rambow and his two sergeants went through the door the press people, already assembled in quantity outside but kept at bay behind several large uniforms, started in on their litany of questions.

Rambow loudly shouted and even-louder repeated his claims that it was all a horrible mistake, a complete violation of his freedom-of-religion rights, his right to peaceful assembly, his freedom of speech rights, and that he would be suing the city of Las Vegas, the state of Nevada, the United States of America, and everything and everyone connected, in any way, to those political bodies, in addition to each and every cop and DA's man involved in the obviously illegal arrest proceedings, and, finally, to most of the now-large crowd of bystanders watching the drama unfold.

A few newspaper reporters started jotting down his statements, but the TV guys just relied on their experienced cameramen getting it all on tape.

Following careful instructions earlier, the police didn't waste any time in getting Rambow and his two uniformed escorts loaded into the back seat of a cruiser. Shepherded by all the other cop cars the procession this time headed west, then turned north on LV Blvd.

There was no need now for anonymity, and every news hound, and most of the tourists patrolling the Strip, knew that "a well-known preacher" had been arrested.

He was charged, according to which open mouth you listened to, with sodomy, rape, public masturbation, theft of church funds, screwing the hated IRS, fondling young boys, terrorism, pinching and caressing numerous young girls' behinds, and even, from a few, murders most foul.

Mike looked at Pap as the police procession wended its way out of sight towards the LVPD booking and processing offices.

"Did you get some goodies, Pap?"

"More than you'll ever need to illustrate your super-scoop article, my boy. And now that I've put in a full day's labor, may I suggest that we have a celebratory beverage?"

"I vote yes," Mike answered. But I don't think we have to be so parsimonious as to limit our intake to one, old partner.

"Let's phone Alison and arrange something in the nature of a 'well done' fiesta."

Pap grinned.

"Maybe you could ask Alison to come in the same costume we rescued her in?"

"I sort of doubt that she'll be willing to don that bra and panties again, Pap.

"She'll probably want to preserve them as fond mementoes of an interesting time in her young life."

"That's too bad, Michael. I have my older life to think about, too, and I can certainly stand having wonderful portraits of a doll like Alison stored in my memory banks. I'm just sorry I didn't get some more revealing pix of Ali that day. More character revealing," he hastily added. "Just for my own personal files, of course."

Shant nodded, wisely said nothing more on that subject, and then pointed to a nearby saloon.

"Let's finish this discussion of Alison's clothing choices in there."

CHAPTER 40

Later that afternoon Shant reached Alison on her cell.

"Hey, cutie, I'm here with Pap at," he glanced around but couldn't see any name, "well, some drinking eshtablishment on LV Boulevard. You've probably seen on TV the take down of Mr. Rambow?

For the next six minutes Alison went into exquisite detail on how thrilled she had been to see Rambow physically arrested, how excited she was to see on local television such a satisfactory conclusion to her terrible imprisonment ordeal, and how she was going to bring Pap such an armful of liquid and food goodies. As for her hero, Shant, she started to describe the physical pleasures she planned to rain on his body, but he rapidly realized the effect this lurid description would have on his visible clothing, he stalled her in mid-gush.

"Yes, it was truly wonderful, Alison. And that's one reason old Pap and I are having that celebray, celebrish, well, these drinks.

"But the reason I called, young lady, was to invite you to my motel this evening."

He grinned broadly at her reply.

"Yes, that for sure, and a mini fiesta as well. You, me, and Pap. And I'm hoping that two of those fine people may be able to spend the whole night, even breakfast, there."

He listened and grinned even more broadly.

"Wonderful. Grab a cab any time after eight. We'll probably have started without you but there will lots, food and booze, left. See you soon."

That evening, promptly at eight on the dot, she rang the motel buzzer on Shant's suite. As soon as she entered, Alison rushed up to Pap, dropping two loaded shopping bags at his feet, and hugged him so tightly that his cheeks turned red.

Then she kissed him right smack on his lips and his cheeks got even redder.

"You old fake, Pap," Mike chortled. "Your face acts like it's never been bussed by a reasonably attractive broad before."

As soon as his breath returned Pap rushed to his own defense.

"Oh, I'm not a complete virgin, it's just that I rarely get hugged so affectionately."

He turned to Alison.

"That was lovely, dear. Shall we do it again?"

She laughed, then put a serious look on her face and turned to Mike.

"Just what do you mean calling me a 'reasonably attractive' broad? And what do you mean even calling me a broad?"

Mike threw up his hands in surrender.

"Okay, I retract that 'reasonably attractive broad', the whole schmear.

"You're a really attractive female. No, an outstandingly attractive female, in fact a knockout. More than that, you're...."

"Let me put an end to the BS," she said, and kissed him on his lips. And held the position long enough that his cheeks reddened.

"Aha. Now who's the virgin?" Pap chuckled.

"That was just a small, a tiny, repayment for the wonderful rescue you guys did," Alison said.

"If you two shining knights hadn't come charging in, I would still be there, clothed in just my bra and panties, and wondering what evil ideas Rambow was planning to implement."

Pap came alive.

"Speaking of those panties and bra, my dear, we", Shant looked ready to sock him, "well maybe me, or I, was wondering if you were going to model them for us, you know, just so that we could relive for our memories how sad and unhappy...."

"And almost naked," Mike interjected.

".... you looked as we did rescue you?"

"I'd be glad to, Pap old dear, but those items are no longer in my wardrobe. In spite of the wonderful memories attached to them, I was forced to dispose of them in my apartment building's incinerator."

"Maybe you could at least send me a pair of your current style, perhaps autographed in some significant place."

She laughed loudly. "Sure, I'll put that on my To Do list, Pap."

CHAPTER 41

"And now, if we are through with all this titillating talk of girlish undies, I have some news, good news, for all of us."

Instantly both Pap and Alison shut up.

Shant stood up, and assumed a political speaker facade.

"Ladies, especially the outstandingly attractive ones in this room, all old farts who claim to be photographers of high quality, and magazine scribblers who know only 38 words total in his native tongue, gather round and give praise to far away editors in cold northern cities from whom all blessings flow.

"Just today, this afternoon in fact, I was able to communicate with said editor. After the usual greetings and requests for local weather conditions, that same far away editor praised this assembled crew for a 'most wonderful article and pix'. It is to be the cover story in this month's issue.

"But beyond the effusive editorial praise, for writers, photographers, and superb investigative researchers, this very same editor bestowed praises in a more tangible fashion.

"As of this afternoon, in that remote editorial office high in the clouds, a series of short written messages were transcribed, put into envelopes of superior quality, and dropped in a little red box, on their way to a city known as Vas Legas, or something."

"So, we're getting a message of appreciation for our efforts?" Pap asked cynically.

"Sort of," Mike replied. "This particular editor isn't much for friendly notes, so I was advised that those quality envelopes actually bore simple pieces of quality paper, with just a few words on them."

Shant paused and gazed at his friends.

"More important, perhaps, is that the few words were merely a segment of other more useful data.

"That data was comprised solely of the same data we feed into computers, just a series of 1s and 0s.

"But in this case the higher numbers, 5s, 6s, and even 9s, were the message."

Alison twigged first.

"Oh, that sweet editor in that faraway foreign land. You mean we're to receive, if the US Postal Service doesn't disappear, checks? Checks which we can cash for real coin of the realm?"

"Yes, dear Alison, checks with fairly large numbers on them. I was advised to not spend mine all in one place.

"The editor was under the misapprehension that the famous Mustang Ranch was here in southern Nevada. She didn't even know that good old Mustang, of one-time Reno fame, was no more, having been driven into the ground by the feds who obviously can't even operate a world-famous whorehouse (foolishly seized for taxes owed), on a profitable basis.

"In any event, I was advised to spend my bonus on something of more uplifting value than behinds.

"And I so advise each of you."

Pap did his famous jig, almost stumbling on the frilly rug.

"A bonus, a bonus! The sweetest words in English. Except, perhaps, a feminine 'Of course I will' as the evening wanes."

"Men. Always one thing on their minds," Alison said. "And thank god for that."

"Now to the important part of this lecture," Mike said. "The drinks". His audience applauded wildly.

The evening continued. Drinks were drunk, clever sayings were misquoted and slurred, good times were remembered and shared.

At one point Mike resumed his political speaker pose.

"I would like to quote a long ago general, now dead, who on the occasion of sneaking out of a very sticky WW2 Japanese situation in the Philippines, said to his friends left behind, 'I shall return.'

"Short and sweet, and the nice thing is that he did, several years later.

"As a professional traveler I must say those same words, but the important thing is that, just as the general did, I too shall return.

"And that means this pocito fiesta we're sharing and enjoying will be repeated sometime. Remember that, because when we next meet, I may give you a pop quiz on your activities since this party."

Six eyes moistened, but another drink for all soon took care of that.

The evening carried on, but like all good times it had to end. Even Pap reached his limit, and when he made his goodbyes, stumbling on all the one syllable words, he insisted he could drive home.

"Sure you could, Pap, but you don't have a car. Maybe it's best that we call you a cab."

Pap agreed and in due time was transported away.

"Well, I guess I need a cab too." Alison didn't sound thrilled by that disclosure.

"I may be a few years over the hill, Ali, but I've never heard of a really attractive girl needing a cab. Is this some kind of new sexual ritual involving major equipment?"

She started to say 'You idiot', but this time speedy Shant closed her lips with his.

After what seemed like 10 minutes to both of them, Alison came up for air.

"You know, I wasn't totally truthful to Pap earlier. I said that that infamous bra and panties set were gone forever. Well, technically they were, but I just happened to have an identical pair put away for emergencies."

She hesitated, looked right at him. "I hope this qualifies as an emergency?"

Shant nodded enthusiastically.

"Certainly does, sweetie. Do I get to see those goodies or are we going to only talk about them?"

Alison answered silently by kicking off her heels, and reached around to find the zipper on her ultra-short skirt.

"Here," said the gentleman Shant, "let me give you a hand. In fact two of them."

As if to prove his offer, one hand found the zipper very quickly. The other hand was equally dexterous, and located the topmost button which controlled her sheer blouse.

In just the nick of time Alison turned around to help him. With her chores completed she repaid his assistance by finding his key zipper and somewhat hurriedly starting its downward slide.

"You know, that is an attractive bra. And the panties are a wonderful match. Maybe I could examine them a little closer, it's always useful to know what kind of undies friends wear."

"I guess that's my next line too, Michael.

"And seeing that we're no longer teenagers, and trying to set new individual speed records, may I suggest that we adjourn to a far more comfortable location where experience and a willingness to learn have great values?"

"Like the bed?"

"Exactly."

And so, they did.

The end of this adventure,

But soon, the start of Shant's next thrilling exploit.

www.ingramcontent.com/pod-product-compliance
Lightning Source LLC
Chambersburg PA
CBHW022012010726
47494CB00003B/1009